TOUCHED BY A GODDESS

Farris threw a startled glance to his right. The white mare blew through her nose and winked at him. In front of his eyes, her form shimmered as if he looked through a summer heat wave. No. It couldn't be. There was not a woman at his side, a woman with long silver-white hair as coarse as a horse's mane.

But his eyes insisted there was such a woman, his nose caught the fragrance of perfume instead of mare, and his hand felt the pressure of a firm warm palm and fingers instead of a lead-rein. She smiled at him, slowly and seductively.

"Well?" she murmured. *"Do you know me, Farris?"*

"I know . . . what I think I see, mistress."

Her mouth twitched in a stifled laugh. *"I shouldn't tease you mortals, but it's such fun. Know, My child, I am Ydona, Lady of Horses and Mother of Mares, and today I claim you for Mine."* She ran a fingertip over his right shoulder and down his arm; a stinging sharp pain followed in its wake.

"If I am Yours, my Lady, why am I a slave? What must I do to earn Your help?"

"Help yourself . . ."

PRAISE FOR
LEOPARD LORD

"Ms. Morland is off to a hot start in fantasy. Her knowledge of the middle ages is impressive . . . Her story is exciting and fast-paced . . . I'm looking forward to reading more by Ms. Morland."

—Anne Logston,
author of *Waterdance*

SHACKLE &
SWORD

———◆———

ALANNA MORLAND

ACE BOOKS, NEW YORK

SHACKLE AND SWORD

An Ace Book / published by arrangement with
the author

PRINTING HISTORY
Ace edition / September 1999

The Penguin Putnam Inc. World Wide Web site address is
http://www.penguinputnam.com

Check out the ACE Science Fiction & Fantasy newsletter
and much more on the Internet at Club PPI!

ISBN: 0-441-00646-9

ACE®
Ace Books are published
by The Berkley Publishing Group,
a division of Penguin Putnam Inc.,
375 Hudson Street, New York, New York 10014.
ACE and the "A" design are trademarks
belonging to Penguin Putnam Inc.

PRINTED IN THE UNITED STATES OF AMERICA

10 9 8 7 6 5 4 3 2 1

This one is for the filkers
who inspired it and
for my sister Lynda
who introduced me to them.

SHACKLE &
SWORD

———————

PROLOGUE

THE CELL

Year 418 D.S.: Fifth day of the month of Greenleaves

Gut-twisting terror drove Farris to his knees. The stone blocks of the prison cell were cold and damp, but he no longer felt them. Despair clamped its shackles around his soul, burning worse than the iron band of the slave-collar around his neck.

When tomorrow's sun rose they would drag him out of here and begin the agonizing torture that would end with his death. If ever there was a time to pray to his patron goddess, this was it.

"Ydona, Lady of Horses, I've worshiped you all my life! You claimed me when I was sixteen, You put Your brand on my arm with Your own hands—help me now!"

A pale silvery shimmer appeared, a shimmer that transformed itself into a woman with white hair as coarse as a horse's mane. She tossed Her forelock out of Her eyes and smiled at him, a smile as warm as a summer's day. *"And do you remember what I told you then? You asked Me what you must do to earn My help. Look into your heart, My son, at your life. And then I say again—help yourself.''*

She shimmered again, and was gone.

His belly clenched tight as the fear that had ridden him all day finally triumphed.

1

FARRIS

Year 410 D.S.: First day of the month of Yellowgrain

"Here they come!" The boy perched on top of the fountain stood up to see better, holding onto the marble griffin's ear to steady himself. The noise of marching feet came clearly to his ears.

"Hey, get down, Farris, before the City Guards come and chase us off and we can't see at all," complained a second boy.

Farris slid down to perch on the griffin's neck as if riding the carved beast, but did not relinquish his place. The celebration of a king's twenty-fifth year on the throne of the fair kingdom of Dur Sharrukhan came around once in a lifetime, and he did not intend to miss a moment of it. This parade was the highlight of three days of celebrating, and he and his friends had been in possession of the fountain for two hours to have the best view. "They're too busy to chase a gang of kids off, Braden, or we'd be gone already. Hey, look!"

It was a most satisfactory parade. The first troops of the royal army marched past, brave in the royal colors of blue

and red with the insignia of the silver griffin on their surcotes. Drummers pounded to keep them in step, and the eerie
wailing of pipes trailed along like the cries of vanquished
monsters. Barred wagons displaying beasts from the royal
menagerie alternated with more troops of the royal soldiers
and the retinues of nobles.

Finally, in the place of honor, came those for whom the
boys waited. Surrounded by the mounted troops known as
the Kings' Elite, on white palfreys barded with red, blue, and
silver, rode King Tiorbran and his queen, Elashava. Following them rode two young men, their sons Gardomir and Alnikhias.

The group of boys on the fountain set up a howl of approval. They were drowned out by a rising tide of cheers
that flowed along in a wave to parallel the monarchs' route.

His Gracious Majesty had the love of his people as few
rulers did; he considered his people his children to protect
rather than his slaves to exploit. Farris and his friends
watched as the king and queen acknowledged the adoration
of their subjects, as did the princes. One of them laughed
and pointed to the fountain as he turned and spoke to his
brother. Then the young man reached into one of a pair of
pouches slung in front of him and withdrew something.

He looked up at Farris, and called, "Griffin rider! Catch!"
Something flew from his hands; Farris gripped tighter with
his knees on his unorthodox mount and leaned out to catch
it.

Still, he did not open the small leather pouch immediately.
His eyes, like those of his friends, were fixed on the riders
around the royal family. Royalty was all very well, but the
bastard son of an innkeeper could not hope to be one of *them*.
But he could aspire to be one of the King's Elite. All it took
was superb knowledge of sword and horse, and Farris believed that he was well on his way to mastery of both. He
pictured himself on one of those magnificent black horses,
dressed in that gleaming armor and scarlet-plumed helm.

So intent was he in his hero worship that he did not even
see the last riders in the parade, servants who scattered coins
for largess to the populace.

"Hey, come on, Farris, what's in it?" someone asked.

"Huh?"

"What's in the pouch?" the boy repeated. "If it's coins, will you share? We wouldn't stand a chance with that crowd down there."

Farris slid to the ground with his friends, pulled loose the knots that held the pouch closed, and spilled the contents into his cupped hand. They were coins, mostly small copper pieces. But there was one shining silver piece, stamped with the royal griffin. This was value indeed, over a week's wages for a peasant or common laborer. He slipped it into his pocket and counted out the rest.

The boy who had asked him to share stared sourly at the few coins allotted to him. "How come you kept the silver and gave Braden more'n the rest of us, Farris?"

"The silver's going in with what I'm saving for my sword," Farris said defensively. "The prince gave it to *me*, y'know. I could have kept it all for myself."

"Like you're going to need a sword, Farris. Innkeepers don't."

Farris stared at him coldly. "I'm going to be King's Elite. Amethyst can catch a husband to be innkeeper in my place."

"Hah! King's Elite have to be eighteen. You've got five more years to go. Maybe by then you'll be good enough that they'll let you join as a horseboy."

"Four. I'll be fourteen next month, a man while you're still a kid, Javan." Farris ignored the jibe about the horseboy. Horseboys were slaves. "I'm already a good enough swordsman for City Guard if I wanted. Rykard said so."

"That's because your mother pays him for your sword-training in free ale. And free tail."

"What did you say?" Farris turned to face the other boy, his eyes narrowed.

"I said your mother lets him swive her, like any other whore. Want to make something of it, you half-breed bastard?"

Farris' only answer was a growl of rage as he launched himself at Javan. The other boys gleefully surrounded them, but their shouts were only a background noise to the two young brawlers. Although Farris was the smaller of the two, he was also the quicker. Before long, it was clear he was the victor, too. Throwing Javan onto his belly, he straddled his back and fastened his hands in the other boy's hair.

"Take it back! *All* of it!" he said fiercely, and ground Javan's face in the dust.

A hand came out of nowhere and grabbed Farris by the shoulder. "Run, Farris! City Guard coming!" his friend Braden yelled.

With a last vicious shove, he released his prey and bolted. Everyone knew that the City Guard was cracking down hard on disturbances; nothing was to be allowed to spoil these celebrations.

City Guardsmen were no match for an active boy. He ran down one alley, vaulted a fence, slid into a shop by the back way and out again by a side door, oozed through another narrow passage between buildings, and into a warren of branching narrow lanes.

When the streets became broader and somewhat cleaner, he was well away from any pursuit, so he slowed and took his time. The dirt on his clothes and the blood seeping from his nose rather spoiled the look of a young man out taking the air and minding his own business, but a brief stop at a public fountain washed away the worst of the evidence on his face.

The inn that was his destination was only a short distance from the North Gate. His mother rigorously insisted that her inn was a respectable place, and he knew that if he swaggered through the public rooms in his present condition he would be in deep trouble. Fortunately only the stableman was visible in the yard when he entered, and Farris managed to slip past him unseen to his own quarters.

His room over the stables was a tiny one that had once been a storage room, but it suited him just fine. There had been no need for his stepfather to go on bellowing about "any boy who sleeps under my roof." His roof, hah! The Black Dragon Inn was his mother's, as it had been her father's before her, and his father's before that. But even pride in his heritage would not keep Farris here once he was old enough for the King's Elite. Jared had told him often enough that a bastard like himself would be lucky to be allowed within pissing distance of their headquarters. He'd show *him!*

Meanwhile, there were horses to tend. Farris changed into his grubby work clothes, although from the look of his good clothes there was now little difference between them.

He supposed that if they were well-to-do innkeepers the son of the house would not be doing stable work, but greeting guests and ordering about servants or slaves. A smile curved his lips at the thought of Gilar, the stableman, thinking of himself as a servant. He was a professional, a retiree from the king's messenger service, and he had done less work in the last two years than Farris himself. Farris hadn't minded; nobody could teach him more about horses than Gilar, and if his labor was the price of the lessons, it was a price he was more than willing to pay.

Gilar grudgingly admitted that Farris had a knack with horses. Any one would come to his whistle or chirruped signal, and even the most skittish was calmed by his presence or his voice. Horses were the other love of his life; sometimes he wondered vaguely which deity would choose him when it came time for him to be dedicated to the gods—Likarion the Warrior, or Ydona, the Lady of Horses?

Swords and horses; the influence of both had fixed his desires on the King's Elite.

Although Farris washed again before he went in to supper, his sister still wrinkled her nose at him.

"Can't you wash better than that?" Amethyst demanded. "Your neck and your wrists are still filthy, and you stink of horses."

"Who made you queen of the world, little sister?" he retorted.

The two children standing belligerently nose-to-nose were twins, but looked no more alike than any other pair of siblings. Amethyst was slender with soft light-brown hair; Farris was somewhat shorter, although he was older by a quarter of an hour, with wheat-blond hair. Only their eyes, the red-brown of dark amber, were alike. Those eyes and something vaguely exotic about their cheekbones were the only things that betrayed their unusual heritage. Their father was not human, but one of the fai, the uncanny forest people who were said to be magical. Farris privately had his doubts about that. *He* certainly couldn't do the kind of magic that was claimed for fai—the stories said that they could make the trees dance to their music, and change time itself. Amethyst had no magic either, although lately she claimed that she could "see" people's emotions as colored auras.

Whatever the truth, Farris hated the being who had sired him as much as he had ever hated anything in his young life. The fai had seduced his mother and then abandoned her, leaving her to bear his bastards alone. The worst of it was that his mother still claimed he had been her lover, not her rapist.

"Here, you two, get to work!" growled a rough voice. Their stepfather Jared lumbered into view and cuffed Farris, then disappeared through the door into the common room before his stepson could do more than glare at him.

"Bastard," Farris muttered at the closed door. "I've done my work for the day and I'm getting something to eat."

"You have *not!*" Amethyst screeched. "Everybody is running their feet off trying to take care of all our customers, and *you* can't go lounge around like a lord and stuff your face while the rest of us work!"

"Oh, yeah? Just watch me, little sister," Farris shot back.

Amethyst flushed bright red and bit back a scream of frustration. Instead her hand whipped out, and the heavy pewter mug clenched in her fist caught him smack over his left ear. He bellowed like a bull calf and clutched at the side of his head, then glared at her as his fingers came away bloody. "You could have killed me with that thing!"

"Since when does pewter hurt solid rock? I'm lucky it didn't break!"

"Children!" snapped their mother's weary voice. "The last thing we need right now is quarreling. Farris, let me see your head." He submitted to Tamsina's examination with a growl, and continued to scowl at his sister.

"You'll live," his mother said dryly. "Go hold a dry rag

on it until it stops bleeding. I'm not up to stitching it right now.''

"Are you feeling sick again, Mother, with that pain in your stomach?'' Amethyst asked worriedly. The look she threw at her brother said as clearly as words, *See,* you're *making her feel worse.*

"Only a little, darling. I'll manage. Everybody will go home tomorrow and then I may treat myself to a day in bed.''

All of their guests were planning to leave for home the next day, but breakfast their last morning was not up to the Black Dragon's usual standards. When Farris came in to breakfast, he found Amethyst presiding over the kitchen instead of their mother.

"Ma isn't any better?'' he asked and looked suspiciously at his plateful of eggs scrambled with fried onions before taking the first bite. There was no telling *what* Amethyst had done to it.

His sister turned a tearful face to him and shook her head. "She's worse. I've sent Beka for the healer. She's burning up with fever—she didn't even know me. How can you just sit there stuffing your face like that?''

Farris looked up from his breakfast, his face worried, although nothing stopped his rapid consumption of the food in front of him. "Thysta, what else can I do? I've got work to do, and my going hungry won't help Ma.''

Her lip trembled, and she bit it fiercely and turned back to her cooking. "I know,'' she whispered. "I'm sorry.''

He was hard at work when the healer came. His first hint that his mother's illness was more serious than a bellyache from bad food came from Gilar. "I'll take over here, boy,'' the stableman said gruffly. "You go up to your mother. Don't waste time changing clothes.''

Wear his working clothes into the house? His mother would kill him. If she was so sick that she wouldn't . . . Farris bolted, up the back stairs to the third floor where the family had their rooms.

Amethyst met him outside the door of the room their mother shared with her husband. Her face was white and tear-streaked. "She's *dying,* Farris. The healer says it's belly-rot, and there's nothing they can do."

His own belly clenched tight with fear. "There must be something!" He burst into the room, and both Jared and the healer glared at him. Tamsina's body was a still lump under the coarse blanket, and the sheet was pulled up over her face.

"Have a little more respect for the dead, boy," Jared snarled.

"No. *No!* She can't be—Master Healer, *please.* She was just a little sick yesterday, and she was getting better."

"There's nothing anybody can do when someone has belly-rot, boy," the healer said brusquely but not unkindly. "This is a clear-cut case—pains in the lower right abdomen that get worse and then go away for a day or two, then death from belly-rot. I'm sorry."

"No." Farris shook his head, his face as white as Amethyst's and with a similar stunned look. "*No,* not my mother." He didn't hear his sister come up beside him, but suddenly her hand was clasping his, hard enough to hurt.

"No bawling from the pair of you," Jared ordered. "I'll not have you upsetting my customers with the news of a death in the house."

Tears blurred Farris' eyes, and he started to shake. Amethyst's hand pulling on his was the only thing he felt until her arms went around him, seeking desperately for the only comfort available to her. Neither noticed when the door to Amethyst's room closed and locked behind them.

Farris cried the last tears of his childhood the day his mother died. The next day he followed her coffin to the graveyard with a cold, still face. Amethyst cried enough for both of them.

Let her cry. Let her think that their mother's death was the worst thing that could happen to them. There was time enough to tell her that they were dependent now on the charity of a man they hated. Jared had lost no time in telling his stepson that the inn now belonged to Tamsina's husband, not her children. Farris could not read the paper Jared said was her will, nor was it likely his mother could have written it, but the seals of the lawyer who had were clear on the bottom. The look of glee on Jared's face did not bode well for proving that he was lying.

Nor did the arrangements Jared had made for his wife's funeral. Byela's priestess released only one white dove over her coffin, not the cloud of them that had taken the soul of the children's grandfather to the heavens the year before. The only mourners were the children and inn servants; Jared was shut up in the tiny room that served as his late wife's office with Gilar, who could read, helping him make sense of the ledger books.

From the graveyard Farris went straight to the stables and his own room. He checked over the pitifully small sack of coins hidden under his mattress, then wearily pulled on his working clothes. The horses in his charge still needed care, even if his world had collapsed around him.

The familiar work gave him plenty of time to think. If Jared threw them out his money would last the two of them for perhaps three weeks. They would not be fourteen until late next month, and could not legally sign a work contract until then, not without a parent's approval. He would be damned if Jared could drive him to beg in the streets, or take the charity of one of the temples.

Maybe . . . Rykard. Maybe his swordmaster could help. He'd ask tomorrow at his lesson. Rykard could give him a recommendation to the City Guard. He was too small, he suspected, even for a green recruit, though he would soon legally be an adult. But surely they could use a tyro, someone in training to take care of the horses and polish the armor and do other things like that, until he hit his growth spurt.

But Jared made no effort at first to evict his stepchildren. Whether it was fear at the loss of outraged customers, or his realization that their work was valuable, Farris didn't know. The days dragged on.

Very late one afternoon in the middle of the month, three men rode into the yard, and Farris went to take their horses. "Just tie them, boy," said the one who, from his clothes and badge of office, seemed to be a magistrates' official. The other two appeared to be merchants. "We'll be here only a short while. Where would I find a man called Jared?''

"In the common room, sir.'' Farris gestured to the big main doors. "Right through the doors there. If he's not, ask one of the servants.''

He gazed after them in puzzlement, wondering if there was something wrong with Jared's claim to the inn. If so, he needed to find out about it. But how?

Amethyst. He couldn't spy on them from the stable, but Amethyst could.

Farris tied the horses in reach of the watering trough, then slipped through the side door into the kitchen. "Beka, where's Amethyst?''

The kitchenmaid rubbed a smudge of flour off her cheek and nodded to the door to the office. "Some high-and-mighty visitors wandered in asking for Jared. Amethyst took them some cakes and wine.''

Good, so his spy was in place already. "Tell her I want to know what they talked about, Beka. Have her meet me in my room after supper. I've got to leave now. My sword-master will skin me alive if I'm late.''

Amethyst poured out the wine slowly and carefully. Let them think that she was clumsy or nervous, let them think anything just so long as they let her stay and find out what they wanted.

"Well, innkeeper Jared?'' the magistrate's representative said. "These gentlemen have legitimate debts to collect against you, and you have put them off again and again, asking for more time. Did this recent inheritance allow you to come into any more cash?''

"No,'' Jared mumbled. Amethyst could tell that he was half-drunk already.

"But the inn and its contents are yours now?''

"Yeah, she left me everything. Her will is in that box there, if you don't believe me.''

"We have no reason to disbelieve you at this point,'' said one of the merchants dryly. "But the fact is that you gambled with money you didn't have, and we want our debts repaid *now*.''

"If you cannot raise the cash any other way, you can always sell this inn. It appears to be a rather valuable property, worth far more than the amounts you owe, and that would leave you enough cash to settle somewhere else," pointed out the magistrate's man.

"And what if I don't want to sell out?" Jared demanded belligerently.

"Then the law has the power to force the sale, or turn the inn over entirely to your creditors." The representative stood, followed by the merchants. "We will leave you to consider your options, and return in two days for your decision. Good day."

Amethyst tried to slip out after them, but Jared's hands snatching her braid stopped her. "Oh no, girl, you stay here. This is *her* fault, your bitch of a mother." She stood trembling in his hand, his anger clearly visible around him like a dark-red cloud. Nothing she could say would defend her mother.

Jared picked up an abandoned wine goblet, drained it in one swallow, and continued to rant. "Yeah, all her fault. This place was *mine* by right as her husband, and do you think *she* would let me run it the way it ought to be run? No, she was happy for it just to bring in bits and dribbles instead of the money it could have. And then she up and died on me, just to make things harder. No cook but a skinny little girl and her bastard brother. Can't even put you to work where you should be, you ugly little bitch, in the bedroom on your back. Not as much use as a slave."

She stared at him in mute terror, for the red aura of his anger was fading out as he stared at her, replaced by an ugly blackish-green, as ugly as his laugh.

"I'll teach that bitch mother of yours a lesson. You and the other little bastard are worth good money, too. You're mine now, legally mine, and I won't give up my inn. I'll sell *you* instead."

Farris slid into the darkened kitchen, hungry, tired, and discouraged. Rykard had been no help. The City Guard didn't take tyros, and as he had feared, he could not yet meet their height requirements. Worse, Rykard had told him that there would be no more swordsmanship lessons.

As Rykard explained it, he had come around for the drink that was his payment, and Jared had all but tossed him out. "A cadger, he called me, Farris! Said I couldn't mooch off him any longer. I'm sorry, boy, but I can't keep on teaching you for free. If I gave free lessons to you and word got around, soon nobody would pay me."

Farris must have let his face show his dismay, for the swordmaster had patted his shoulder in rough sympathy. "Ah now, lad, buck up. There's nothing much more I can teach you anyhow. It's just practice you'll need from now on. You'll hit your growth spurt soon, see if you don't, and then the City Guard will be fools if they don't snap you up. A left-handed swordsman like you is worth his weight in griffins."

The kitchen was dark, with only the fire to give any light. Amethyst was not in sight, nor were any of the servants. Was it that late? He had wandered down to the Grand Plaza and loitered there, trying to think what he could do next. He must have spent more time there than he thought.

The square of spicebread and the mug of milk were on the table just as his mother had always left them for him. Amethyst must have remembered and put them out for him. He ate with only half his attention on the food.

The mug of milk tasted bitter, but he drank it anyway. No use turning down *Jared's* food, in *Jared's* inn. He earned it with his own sweat, damn him, every mouthful!

Farris sat staring at the fire and brooding until a huge yawn made his jaws crack. So tired. The last few days must be catching up to him; he could fall asleep right here. He stumbled groggily through the yard and up to his room. Kicking off his boots was exhausting, and taking off his shirt even more so. He fell across the bed still wearing his breeches, too sleepy to pull up the blanket.

2

SLAVE

He dreamed. In his dreams two men came into his room just before daybreak. "He's waking up. Get that stuff down him, quick." Someone pried his mouth open and poured a thick, sticky syrup down his throat. He went back to sleep, and then dreamed again. Jared was in the room, and in the way of dreams it did not seem strange that he should be there. He pulled Farris to his feet and jerked his arms behind his back. Cords bit into his wrists as Jared tied his hands, and he thought about resisting him, but it was too much trouble.

Jared prodded him down the stairs and there was Amethyst with her hands tied, too. She was crying, held firmly in the grip of another man. "Farris, wake up, please, you've got to!" she cried before the man put his hand over her mouth.

Why was she crying? Dreams weren't anything to cry about.

He floated down the street, his bare feet barely touching the ground. Behind him he could hear his sister struggling to get away from the man. Silly Amethyst. Just let the dream end, and she would be all right.

Where in Ardesana were they? That was the fountain that

marked the Slaver's Quarter. Funny. He had never been here. How could he dream about somewhere he'd never been?

"Any particular place?" asked the man who was holding Amethyst.

Jared shrugged. "Start with the first one and take the best offer. In here, you."

The stone floor was cold on his feet after the warm dust of the street, and the room was dark after the sunlight. Voices boomed and whined around him, only some of the words making sense. "Free youngsters? . . . too old . . . if they were five years younger . . ."

Sunshine and shadow again, and yet again. He'd never had a dream go on this long, or felt one so real.

"Twins? They don't look it. Too bad, a matched pair would be worth my while. I'll give you fifty silvers for the boy, and eighty for the girl, if she's a virgin."

"You can't cheat me like that, slaver," Jared snarled. "I know what slaves cost. No sale."

The light on the street was even harsher this time. Farris blinked and shook his head. He'd never felt like this in a dream. Hot and cold, the rasp of the cords binding his wrists, the dazzle of harsh, hot summer sun on the whitewashed buildings—all of it was too real. Jared stopped and looked up at one building.

"This is the largest slave-dealer in the city," the other man said. "If he won't take them, I don't know who will."

As Jared pushed him through the door, Farris' toes banged against the doorsill. The pain exploded into his mind; as minor as it was, it was enough to bring him out of his daze.

Slave-dealer. It was real, then, not a dream. Jared's demands to see the proprietor were real, as was the heavyset man in the garb of a merchant who appeared.

"Yes, I handle adolescents. Thirteen? You are certain? I would have said the girl was fourteen, the boy twelve." The slave-dealer reached out and took Farris' head in both hands, twisting his face upward to look at his eyes. "This boy's been drugged."

"Easiest way to handle him. What sort of offer can you make me for them? The girl's a virgin."

"Hmm. Freeborn adolescents are a lot of trouble to break, especially boys. If you had to drug him to get him here . . ."

"I don't need to tell you your business, do I? He responds well enough to my belt. Give him a few lashes and he'll come around. Look at the girl again." Jared reached out and pulled the neck of her blouse down to expose one breast. "Pretty as they come. I tell you, I've had a time keeping my hands off her." He cupped the breast and teased the pink nipple with his thumb, then pulled the blouse back into place again.

How *dare* he do that to Farris' sister? She was no whore to be pawed over! Jared would die. Farris would kill him, slowly, and enjoy every moment of it. He held his body in check and concentrated on regaining proper use of it.

"Eighty silvers for the boy, one gold for the girl. Take it or leave it," the slaver said bluntly.

"What you take me for is a fool!" exploded Jared. "Slaves are worth five or six golds apiece!"

"Adults, yes, properly trained and broken. Children are cheaper, and you don't get full retail, you get wholesale. Nobody will give you any more."

"Three golds and fifty silvers for both of them," Jared insisted.

"One and ninety. Final offer."

As they bargained, Farris felt both strength and wits coming back to him. The grogginess that had made everything seem like a dream was wearing off.

Jared looked down at the two gold pieces that the slaver offered, and then back at his companion, who nodded grimly. "Next time don't gamble with borrowed money, Jared."

With a scowl, Jared picked up the coins and shoved them in his pocket.

The slaver smiled, not pleasantly. "Go with my scribe there, and he will take the information on the slaves and make you out a bill of sale. Good day. Jamus!"

A guardsman in the slaver's colors appeared, and took Farris' arm. With a knife, he severed the cords around his wrists, and eyed Amethyst with approval as he cut her hands free as well.

"Please, no!" she whispered as the same knife severed
the cord holding the amulet of Palona around her neck. "It
was my mother's—it's all that I've got."

"The Goddess of Childhood doesn't worry Herself about
slave-children," the slaver said dryly as the guardsman
tossed him the amulet.

Jared had wasted too much time dragging them from
slaver to slaver. The drug had nearly worn off by now. Farris
pretended that it was still working and allowed them to shove
him down a long, bare passageway. He could hear his sister
behind him, fighting back sobs.

They came to a room that should have looked more fright-
ening than it did. Muddy brown slave-tunics sat folded me-
ticulously on shelves, and black iron collars sat on others.
Slave-whips of various sorts hung neatly on pegs in the wall.

If they escaped, it must be now, then. Once they locked
those collars around their necks, it would be too late. Farris
dragged his head proudly erect and stared balefully at the
man who claimed to be his master. "We are *not* slaves!"
Amethyst echoed him a heartbeat later.

The slaver gave an exasperated sigh, muttered something
about "freeborns," and cast a significant look at the guard.
Both of them advanced slowly on Farris, ignoring Amethyst.

He stood his ground defiantly. If he could snatch the
guard's sword or dagger from its sheath, maybe he could
hold them off long enough for his sister to get away. They
wouldn't expect him to know anything about swordplay.

If he had been capable of his normal speed, his plan might
have worked. As it was, his fingers brushed the hilt of the
sword just as the guard backhanded him across the face. The
blow knocked him to the floor and the slaver stepped hastily
on his hand. Amethyst flew to her twin's rescue, but her
slight weight shoving him was of little consequence. She too
was slapped aside.

The slaver was a big man, with big hands. He reached
down to Farris, grabbed him by his free wrist, and as he
removed his foot deftly trapped the boy's other wrist in the
same hand. That left him with one hand free to fasten in
Farris' hair. He hauled him snarling and struggling to his

feet and pulled him belly-down across a table. "Look you, boy," the slaver growled. "The pair of you were slaves the moment your father took my money. Jamus, prove it."

Farris heard a shriek of rage from Amethyst, then lines of blazing pain streaked along his back. He continued to fight, the pain only spurring him on. This was no worse than Jared's belt on his back. That hadn't broken him, and neither would *this!*

"Well, boy?" the slaver challenged.

"Free!" Farris spat back.

"The twoblade, sir?" the guard's voice rumbled behind him.

"No. The four. I went easy on you at first, slave, because little boys can be foolish. Now you get a real lashing."

He did not hear the whistle of the lash in the air; he was fighting too hard and swearing too loudly. The four-bladed whip landed on his back with a stunning blow. Fire burst over his whole back, as if they had hit him with a burning log. The earlier blows of the other, lighter whip were nothing compared with this; this was sheer nightmarish agony. The lash fell again, and this time he could not bite back a scream.

The slaver must have released his wrists, for he found himself huddled on his knees, gasping for breath. It was too much. If they beat him any more he would die. *Let them kill me, then. Better to die free than live as a slave.* He forced his mouth to say the word, although it came out only a whisper. *"Free. . . ."*

"Again, sir?"

"No. The girl this time."

The girl this time. In his pain, the words did not have any meaning at first. Then he heard Amethyst's cry of terror and the rip of fabric as they tore off her blouse to bare her back. Farris made a convulsive move toward her and sank down again, fresh agony lancing through his lacerated back.

"Noooo!" This was no whisper, but a long, drawn-out cry of torment. No, not his sister, not Amethyst. Not his torture repeated on her fragile body. "No, *please!* I—yield."

Hands fastened in his hair again, jerking his face up to

meet the slaver's eyes. "Fighters yield, boy. Slaves submit to their masters. Do you?"

Anything, even submission for now, to save his sister. He could die later. "Yes."

"Yes, *what?*"

"Yes, I submit."

The slave dealer sighed again. "Jamus. The twoblade."

Both of them knew their jobs, knew just how much punishment a young human body could take. The guard reached out a long arm and picked up a smaller whip with only two blades, then applied it accurately to the boy's back. The lashes bit across the earlier ones at an angle. Farris made a strangled noise, halfway between a gasp and a scream, and his body jerked in a convulsion so strong that a chunk of his hair ripped away in the slaver's fist.

He had been wrong. His body could take a lot more pain without dying. What did they want? He had already submitted.

The slaver told him. "Say 'I submit, *master.*' A slave always gives his master his proper title."

Call these men "master" because they were bigger and stronger and could beat him? *Or they could beat Amethyst,* he thought. "I submit . . . master."

The slaver released Farris' hair and returned his attention to Amethyst. "You, girl. Finish stripping."

She stared at him mutely, her hands shielding her breasts, and blushed bright pink. The guardsman laughed. "A virgin, sir?"

"Supposed to be. If she is, she stays that way, Jamus. But anything else . . ." He shrugged indifferently. "Strip her and collar her. I expect she'll put the tunic on fast enough on her own."

Farris dropped his head and closed his eyes, and wished he could close his ears to his twin's muffled sobs. The rip again of fabric and the click of the collar locking around her neck were all too clear.

But the click of the collar locking on his own neck was not. Sight, sound, *everything* was swallowed up in a new wave of pain. Cold iron alone on his bare skin would have been painful but tolerable. On top of the pain from his lashing, it was not. He screamed again and fell to the floor, clawing desperately at the band of torturing pain around his throat.

"Bloody hell!" The slaver reached down and checked the fit of the collar on the convulsing boy's neck, then turned to the girl in the guardsman's arms. "Tell me the truth, girl. Is he fai?"

Her voice was only an agonized whisper as she watched her brother. "Yes, half-fai, m-master, both of us. *Please*, take it off him!"

He cursed viciously. "Damned weakling fai, if he dies on me, I'll have that bastard who sold him up before the magistrates so fast he won't know what hit him! Everyone knows they can't stand iron touching them. Jamus, leave the girl and take him to an isolation cell."

The guard obeyed, handling Farris with practiced ease. Amethyst bit her lip as she watched, her last sight of her brother, unconscious now, slung over the man's shoulder as he took him away.

"Poor child. Is this really necessary, Likarion?"

If the boy in the isolation cell had been awake to see the two deities looking down at him, he might have thought they were human. Then again, he might not, for they trembled on the very edge of visibility. The female shifted from something that might be woman to something that might almost be horse. The male's form wavered between that of an armored warrior and a sheet of flame.

"Since when do you concern yourself with human children, Ydona? 'The fire that melts butter hardens steel,' the humans say. This one must be strong if he is to be one of Mine. I wish to see what the forging does to him."

"He would not need to be warrior-steel to be one of Mine. He has the Gifts, even if they are not of Our giving," Ydona retorted.

"Then we will see what he makes of them."

• • •

Farris came awake slowly, sliding in and out of consciousness the way an otter plays in a quiet pool, barely breaking water and diving again beneath the surface. One rise took him too close, and he broke into full consciousness and a rush of pain. He tried to roll back beneath that quiet welcoming dark surface, where pain is only a dim memory and fear is nothing at all, but entry was denied him.

He lay still for some time, taking stock of his body. His back was stiff and horribly sore, and the band of pain that was the collar still burned. The collar—the collar that now marked him as slave. "Gods—Likarion, help me!" he whispered. "I can't be a slave! I'll die first."

"Then die, little weakling," a man's voice said. *"Let them break you. Worthless little half-breed bastard, not the warrior you thought you were. Can't take what defeated warriors have done for centuries. Can't take submitting to the lash and living through it, until your masters make that one little mistake that gives you your revenge."*

The words were in his head, but he wasn't thinking them. It was as if someone else was in there, speaking to him in tones of deepest disgust. The words burned deeper into his soul than the collar burned into his neck. *Revenge.* A wave of red anger swelled up and broke in his mind at the thought of revenge, and the backwash spread itself to his numb limbs.

Gasping with renewed pain as he moved, he levered himself up to a sitting position and looked around for the source of the voice. He was alone in a tiny cell of cold gray bricks and heavy bars. Was someone on the other side of the wall, or was it really in his head? *"No!"* he rasped. "I am not a weakling! I *can* take it, and *I will!"*

There was no answer, either from the voice or from anybody else.

3

LOARN

Once again Farris knelt in front of a new master. This man was tall and thin, with graying dark hair and a hawk's-beak nose over a thin mustache. A faintly dissatisfied expression spread over his face as he read over the sales papers. A frown wrinkled his brow as he finally looked at Farris.

"I am Stablemaster Roldan, in charge of all the Outside slaves and servants here in Loarn. Your name is Farris, and you are sixteen?"

"Yes, master."

"How long have you been a slave?"

"Almost three years, master." They hadn't been easy years. The evidence of that was plain to see on his back. It was heavily striped with scars, some of them just now fading to white lines, some plainly red though well-healed, and a few still welted, raw lash marks. The other scars, the ones on his soul, didn't show.

"Well, Farris, what experience do you have with horses that prompted the steward to buy you?"

"I worked at an inn stable from the time I was six, master.

My first master bought me to ride his racing horses, but I got too big in just a few months.''

"Too big? You can't be more than a hand over five feet tall."

Farris shrugged slightly without saying anything. There was no need to tell him he was short. He knew it every time he looked up at a bigger man.

"Go on."

"He sold me to a horse-dealer who traveled with the merchant caravans. I worked for him for more than two years, riding and driving his horses. He died in a bandit raid on the caravan, and his brother put me up for auction at the Beast-Fair."

As Farris reported his history, he covertly studied his new master. His face said that he was a stern but not cruel taskmaster. His hands were as rough and scarred as Farris' own, although the nails were better kept. Clearly he did not sit back and give orders while leaving all the work to underlings.

The stablemaster nodded. "So you have general stable and riding experience. The work you will do here will be somewhat different. Loarn is a breeding estate; we raise palfreys to satisfy the demands of the noble ladies of the kingdom. Besides doing usual stable work, you will be working with the brood mares and their foals, and if you show an aptitude for it, breaking the young stock. I prefer a smaller man such as you for that, so that my young animals are not injured by trying to carry too big a rider too soon."

Roldan shifted slightly in his chair, then ordered, "Stand up and strip, completely. I want to have a look at you." As Farris silently obeyed, he critically examined his back as well as generally looking over his body.

"Turn," the stablemaster directed. "You may put the breeches back on. Why were you beaten so often?"

"Master Brenen enjoyed beating his slaves when he was drunk." *And worse.* Farris forced his thoughts away from that track. Brenen was dead, roasting in the worst of the hells, if there was justice in the afterworlds. But Jared, now—*Jared* was still alive. Someday he would pay for every one of those scars, pay for every hour of pain and shame and suicidal despair.

"Hmm," Roldan said thoughtfully. "Not because of runaway attempts or troublemaking?"

"No, master." *I may be a slave, but I'm not stupid. Head shaved, collar locked on my neck so anybody who sees me knows I'm a slave—where could I run to? And troublemaking? When your master orders you to learn to fight, is that troublemaking?*

"Good. You don't look foolish enough to try something so useless as running. Now, I expect hard work from all my people, no slacking or excuses. You do and you'll feel the lash. But I like to think of myself as a fair man. Do your work well and stay out of trouble, and you won't need to be punished.

"Standard respect is expected of you at all times. You will call me Master Roldan and you normally need not kneel in my presence. You are the property of Duke Launart of Draksgard and his son Torkild. Loarn is the heir's holding, so you will see Lord Torkild much more often than you will His Grace. Unless you are trying to control a horse, you will kneel in the presence of either of them.

"Is there anything that I have said so far that you do not understand? If you have any questions about your work or what is expected of you, you have standing permission to ask me; I prefer intelligent questions beforehand to punishment afterward."

"No questions, master." Farris had questions, yes, but not ones that he was willing to ask the man who held lashing rights over his body.

Master Roldan nodded, and reaching out a long arm, opened a door in the wall. *"Kiam!"* he shouted.

A voice yelped back, "Yes, master!" closely followed by the body of another young slave.

"Farris, put your boots back on. Leave that old tunic. Kiam, take him around and get him settled in. Stores for a proper tunic, servant's hall, barracks. You know the routine. Both of you are dismissed."

Kiam was a year or so younger than Farris, with a thin

freckled face and bright blue eyes. His stubble of hair was bright coppery red. He was delicately boned, and small enough that he made Farris feel big and gawky for the first time in his life.

"Stores first," Kiam said. "Then we can go out by way of the kitchen and see if we can maybe cadge something to eat." At Farris' continued silence, he glanced at him out of the corner of his eyes and added quietly, "You don't need to be scared of Master Roldan. He is a fair master, just as he says."

"Who says I'm scared?" Farris asked belligerently.

"Nobody. But from the looks of your back you've had a hard time of it in the past."

Farris shrugged neutrally. This Kiam seemed friendly enough, but he wasn't willing to open up around him yet. Better find out the lay of the land first rather than make friendships too quickly.

Kiam ignored his indifference and dropped back half a step to walk at his elbow. "If you're going to be scared of anybody, be scared of *him.*" He motioned slightly with his head at another slave who was sweeping horse dung off the cobbles of the yard. "That's Lurkar. If you don't have a protector, he'll try to swive you, out of sheer meanness, just to make you cry. He likes to make young ones like us submit to him."

"He does, huh," Farris said softly. This was exactly the kind of thing he needed to know but wouldn't find out from the stablemaster. "Thanks for the warning. When? Where?"

"In the barracks, after they lock us in for the night. He doesn't dare try it anywhere else."

"No telling the masters?"

" 'Course not. You tell and you're asking for big trouble from everybody."

Farris grinned wickedly at him. "Good. He might find out he needs a protector from *me.*"

A "proper" tunic turned out to be rust-brown with a yellow stripe from each shoulder to the hem. In addition, the storesmistress thrust a coarse gray wool blanket into his arms. "That's the only one you'll get, boy, so don't lose it. You are dismissed."

In the kitchen it was obvious that Kiam was a favorite. The kitchenmistress readily granted him permission to take two chunks of slightly scorched spicebread but laughingly warned him to run along before they put him to work. The bread was sweet and spicy and still warm. As he continued to follow Kiam, Farris carefully savored every crumb of the first treat he had had in almost three years.

After he had licked his fingers clean, Farris asked, "Do you go all over like this all the time? What's your job?"

"I'm a dogboy. And since the dogs have to get used to going all over and being around people, I go everywhere, too. It's real useful to pick up all the gossip going around. The masters can't hardly sneeze without the whole castle knowing.

"This is our barracks. Throw your blanket on the pile with the rest of them. It won't matter if they get mixed up, they're all the same."

The barracks was a long, low-roofed stone building that turned a blank face to the yard. Inside bunks jutted from the wall, supported at intervals by posts. Straw for beds was piled both on them and under them. Several sets of shackles hung from large rings in the wall, and other empty rings were set at intervals.

"We're shackled at night?" Farris asked.

"Not usually. Only if you're really being punished for something. Master Roldan feels that locking us in is enough control. Why? Did your last master shackle you?"

"Sometimes," Farris said shortly. Maybe someday he could forget what Brenen had done when he'd shackled his slave.

Kiam led Farris through the whole stable compound after that. Hawkmews and kennels were closest to the gate, with stables next and byres, barns, and pigpens farther back, so as not to offend the delicate noses of the nobility.

He paid the most attention to the stables, of course, and the paddocks around them. There was also a large smooth grassy area for exercising the horses. At one end was a heavy

post with a crossbar at the top, just over Farris' head. Shackles swung at intervals along the bar. Kiam said nothing about
it. Farris didn't need to ask him; it was clear enough what
happened there, and to whom.

Since Roldan had not assigned Farris any duties yet, Kiam
eventually took him back to the kennels. They settled down
on the floor in front of one of the stall-like boxes where the
bitches had their litters. A very large hairy dog and her seven
puppies occupied this one. She jumped over the low barrier
that kept the puppies in and licked Kiam's face, waving her
tail happily.

As he took each puppy out to pet and play with it, Kiam
continued to chatter about Loarn, warning Farris of the hazards of life there as a slave.

A bell rang faintly. Kiam put the last puppy back in with
its anxious mother and scrambled to his feet. "That's the
first bell for supper. We need to get washed up. The Inside
steward doesn't like us coming in smelling like the animals."

In the barracks that night, the man Kiam had called Lurkar
didn't bother Farris. Whatever work he did, it appeared he
was too tired this night to bother anybody. He settled down
on a pile of straw across the room from Farris, next to another man, and the two of them exchanged a few quiet words,
occasionally glancing in the direction of Kiam and Farris.

The other man did approach them. "Want some company,
boys?"

Farris refused, saying "No," dismissively, and Kiam
scowled at him. "Leave both of us alone, Fedor."

"Haral's got enough to do to take care of you, boy. He
can't take on your new friend, too. Besides, that'd be self-
ish." Fedor ran his eyes over them in a way that made the
hair prickle on Farris' neck. It was the same greedy posses-
sive expression that Brenen had always worn when he forced
Farris to his knees.

"I said *no*," Farris growled, staring aggressively up at the
taller man.

"Feisty little gamecock, aren't you? Keep us in mind. You

may regret it later.'' Fedor turned and swaggered back to his own sleeping area.

Farris kept his eyes on both men as he braced both hands on the bunk behind him and pushed straight up. It wouldn't hurt to display his strength, he thought, although he suspected that their impression of him as a youngster who could be easily intimidated might be hard to shake.

He settled down in the straw so that he could keep an eye on them. Kiam sat next to him, his legs swinging over the edge of the bunk. ''Are you sure you want to sleep alone, Farris?'' he asked quietly. ''You can come down with me and Haral. I told you Lurkar's a mean one, and Fedor's almost as bad.''

''Not now, Kiam. If they think I need a protector it will be worse than trying to fight them off right now. And I can.''

Kiam said doubtfully, ''Well, if you're sure.'' He hopped down and disappeared out of sight under the bunks, presumably to his place with his protector Haral.

In spite of his assurances to Kiam, Farris watched the two across the room until he was sure they were asleep before he closed his own eyes.

He slept more deeply than he had intended. He woke to rough hands dragging him from the bunk. Two men were holding him so that his toes barely touched the floor. After his first instinctive movement of resistance, he went limp in their hands, simulating fear, and the tremor of his body convinced them.

''Damn you, Lurkar, you said I could use him first if I helped you,'' whined Fedor's voice in his ear.

''No time now. I'll help you with him tonight.'' Lurkar pushed him away and let Farris fall.

For Lurkar, it was the wrong move. As soon as Farris touched the floor fully, he lashed out in quick aggressive action. Lurkar doubled over, holding his belly and gasping. There was the sound of a snap and a yowl from Fedor, who stumbled back clutching at his broken wrist.

Lurkar lunged forward and grabbed one arm, trying to pull Farris off balance and force him to his knees. Farris twisted in his grasp and chopped at his restraining hand, jerking his arm free as something snapped. He lashed out again, stabbing with stiffened fingers at Lurkar's eyes. The bigger man screamed and clutched at his face as blood burst from between his fingers.

"Want any more, Lurkar?" Farris snarled.

"Not from you, boy," said a sharp voice from the doorway, and Farris whipped around to face this new threat. Master Roldan stood outlined against the light from the opening. "What's going on here?"

"Your new boy attacked us, master," Fedor whined. "We were just trying to be friendly, master, and he broke my wrist and poked Lurkar's eye out!"

Lurkar, his head down but still clutching at his eye, moaned out a loud agreement.

Farris, his face unreadable, said nothing. The blood on his hands told its own story, and he had no proof of what they had intended to do to him.

"Haral? What did you see?" snapped Roldan.

"They were trying to bully him, master." Haral's face was equally unreadable, as was his voice.

"It looks like he bullies better than they do. Kiam, run for the healer. You three stay. Everybody else, out."

The subdued slaves obeyed. When the others had gone, Roldan turned a cold eye on Farris. "Learn right now, slave, that any disagreements you have here you settle without damaging your master's property. These men won't be able to work today, but after your punishment you will."

Roldan did not delay punishment for the master's property either, Farris discovered. The ten lashes Roldan laid on his back were efficient, methodical, and painful, but over quickly. Then; ignoring his bloody wounds and stumbling walk, Roldan drove him to the morning lineup with the other slaves and issued them all with their orders for the day.

Kiam, at breakfast an hour later, complained on his behalf. "How come he didn't lash Lurkar and Fedor? They started it."

"Drop it, Kiam, and keep your voice down," Haral ordered quietly. "You know what we'll all get if you bring

Master Roldan down on top of us. He probably figured that what Farris did to them was punishment enough. I heard the healer say that Lurkar's lost that eye.''

"Good," Kiam muttered, and spooned up the last of his porridge. "Hey Farris, aren't you going to eat?"

Farris shook his head and pushed his scarcely touched bowl toward the younger slave. If he ate anything now, it would likely come back up, and his back hurt enough without adding the convulsions of vomiting to it.

In spite of his pain, though, he felt a heady sense of triumph. He could hold his own here, and *nobody* could force him to submit that way again!

That night in the barracks, Roldan shackled all three fighters from the morning as further punishment.

Kiam watched him closely, noticing the barely perceptible flinch when the shackles closed about his new friend's wrists. With his eyes down but his chin stuck out stubbornly, he slid over and dropped to his knees in front of Roldan. "Please, Master Roldan, may I speak?"

Roldan looked at him sharply. Kiam was a favorite with almost everybody, free and slave, but shrewdly made little use of it. "Go on."

"Please, master, don't shackle Farris like that. If someone else tries to bully him, he can't protect himself."

"Oh? And should I leave him loose to practice his own kind of bullying?" Nevertheless, the stablemaster looked thoughtfully around the barracks at the other slaves. "But you may be right, boy. Go in the tack room and get me that long piece of light chain and a small padlock."

He released Farris from the shackles and knelt him at one of the empty wall-rings. When Kiam returned with the items he had ordered, he looped the chain through the wall-ring and locked it to the ring on Farris' collar. "There, Kiam, does that make you happy?"

As soon as Roldan had gone, Lurkar started blustering. "When I get out of these shackles, boy, you'd better watch out. I'll get you for this, and Fedor isn't too happy, either."

"I'm scared, Lurkar, I'm real scared," Farris sneered.

With an assertive eye he measured the distance to the nearest
bunk-support post. The chain was long enough to let him lie
down comfortably; it should be long enough, and there was
just enough light left to make things out. "You and Fedor
just sit there and watch what I'll do to you if you touch me
or anybody else again.

"Kiam, move away from that post. I don't want to hurt
you. You see that post, Lurkar? That's your back." A swift
chopping blow of his left hand connected squarely with the
post. There was a sharp *crack* as it splintered and broke, and
the section of bunk it supported sagged a little.

"Choose right now, Lurkar. Your other eye, your back,
or your neck. I can kill a man that way; do you want to be
my first kill? How about you, Fedor? Are you volunteering
also? Maybe I should just rip your balls off and stuff them
down your throat. It's worth a lashing to me to take you two
out."

"Believe him, and leave him alone," Haral growled.
"We're all tired of your threats. I'll let him kill you and help
him cover it up afterward."

"Me too," Kiam said fiercely, and other slaves muttered
agreement.

Lurkar and Fedor subsided, mumbling vague threats. Neither was willing to admit that the balance of power in the
barracks had just shifted with the appearance of this aggressive young fighter.

Farris ignored them and turned to his own bed, trying to
find some way to use the blanket without letting it touch his
back. Kiam appeared to be about to offer to help him, but
joined Haral in their own pile of straw three places down at
the other slave's signal.

He was nearly asleep in the darkness when an odd noise
broke into his drowsiness. That soft protesting squeak had
surely come from Kiam, and now there was a deeper laugh
from Haral. Their voices were too low to make out words,
but the sounds that followed were unmistakable.

So that was what a protector was, a man who defended
you against gang rape so that he could use you himself.

As Kiam's soft moans became louder, Farris grew tenser.

Kiam was his friend, the only one here who had been friendly; Kiam had just tried his best to help him. How could he just lie there and do nothing? Haral was not their master, and he had no right to use Kiam like that. Finally he couldn't stand it any longer and came to his feet with a jangle of chain. "Haral!" he growled. "Leave him *alone!*"

Haral's voice was a growl, too. *"I'm* his protector, little gamecock, and that means I'll protect him from you, too. You think you can swagger in here and just take anything you want?"

"N-no, wait, Haral. I d-don't think he meant anything like that." Kiam's voice was muffled and shaky. "Farris?"

"I meant exactly what I said. I won't listen to Haral rape you any more than I'll let someone do it to me."

To his astonishment, Kiam laughed softly. "Turn me loose, Haral, and clear everybody out of this end. I want to talk to Farris in private."

Haral growled again but from the sounds complied; Farris could hear sleepy grumbles as small bare feet padded toward him. Kiam's body radiated heat as he pulled Farris back down onto his bed and sat next to him. His voice was low as he said, "He wasn't raping me, Farris. We both enjoy what we do for each other." He waited a few heartbeats longer, listening as if to make sure they had as much privacy as possible, then whispered in Farris' ear, "But I think some-one must have raped you, maybe your last master? And that's why you fought like that this morning, and challenged Haral just now, isn't it?"

Farris said nothing. He would never tell anybody how Bre-nen had used him, or of the merciless beatings beforehand that had intensified his master's pleasure.

"It's all right, Farris. I'll explain to Haral. I don't want the two of you to be enemies. But please, believe me." Kiam's voice was soft, but full of affection. "It's different when you . . . when you care about each other."

"He was hurting you, and you *like* it?"

Kiam chuckled softly. "I guess it must have sounded like it to you, but I wasn't being hurt. I'm always noisy."

"I'll gag him with his own tunic next time," said Haral's

deep voice out of the darkness. "Come on back to bed, Kiam."

"Kiam?" asked another voice. "Nobody will be able to sleep for a while now. Will you sing for us?" Other voices murmured approval of that idea, too.

"I guess I can. What do you want?"

"Briunal's song," said Haral.

Kiam hummed softly for a few notes, then began to sing, and Farris knew why the young man next to him was such an obvious favorite. Kiam could *sing*. Oh, anybody could sing in the ordinary way, he did himself at times, but Kiam's voice was the most beautiful clear pure tone he had ever heard.

The song was one that he had never heard before. It told of the slave Briunal over a hundred years ago, trained to fight with sword and dagger for the pleasure of his masters. Matched with another fighter in the pit of sand, he had rebelled and killed the lords assembled to watch them fight to the death. The song went on to tell of their escape, the spread of the rebellion, how their masters walked in fear and learned, in the words of the repeated chorus, that "by no man could they be controlled."

It told, too, of Briunal's capture and cruel death, and the suppression of the uprising. But even Briunal's death could not kill the rebellion that lived in slave hearts, for the last verse promised,

> *And slaves we'll not be, says Briunal's ghost*
> *For he is a hero so bold*
> *Our masters will die, for mercy they'll cry*
> *And by no man shall we be controlled*
> *Aye, and by no man shall we be controlled.*

4

---❖---

YDONA

Farris was beginning to think that being a slave at Loarn might not be so bad, when one day Duke Launart swept down on the castle with all his household in tow. All the servants and slaves assembled while their lord and master addressed them.

The duke surveyed his domain and his people, their faces pleased or wary or carefully blank, and smiled benignly down on them.

"All of you know my son and heir, Lord Torkild." Launart indicated the lordling standing next to him, a haughty smile on his young face. "He comes of age this week, and takes the reins of his beginning responsibilities. When he has been dedicated as an adult, he will be your lord, not I. You will witness this, for he will be dedicated here on his own estate, as it has always been and will ever be."

Torkild stepped arrogantly forward and, as they had been coached, his people broke into cheers. Farris had never felt less like cheering. This cocky brat might be his master, but he didn't have to like it.

He liked it even less when he heard the details of the dedication ceremony. Not only would Duke Launart's household be invading the quiet of Loarn, but delegations of other lords and ladies would be guests to celebrate Torkild's dedication as well.

Rumor said that even the king would be there. Not King Tiorbran; even slaves had heard of the battle almost three years ago that had ended in the deaths of both Crown Prince Gardomir and Tiorbran himself. The old king's second son, Alnikhias, sat on the Griffin Throne now.

Priests of the many gods and goddesses would come, too. The son and heir of a duke did not go as supplicant to them, as if he were a peasant. They would come to him.

Long ago the gods had decreed that when a child became an adult, he must draw one of the lottery-stones from the Bowl of the Gods, each marked with the name of a god or goddess. The deity who would be his patron would guide his hand to the correct stone, revealing that name for all to see.

When a day dawned bright and clear and the priests determined that the omens were good, Launart ceremonially elevated Lord Torkild to his rank of heir and dedicated him to the gods as an adult. Important guests sat where they could observe the rites in comfort. Servants and slaves stood behind them to watch, except Farris and Kiam. They had work to do.

Torkild, as expected, drew the name of Likarion, God of Warriors. The sacrifice Launart dedicated for him was not the dove or lamb of a peasant, but one each of Loarn's finest mares and fierce hunting dogs.

It was too much to ask that free servants should handle the creatures; that was why the gods made slaves. Farris and Kiam, as the animal-handlers closest in age to the new lord, were conscripted for this important duty. Freshly bathed and shaved and wearing stiff new tunics in Launart's colors of rust-brown and gold, they stood to one side holding lead-rein and leash. Farris was relieved that the sacrifice did not include killing the animals; Loarn horses and dogs were much too valuable. Instead the priests of Likarion would sell them later. For now, they merely clipped a lock of hair from each animal to burn symbolically as sacrifice.

Lord Torkild, too, would provide part of the burnt offering. Officially his first shave was the one the priest was now giving to him; such beard fuzz as could be collected was burned in the same sacred fire.

As they stood and listened to the prayers offered up to Likarion during this part of the ceremony, Kiam nudged Farris. "Hey, Farris, what did they say when you got your first shave?" he whispered.

Farris muffled a snort. "They said, 'Hold still, slave, unless you *want* your throat cut.'"

"I wouldn't have let them do that," whispered a woman's voice in his other ear. He threw a startled glance to his right. The white mare blew through her nose and winked at him. In front of his eyes, her form shimmered as if he looked through a summer heat wave. No. It couldn't be. There was not a woman at his side, a woman with long silver-white hair as coarse as a horse's mane.

But his eyes insisted there was such a woman, his nose caught the fragrance of perfume instead of mare, and his hand felt the pressure of a firm warm palm and fingers instead of a lead-rein. She smiled at him, slowly and seductively.

"Well?" she murmured. *"Do you know Me, Farris?"*

"I know . . . what I think I see, mistress." He didn't speak aloud—the sudden dryness of his mouth would have prevented it even if he had wanted to, but she seemed to understand him nevertheless. "You are . . . if you are really here, and I am still sane, a goddess."

Her mouth twitched in a stifled laugh. *"I shouldn't tease you mortals, but it's such fun. Know, My child, I am Ydona, Lady of Horses and Mother of Mares, and today I claim you for Mine."* She ran a fingertip over his right shoulder and down his arm; a stinging sharp pain followed in its wake.

He restrained the urge to go to his knees. If he was feverish and dreaming, he wouldn't be able to control the mare that was really there instead of this woman. "Yours, my Lady? But I'm a slave."

"My son, not My slave," she corrected with a smile.

"You have always been Mine. You care for My horse-children as I do Myself. And I had a good deal to do to claim you. Likarion wants you, too, a great deal more than he wants that silly Torkild. Perhaps it is fortunate for Me that He is always willing to gamble."

The deities *gambled?* Could he, with this woman? Even from a goddess, he wouldn't beg. "If I am Yours, my Lady, why am I a slave? Likarion wouldn't leave one of His own like this. What must I do to earn Your help?"

"Help yourself." Her eyes were enormous, dark, and long-lashed. They filled all his vision as She began to laugh; then the world shimmered again and Her laugh became a whinny. A white mare stood beside him on the end of the rein.

Nobody appeared to have noticed anything. Kiam still had his eyes fixed on the figures of their young master and the priest of Likarion. Farris dragged his own eyes back to the ceremony also.

The warrior-priest finished his invocation with the words, "God of Warriors, accept this, your new son." He lifted a slim wand of metal from the brazier where it had been resting throughout the ceremony; the tip, cast in the shape of a tiny sword, glowed cherry red. As the acolyte held Torkild's wrist and elbow firmly, the priest pressed the iron to the lordling's upper arm, just below the shoulder. It sizzled briefly before he yanked it away. Torkild did not move or make a sound.

Farris grudgingly admitted to himself that he didn't know if he could have taken branding unflinchingly, and he wondered if they had drugged Torkild. But his responses had been clearly spoken; he wasn't mind-fuzzed, it seemed. "More guts than I gave him credit for," he whispered to Kiam.

Kiam snorted softly. "They numbed his arm with wound-salve. He'll hurt worse later, doing it that way, but they couldn't risk having him faint."

Farris' own arm hurt where the goddess had touched him, but it must be his own imagination that it burned. She had scratched him, that was all. He surrendered the lead-rein of the white mare to an acolyte as the priest led the new "warrior-lord" in procession to his new holding. The nobility and free servants followed, heading for the feast prepared in celebration, and the slaves returned to their work.

As soon as he could, Farris looked at his own right arm. A handspan below the shoulder was a mark burned into his flesh; there, small as a woman's fingernail, deep and black, was the hoofprint that was the symbol of Ydona.

3

VIVEKA

Year 417 D.S.: Eighteenth day of the month of Treebloom

Out of long habit Farris woke well before the clang of the bell that announced morning to the castle. His dreams that morning had not been nightmares, but deeply satisfying ones. At least, in sleep they had been satisfying; Jared ran before him whimpering in terror as Farris rode him down to take his revenge. He dropped to his knees and begged for mercy, but Farris' sword took his head off. As it rolled along the ground spraying blood, Amethyst ran from the woods, reaching out to hug him. Just as her hands touched him, he'd awakened. He always did, in these dreams, and every time the loss of his twin was for a moment as sharply painful as if it had happened yesterday.

And at that, dreams of losing her again were easier than the ones that haunted all too many nights. Those dreams—nightmares of Amethyst stripped naked, raped, lashed as he himself had been, or worse—only strengthened his bone-deep hunger for revenge. During the day he forced himself not to think of his sister, not to imagine what might be happening to her. It hurt too much otherwise. It was easier to imagine what he would do to Jared someday.

No point now trying to go back to sleep. Get some exercise, before Roldan comes in. Farris slid out of his bunk and padded across the barracks floor to nudge Kiam's bare foot with his own. The younger slave raised his head sleepily, smiled at him, and carefully disentangled himself from Haral's embrace.

"Love" was not a word used in the barracks, but everyone knew that Kiam and Haral meant more to each other than just sex partners. Alone among the male slaves, only the two of them never talked about women or plotted some way to engage the interest of one or another of the female slaves. Their relationship was enough; at times Farris wondered if they thought of themselves as "married," and even envied them. His intimacies with girls were brief and infrequent, and any kind of permanent relationship was impossible, but Kiam and Haral had each other.

Both young men stretched and began to run through warm-up exercises, then faced off and began a slow-motion fighting that looked like dancing. Kiam had asked for fighting lessons shortly after Farris started exercising alone in the barracks; those lessons had cemented their friendship.

Farris went flying over Kiam's shoulder just as Master Roldan unlocked the barracks door. He also had watched their fighting with a suspicious eye, but did not forbid it. They were first out the door and continued their mock battle as Roldan herded the other slaves into the morning lineup.

"I'm happy to see that the two of you have so much energy," the stablemaster said somewhat sourly. "Maybe you can put it to your work instead of playing."

Farris was working, counting out scoops of grain, when a woman's voice broke into his concentration.

"You there, stableboy, I want my horse brought out immediately," she said imperiously.

He ducked his head as he turned, seeing in a single sweeping glance a small blonde figure in a heavily embroidered white blouse and full blue riding skirt.

"Yes, mistress?" Farris stared at the floor in front of the girl's feet. He had learned quite painfully that some free women objected more to a male slave's eyes on their bodies than on their faces.

"I want my horse, slave," she snapped impatiently, and lightly slapped her own palm several times with her riding whip.

He pretended to flinch and said hastily, "Yes, mistress, of course. If you would tell me, please, which one is yours?"

Instead of answering, she looked at him in a way that reminded him uneasily of being on the block again, a slow, deliberate survey of his body from head to foot and back again to his bowed head.

"You want to look at me, slave-boy?" she said mockingly. "I give you permission—no, I *order* you to look at my face."

He did as he was ordered. She was tiny, shorter than Farris by more than a handspan, with a dainty oval face narrowing to a pointed chin, and slanted pale blue eyes framed by long, straight, pale blonde hair. She would have been prettier without the sly, speculative look on her face.

"Well, slave, do you like what you see? I suppose—" She broke off abruptly, her face twisting into a scowl before she composed it into empty-headed prettiness. Farris heard with relief other voices and footsteps, the young master's voice among them calling a woman's name, Viveka.

The woman stepped away from him toward the doorway, calling out briefly, "I'm here, Torkild." She tipped her head back to give that young lord a coquettish smile as he came to her side, sliding her hand into the crook of his elbow. Farris, in the presence of his master, dropped reluctantly to his knees.

"Why on earth do you tolerate such stupid stable slaves, my lord? This one doesn't know which horse is mine! He ought to be punished."

The lord laughed indulgently at her. "My dear, we can't punish a whole estate full of servants for not knowing about all of your whims immediately. You, boy, what's your name?"

"Farris, master." *I've been here four years, and you still don't know my name? Is that an indication of my insignificance, or your lack of intelligence?*

"Well, Farris, this is my cousin Lady Viveka, and if our fathers agree, soon to be my wife." Torkild patted her hand and gave the young lady a grin that was even more moronic than usual. "She rides the little palomino mare that matches her beauty. You will know that next time, won't you? Now go fetch it around."

"Yes, master," Farris assured him as he bounced to his feet to obey. Oh, yes, he knew that mare. She had come into the stables the week before when the guests arrived, and had been troublesome ever since. She was hard-mouthed and skittish, quick to try to bite him, and even quicker to kick at him. If horses reflected their riders, he wanted nothing more to do with either mare or girl.

Slaves seldom got their wishes, so Farris was not surprised that during that spring and summer the Lady Viveka became the major irritant in his life, worse in her own way than the constant bite of his collar. Sometimes he came to believe that she spent every spare moment of her time persecuting him, although the gossip he had from Kiam assured him this wasn't so. She spent time bedeviling everybody, from the bath-slave who didn't have the water the right temperature to the mercenary guardsmen who were insufficiently respectful.

But in the weeks that followed, Lady Viveka did seem to have a particular appetite for stirring up trouble at the kennels, hawkmews, and stables, with special spite reserved for Farris. Somehow she seemed to know when Roldan assigned him ordinary stable duties, and she started to demand to inspect his work on her horse and gear, picking and finding fault where none existed—she didn't like the grooming job he had done on her horse, or her saddle had a speck of muck on it. The stablemaster listened with growing irritation of his own, attempted to soothe her ruffled feathers by promising to discipline Farris, and ignored her as much as possible.

And still her visit went on through spring and summer and

Harvest Fair, until the bright leaves of autumn and the swans migrating overhead told Farris that he had lost another summer of his life to slavery.

Autumn winds were whirling dry leaves about when she stepped up her campaign. One brisk morning she said, "It's too windy out there. I don't want to walk out to the mounting block. Help me into the saddle."

Farris murmured a quiet "As you wish, mistress," and laced his fingers into a stirrup for her to set her foot in. As he lifted to boost her up to the saddle, the mare turned her head and nipped him sharply on the buttocks. He jerked slightly, more with surprise than pain, causing the girl to slip and come down with a bump into the saddle.

She gave a little shriek of outrage. "You clumsy idiot, how *dare* you drop me like that? Torkild! *Torkild!*"

Both Lord Torkild and Roldan appeared, drawn by her cries. Farris tried to explain to Roldan but Viveka drowned him out with her shrill complaint. "I want that slave punished, Torkild. He's insolent and deliberately clumsy. First he insisted he would help me onto my horse and then he dropped me so hard I'll be all over bruises for a week!"

"Of course, my dear," the young lord soothed her. "You needn't worry yourself over a stableboy, after all. Roldan, I want this boy given a dozen lashes."

Viveka's face darkened. "Oh, *no,* Torkild, I've complained about him any number of times and it hasn't done any good. I think your stablemaster is letting him off without any punishment at all." She looked down at her horse's mane and allowed her lower lip to tremble, then gazed appealingly at her cousin. "Please, Torkild, make sure he gets those lashes. Do it yourself . . . please? For me?"

He caught her hand and gently kissed the fingertips. "Let it be as you wish, my love. Roldan, see that all of the stablehands and Outside people are assembled after their noon meal. I want them to witness his punishment, and I want him confined until then, so he doesn't try to hide. My lady, shall we go now? Even a short ride will be better than none."

Farris could see the muscle twitching in Roldan's jaw as the stablemaster grasped him by the upper arm and hustled him off toward the barracks. When they were out of earshot, Roldan turned back to Farris. "Dammit, I'm sorry, Farris, but you're in for it now. She's right, I have been letting you off because I know the quality of work you do and that she's got no real cause for complaint. I've been trying to protect all of my people from that conniving little bitch, so now she's going over my head."

He looked for a moment in the direction the riding party had gone and added, almost to himself, "Gods help us all if she becomes lady here."

Farris heard himself saying, in a quiet, bitter voice, "Gods don't help slaves, Master Roldan. I know."

"I suppose you do, boy. I suppose you do," muttered Roldan as he locked shackles on Farris and turned away to his own work.

Farris had never heard the stablemaster apologize to a slave before, nor had he realized that Roldan tried to protect them from the whims of the highborn nobles they all served. After all, he handed out enough punishments himself if he caught any of them slacking!

He mulled it over as he settled himself into a bed. One of the first things he had learned in his life as a slave was "never turn down a chance to eat or sleep," and what else could he do, locked up like this?

6

———◆———

GAULT

A voice hissing his name woke him sometime later. "Farris! Damn you, wake up and take this before I get caught." Kiam handed Farris a waterskin and a chunk of dry bread.

Farris bit off a mouthful, washed it down with two or three swallows of water, and handed it back. "Thanks, Kiam. You eat the rest of it. I don't want that much in my belly now. Last time Roldan lashed me, I puked my guts out."

Kiam grinned at him wryly. "Neither of us would have puked if they hadn't caught us stuffing ourselves with stolen peaches. When was that, two, three years ago?"

Boots rang on the cobbles outside. "Go! He's coming."

To his surprise Roldan was not alone. The other man was Gault, a mercenary from the warband hired as castle guard. He was about ten years older than Farris, more than a head taller, and at least half again his weight. Farris allowed himself a moment of private amusement behind his impassive slave-face. So the lordling thought he was that dangerous a slave, did he? If he had wanted to resist, how many mercenaries would it really take to drag him out to the whipping post?

Gault looked soberly at him as Roldan unlocked the chain

and he stripped off his tunic. "What did you do to get Her Ladyship in such a cat-haired snit, Farris? Forget to kiss the ground she walks on?"

"Dropped her on her little arse, sir," Farris said briefly. He knew Gault well enough to know that the mercenary, like most mercenaries, did not like to be called "master." Gault preferred to tend to his horse himself, so they had often worked side by side. Over the last year the mercenary's gruff friendliness had broken through Farris' wariness of a free guardsman, and they had established a cautious friendship.

"Here, take this." Gault handed him a small scrap of soft leather. "Something to bite down on helps, I hear. And I don't like what I'm about to do, but it's orders straight from the lordling. You're left-handed, aren't you? Turn your back and give me your left arm." With a quick, practiced twist he bent Farris' arm at the elbow and shoved the slave's fist up between his shoulder blades.

They marched him out to the exercise yard where the whipping post stood. Gault maintained the pressure on Farris' arm until the shackle snapped shut on his right wrist.

It was hot from the sun, but the pain from it went deeper, into the bone and shooting down his arm. He battled the urge to fight before they locked iron on his left wrist as well, bit down hard on the scrap of leather, and allowed them to do what they would. It would look like cowardice, like fear of the lash, if he resisted now.

In its way the leather slave-hood that Roldan jerked over his head was a relief. Under the hood, he didn't have to discipline his face into its stoic mask.

Sweat prickled on his forehead and back and streaked down his sides. The silence from the assembled slaves behind him was almost palpable. Then a soft sound, like wind over a wheatfield, moved through them. The lords and masters were here. *She* was here, watching with pleasure.

"This is what happens to a slave that is disobedient and insolent," Torkild said contemptuously.

How would you feel, Torkild, shackled to a whipping post? Farris thought with hatred. The lash whistled through the air;

the pain in his wrists was drowned momentarily in the lines of white fire on his back. One.

Does it make you feel your power, to know you can whip me? The lash whistled and struck again. Two.

Just like that shit-headed lordling to use the fourblade. Three.

Was *she* enjoying the sight of blood running down his back? *Vicious little bitch.* Four.

Get you under the lash, little bitch. Do you bleed red, too? Five.

You too, Torkild. Revenge, someday. Six.

He found another use for the leather in his mouth; it helped stifle any noises that tried to come out. *Thanks, Gault.* Seven.

Red and black clouds swirled in front of him now in the darkness of the hood, and a sudden streaking of bright white stars landed on his back to burn like coals. Eight.

Those black clouds grew thicker. *No. Take it. Won't pass out.* Nine.

Won't. Ten.

Eleven.

Twelve.

Even after they stripped the hood off, he was barely aware of someone unlocking one wrist. His arm dropped limply onto someone's shoulder. Gault. The other wrist. Kiam. *Guts, Kiam. Whip you, too.*

They eased him to the ground, belly-down in the cool, soft grass. He was left to lie there while the rest of the slaves filed past him for a good close look at what happened when they sufficiently displeased the masters the gods had chosen to set over them.

Gods help them all.

He spent the next day on a blanket-covered pile of straw in the barracks. Once Kiam managed to steal time to gently rub his back with an ointment he used on the dogs to prevent infection and speed healing.

Roldan put him to light duty the day after that, and he was contented enough to be set to clean and repair all the assorted pieces of harness, saddles, bridles, and other horse-gear.

Gault took to coming around to the stables often after his own duty shift was over. They talked of many things—or rather, Gault talked and Farris listened while he worked, for Gault was one of those who talked for the pleasure of hearing his own voice. But Farris found he enjoyed listening to Gault's bragging and stories of life as a mercenary. Battles and skirmishes vied with hell-raising, marching through the mud, and practical jokes as Gault made himself the hero of every saga. Sometimes Kiam brought over a puppy as part of his job as dogboy to get them used to many different people, and listened, too.

Gault watched one day in early winter as Farris carefully cleaned and polished a silver-mounted bridle set with jade and opals. "Fancy piece, that," the mercenary commented. "One of the lordling's pretties?"

"Yeah. Worth more than I am, probably."

"Probably," Kiam agreed as he looked up from where he sat on the floor, watching the puppy that Gault was teasing. "You're not worth very much, Farris. Sir, are you hurt?"

The mercenary looked ruefully at his bleeding finger where the puppy had just bitten it. "Fierce little bugger, isn't he? A little scratch like this isn't anything, boy. You should have seen me after Earl Duer's last wargames."

"Were you wounded, sir? I thought in wargames they used wooden swords," Kiam asked, wide-eyed at the thought of facing the steel of a real sword.

Gault grinned. "Oh, I got wounded all right, but not with steel. I wasn't fighting that day; you see, in wargames, some people are marshals to watch that the fighting is fair and nobody gets really hurt.

"Well, the earl is one of those who really cares about his fighting men, so he has slave-girls carrying water out to the battlefield. Or the woods, in my case. Now, the point of a forest battle is to find and capture the banners they have posted, and I was stationed out in the woods near one of them to marshal. I don't know what was going on in the rest

of the battle, but nobody came near me all day. It was just
me and five watergirls, out there all alone all afternoon.'' He
leaned back in his chair and chuckled reminiscently.

"So I had to let these poor girls do their jobs, so they
wouldn't get punished, right? They poured so much water
down me that I thought my back teeth would float away.
And when I went to take a piss to get rid of some of it, they
liked what they saw so much that they attacked me!''

Farris laughed. *"Five,* Gault? What did they do? Knock
you down and ravish you?''

Gault didn't answer, just laughed in his turn and looked
smug.

"How come we never get jobs like that, Farris?'' Kiam
complained.

"What, marshaling? Because we're slaves, beetlewits.''

"No, carrying water,'' Kiam retorted, and slid a coy
glance up at Gault, who looked startled.

"Are you still that pissed off at Haral, Kiam?'' Farris said
with amusement. Kiam and Haral seldom quarreled, but last
night had been a noisy exception; Kiam had abandoned their
bed-place to sleep next to Farris. "Ignore him, Gault. He
keeps trying to get *me* into bed with him, and it never
works.''

Kiam made a face at him. "Spoilsport. I slept with you
last night, and nothing happened but sleep.''

"So you're going after bigger game now?'' Farris grinned.

"Much bigger,'' Kiam agreed. "If the girls can go after
him directly, why can't I? Can I . . . *tempt* you, sir?'' He
stretched his body sensuously as he spoke.

"No. Boys aren't to my taste,'' Gault said curtly.

At his hostile tone, Kiam froze in mid-stretch. Lowering
his head submissively, he whispered, "I—I'm sorry, sir. I
didn't mean to make you angry.''

Farris glanced from Kiam's subdued, frightened face to
Gault's offended one and dropped to his knees next to his
friend. "Please, sir, don't punish him. It's my fault. I
shouldn't have goaded him.''

Gault looked at him sharply. "So you won't beg for mercy

for yourself, but you will for him, Farris? Is he your catamite, then?''

"No. Other men aren't to my taste, either. But he is my friend, and if you demand it, master, then yes, I will beg for him." Farris met the mercenary's eyes with wariness but no submissiveness. "I *do* beg for him. *Please,* sir!"

"Will you take his lashes for him, too?"

"No, he won't," Kiam said immediately, overlapping Farris' "yes." "I take my own lashes, sir." His eyes met Gault's too, then dropped as both slaves waited.

Gault looked at both of them thoughtfully. He'd never known that slaves could have that kind of loyalty to each other. His eyes lingered on Farris, on his knees defending his friend the only way he could. *Where does a slave get that kind of courage? He didn't flinch or beg when that damned soft-handed lordling lashed him, and yet he's willing to take another beating for his friend.* And if he, Gault, punished either one of them, the intriguing friendship between himself and this young man would end. *Oh, bloody hell, what did the boy do, after all? Just asked if I was interested.* "Ah, just don't do it again, Kiam. Now I've lost where I was in my story!"

Both slaves visibly relaxed. "Five insatiable slave-girls were ravishing you," Farris said helpfully. "And you never told us how you got wounded."

"They liked to bite!"

Kiam asked permission to take the puppy away a short time later. Clearly, he was uncomfortable now around Gault, and regretted his impulsive overture.

When he had gone, Gault asked, "Farris, why did he do that?"

Farris shrugged. "Don't know. He's slaveborn, and I can't always figure him out."

So. Another clue to that mystery. He's freeborn, or he wouldn't phrase it like that, Gault thought. The mercenary watched Farris lock the fancy bridle into a cabinet and take out a box of miscellaneous metal pieces, and a small piece of soft leather.

"Last stuff to do, and I'm all done with this job," he remarked. Gault watched idly as he used the leather to pick up an ornament and started polishing with the other hand.

"Push that metal polish over here, would you?" Gault drew his sword and reached for another rag as Farris nudged the polish pot more toward him. "Did I show you my new pretty?"

The sword in his hand was a thing of gleaming deadly beauty. Gault reversed it in his hand to show Farris the bronze pommel, cast in the shape of a stylized raven.

"Ahh, she's a beauty, Gault!" Farris whistled enviously. He was being a damned fool, he knew, but he wanted to hold that sword, to recapture just for a heartbeat the feeling that he was a swordsman and not a slave. That desire must have shown in his eyes, because Gault impulsively held it out to him.

"Go on, Farris, take a swing. There's nobody here but us, and I won't tell." He watched the lights flare briefly in Farris' eyes before the slave shuttered them behind a blank mask.

"I can't risk it, Gault. If someone walks in on me . . ." His voice was quiet and resigned.

"They can't if I lean against the door like this." Gault put the sword on the table and stepped over to put his back to the tack-room door.

Farris hesitated a heartbeat longer. The windows were set high in the walls, to provide light but lessen the risk of someone breaking in; nobody could look in to see him. And Gault meant it. If he wanted to get Farris in trouble, all he would have to do is say he saw him touching a sword.

Slowly he let his hand creep forward and close on the leather-wrapped hilt as he stood up. He raised the sword, drew it back past his head, and swung it carefully. The merest thread of "ahh" broke past his lips as he felt the perfect balance and play, so that it seemed almost as if the sword swung itself.

Gault watched him with a spark of astonishment. *Bloody hell! He's had sword-training!* he thought as Farris threw his body weight behind a slashing blow at an imaginary enemy, recovered to block an equally imaginary counterblow, and flowed smoothly into a lunging thrust. He'd expected an aimless amateur waving, just as likely to hurt the wielder as an opponent.

Farris crouched for a moment longer holding the sword as if his unseen foe held him at bay. Then with a sigh he forced himself to put it back on the table. "A little too long for me, but she is a beauty," he repeated. "Did she tell you her name yet?"

"Vessa. Wasp, in the old tongue. She's a Riazan, like me."

"Didn't think she was a northern blade. You southerners like fancier ones." Farris fell silent as he returned to his work.

Gault watched him, also silent for once as he considered asking how it happened that a slave had had sword-training. *No, best leave it. I've pushed his trust enough today over the business with Kiam.* Idly he wondered at the care Farris was taking to avoid touching the iron bit, and then remembered other times where he had avoided handling metal. Just now, for example; he had touched the leather wrapping on the hilt but not the sword itself. He could think of only one explanation for that.

"You're fai, aren't you?" he blurted.

Farris froze into tense stillness. "Half. How did you know?"

"Watching you not touch iron, and remembering that beating you got. When a man flinches and sweats when I put shackles on him and then takes a lashing like that without moving or making a sound, something's funny. And I knew a man who said he knew a fai warrior once, couldn't stand the touch of iron. Said it burned him.

"You can tell me to shut up if you want, Farris, but I was wondering, what about your collar?"

"Shut up, Gault." After a few moments he gruffly admitted, "It burns, like a sunburn. You get used to it."

"You keep quiet about it, don't you? Being fai, I mean. Why?"

It had been a mistake to swing that sword. All the yearning

for his lost freedom was back, as strong and as painful as it had been the first years of his bondage. Farris realized with bitterness that under Roldan's relatively easy mastership he had started to accept that his life must be as it was, that the idea of living out the rest of his years as a slave was becoming tolerable—and that the hunger for revenge against Jared was dying. The bitterness forced out his words in a flood.

"If I tell people, they expect me to do magic! 'Is it true you can understand animals' speech? Can you call fire out of the air or turn invisible? Have you ever bespelled anyone?' " he mimicked savagely. "Gods, if I could, do you think I'd be *here,* with a *slave-collar* on my neck? I'd be out free somewhere doing whatever I damn well pleased whenever I damn well wanted to do it."

"None of us is that free, Farris."

"Yeah. Sure, Gault." He clamped his mouth shut on the rest of what he wanted to say. He had said and done too much as it was.

7

FIGHTER

It was only a few weeks later, on the last night of Yearsend, that Gault swaggered into the stable common room. He was just drunk enough to be very, very happy, but not nearly as drunk as he intended to get.

"Here, Farris, have a coupla good slugs. 'S good wine, filched from the duke's own cellar. Me and my *sabros* been savin' it." He thrust a wineskin under Farris' nose.

Farris took it, squirted a short stream into his mouth to be polite, then tried to hand it back.

"Nonono, you take more'n that. 'S not even enough to get a buzz on."

"Thanks, Gault, but I can't get drunk. It's wasted on me."

"Whatcha mean, you can't get drunk? Not even the duke hisself tries to keep people sober at Yearsend. Or are you such a high-and-mighty slave you *won't* get drunk with a common, low-down mercernanaer . . . mercer . . . fighter?"

Farris sighed and gently eased Gault onto a bench. "I mean I can't get drunk. I've tried more than once, and it's like I'm drinking water. No buzz, no chasing dancing-girls around the table, no hangover, nothing."

"Are y'sure you got enough?"

"We stole a whole keg of wine last Yearsend and hid it in the barracks. After they locked us in, we took turns with it, and I matched them all drink for drink. Eventually everybody else was too drunk to move and I sat there stone cold sober." Then he grinned reflectively. "But it sure made for some interesting fights before they passed out. Kiam had Lurkar down and was pounding his head against the wall."

"Kiam? Lil' bitty Kiam had that big lunk down?"

"Kiam's one of the best fighters in the barracks. He's fast, and a lot stronger than he looks."

Gault mulled this over owlishly while he took another deep drink from his wineskin. "Huh. Wouldn'ta thought it 'f lil' Kiam. Who's the best, then?"

"I am."

"G'wan. I could take a little man like you apart with one hand."

Farris' face and voice went expressionless. "Yes, master, you could." *Damn. I should have known better than to brag around a drunk mercenary.*

"Don' give me that master shit. You know Free Mercenaries hate that. I wan' you t' try to take me on, jus' *try."*

"Is that a direct order, *master?"*

"You bet it is, *slave."* Gault lunged at Farris, swinging wildly. Somehow he found himself on his back with his nose hurting. He rolled over, pushed himself to all fours, and shook his head, spraying drops of blood. "You snuck up on me when I wasn' lookin'!"

Farris crouched in a fighter's stance in the middle of the floor, weight balanced easily and hands ready. A fey light flickered in his eyes and his mouth curled into a half-smile.

Gault lurched at him again. No, he couldn't be that drunk, to feel like he was wading in thick, sticky honey while Farris danced around him. The honey was slowing his swings, too, even the one he landed on Farris' eye.

Farris' hands flew out and tapped him lightly on the forearm. Pain shot up to Gault's elbow and he roared, lunging again at the slave who had somehow caused it. *I'm gonna bash 'is head in, break 'is neck, rip 'is arm off and beat 'im with the bloody end. . . .*

Funny, I didn't know I could fly. A wall appeared and interrupted this new experience. Gault slid down to the floor and sprawled there, thinking about it. *Now what was I doin'? Oh yeah, makin' Farris fight with me. Why?*

"What's all the noise about in here?"

Who'sat? Roldan, yeah, that's 'is name. Stablemaster. Won' be too happy to find one of 'is slaves fightin'. An'ts my fault. " 'S all right, Roldan. I think I fell down. Been drinkin', y'know," Gault mumbled.

Roldan looked sharply at him, then back at Farris standing tensely in the middle of the floor. He was fairly certain he knew just how Gault had "fallen down," but if the mercenary didn't want to complain about it, then that was his affair. "Are you hurt?"

"Arm's hurt. Feels like it's broken."

Roldan huffed with exasperation and checked the arm carefully. "I'm not feeling any bone ends, just a slight lump. Greenstick break, I think. Congratulations, Gault. We won't have to knock you on the head, just put a splint on it."

"Wait. Lemme get my wineskin."

"You don't need it. We don't have to set it, just splint it," explained Roldan with more than a little annoyance.

Gault watched the splinting with dazed eyes. Farris regarded him with some concern. He was a little sorry—but only a little—that he had had to get rough enough with the big mercenary to break his arm. It had felt good to do even this little bit of fighting. Maybe over this winter he should work out more with Kiam. As drunk as he was, Gault shouldn't have touched him at all, much less blacken his eye. "Gault, you don't look too good. Why don't you go back to your barracks and finish off that wineskin tomorrow?"

"Um, yeah, I'm not feelin' too good. I don' think I can make it back t' barracks. You got somewhere I could lie down here?"

Roldan motioned into the darkness. "You can sleep it off in one of the stalls over there. Farris, it's past lock-up time for you. Get moving. I've wasted enough time on the pair of you tonight!"

• • •

A horrible noise woke Gault the next morning, and a blinding light pierced his eyes when he inadvertently opened them. *I must have* really *gotten foxed last night. Where the hell am I?*

The hideous noise resolved itself into whistling and a soft scraping sound. He blinked cautiously and gradually the light became more bearable. It seemed that he was in a stall in the stable. He got gingerly to his feet, which fortunately still seemed to be attached (unlike his head, which threatened to fall off and roll away), and looked around.

Farris was three stalls down, grooming the occupant and whistling softly to himself. He was being closely supervised by a purring black-and-white cat who was sitting on the horse's rump. The slave grinned maliciously when he saw Gault. "So, the dead do walk! How does it go this morning, Gault?"

"I think . . . I don't remember how it's supposed to go," Gault said slowly. "What the hell happened last night? I know I didn't have a splint on my arm when I started celebrating."

Farris looked at him curiously, although the rhythm of his hands currying the horse never changed. "You really don't remember last night?" He disappeared as he crouched down to curry under the horse's belly. "Move over, Featherhead. How can I get your belly if you try to squeeze me against the wall?"

"Do you always talk to them like that?" asked Gault, momentarily distracted. He moved cautiously out of his own stall and to the end of the stall Farris was in so that he didn't have to talk to a disembodied voice.

"Usually. I've been trying not to disturb your peaceful slumbers."

"Arrrrr. Don't tell me you slept any better. Who gave you the black eye?"

The brushing rhythm abruptly stopped as Farris threw him a startled glance. "You did."

"Damn, I thought I just dreamed that we were fighting. I started it, didn't I?"

"Hell, yes! You said you could take me apart with one

hand, and I agreed with you. I'm not fool enough to start a fight with a free man, even if he is foxed out of his skull.''

"Bloody hell. I'm sorry, Farris. I must have been too drunk to think that it could get you in trouble.'' Gault shook his head and immediately wished he could undo the motion. It felt like his brain was sloshing around loose in there.

"I know. That's why I went easy on you,'' Farris said.

The mercenary stared at him in disbelief. "You *what?*''

"A greenstick break in one arm and a bloody nose is a lot less than I could have done. You've still got both eyes, don't you?''

"Both eyes?''

"Ask Lurkar sometime how he lost that one of his. And I was only sixteen then,''

"I don't think I want to ask, but I'll do it anyway. What did he try to do to you?'' Gault had a feeling that perhaps he was lucky at that. Over the last month it had become clear that Farris was not the quiet, subservient young man that he first appeared to be.

"I don't have a liking for rape, especially as the victim. Lurkar and Fedor thought I was young enough and small enough to be an easy lay.'' Farris' eyes glittered and his lips twisted wolfishly. "They found out different.''

So there was a fighter, a dangerous one, that lived behind the slave's often expressionless eyes. Gault had suspected before that Farris hid his emotions behind a blank mask and determined self-control. Now he understood the saying that a man has as many enemies as he has slaves, and the law that forbade edged weapons to slaves. What would this young man do with a naked sword in his hands?

The idea intrigued him. Best move cautiously, or he would chase the fighter back into the cover of the slave. "What happened then?''

Farris shrugged. "I got a lashing and Roldan chained us at night for a while.''

"Huh? They punished you for defending yourself?''

Farris glanced at him with a look that said he didn't know how anybody as old as Gault could be that ignorant. "No. I was punished for disabling them enough so they couldn't work the next day. Other than that, once that barracks door locks on us, our good kind masters don't care what we do to each other.''

"Oh. And that one fight made you the best in the whole barracks?"

"No, I fought everybody but Kiam and Haral one time or another. Most of the time it was just for the hell of it, you know? Not over anything at all.''

"You know, in the old days you'd've made a hell of a pit fighter.''

Farris gave a short bark of laughter. "Don't I wish! I hear they got treated better than some lordlings' wives. Pampering, good food, pretty slave-girls to share your bed, and all you had to do to earn it was risk your life on the sand facing another swordsman.''

The mercenary laughed too. "Hell, I do that on the battlefield without the pampering and pretty girls!''

"Poor you,'' Farris said pityingly. "Want to trade places with me?'' He gave the horse a friendly slap on the rump, dislodging the cat as he left the stall to move to the next one.

"How's your swordwork?'' Gault asked, trying for a note of humor. "With my arm out of commission, the captain might consider it.''

Farris didn't hear it as humor. His face dropped into the defensive emotionless slave-mask. Behind it he felt as if Gault had viciously kicked him in the belly with no warning. *That puts you in your place, slave. Only a barracks-brawler, not the swordsman you thought you could be.* "And get my hands chopped off for touching a weapon? No thank you, master,'' he said flatly.

"Ah, Farris, come on! You know I didn't mean anything like that!''

Farris dropped to his knees and fastened his gaze to the floor under Gault's feet. *If he wants a slave instead of a friend, he'll get one.* "May I go on with my work, master?''

Gault couldn't let it drop. Somehow it was very important that he find out why the mention of swordplay sent Farris bolting for cover like that. "No. Answer me, slave. How well can you use a sword? I know you can. I saw you.''

"I was fairly good as a boy, master."

"Who had your training? How long?"

"A retired City Guard captain, a friend's uncle. Three years, twice a week. About eight years ago." Farris bit the words off so abruptly that they verged on insolence, knowing that speaking so to a free man would probably earn him a lashing. So what? Nothing they could do to him would make him hurt more than he was right now. The hands clasped behind his back clenched convulsively into fists.

"Why?" Gault persisted. "Most boys won't put that much time and effort into anything, much less the dedication it takes to be a good swordsman."

"I had a stupid idea that I could get good enough for the King's Elite, master."

"Dammit, Farris, look at me and quit acting like a slave. If I can get permission somehow, are you willing to resume that training?" *Why did I say that?*

Farris jerked his head up to stare at the mercenary. The amber eyes that met Gault's were burning with a hot, steady light. Hatred? Maybe, but Gault didn't care.

Nor did Farris. *"Yes!* But you can't and you know it. I *am* a slave."

"I don't know. I'll try." He indicated the splint on his right arm. "I need a left-handed partner for a while. And you did break it."

"Uh, Captain?" Gault poked his head through the doorway of the guard room and asked, "Can I talk to you for a moment, sir? I've got a problem."

Captain Garan eyed the splint on Gault's arm and said, "I guess you do. What happened?"

"You know Farris? In the stables?"

"Yeah, he's a good kid. Knows horses. What about him?" His face changed, drawing into a scowl. "Don't tell me you were celebrating last night and smashed him up. He doesn't deserve treatment like that."

Gault looked sheepish. "Well, not exactly, sir. He's *good.* He only got a black eye. I'm still trying to figure out how he broke my arm just tapping on it like that."

The captain gave a sigh of weary patience. "All right, Gault. Start at the beginning. What happened?"

Starting at the beginning meant going back to last fall. Knowing that his captain did not appreciate long, rambling reports, Gault tried to make his story as clear and concise as possible, though he wasn't too clear himself on some of last night's details.

"So you see, sir," he concluded, "I, uh, kind of promised him I would see how he could get more sword training. I . . . dammit, Captain, I think he's a natural."

Garan was silent for a moment, his own face unreadable. "A natural, you say. A swordsman born, trapped in the collar of a slave. . . ." His voice trailed off and he gazed thoughtfully at a scar running across his own palm before he snapped his attention back to Gault. "And?"

"Uh, yessir. I think he deserves a chance. That boy's got guts."

"And how do you propose to give him that chance?"

"Well, sir, if we could kind of . . . kind of bend the law a little? I know he can't touch an edged weapon, like a sword or dagger, but our training swords are just sticks. No edges, do you see what I mean?"

"And who would train with him? You know how most of the Ravens feel about slaves."

Gault's jaw took on a stubborn set. "I will, sir. You can call it my punishment for fighting."

"So you say that last night you were too drunk to think about complaining?" The look on Roldan's face said he didn't quite believe Gault.

"That and, well, I did have kind of a liking for the boy. A broken arm can make you change your mind, y'know."

Roldan rubbed his hand over his eyes. "All right, if you are making a formal complaint to me, how many lashes do you want him given?"

"I'm making the complaint, Roldan, and I had another punishment in mind," put in Garan. "I've got Gault here on the sick list now, sword arm broken and all, who needs discipline for fighting also. A good set of bruises would improve both their attitudes immensely. Why not let them take the wooden practice swords and have a go at each other every day until Gault's arm heals?''

''A slave with a sword? You know the law. I can't possibly countenance it.''

''Well now, Roldan, that law says 'edged weapons.' Our sticks are hardly that.'' Garan grinned wickedly. ''I wouldn't put him up against Gault in proper fighting form, but I'd like to see what a slave who's never held a sword can do against him left-handed. The boy's a leading fighter among the slaves, I hear.''

''And left-handed himself as well.'' Roldan leaned back against his chair and considered. ''He has his own work to do, you know.''

''How much work is there for a horse trainer this time of year? I'll bet you've got three slaves doing the work of one, the same kind of make-work that I have my lads doing to keep them out of mischief. Likarion knows mine can get into enough trouble. Many's the time I wish I could give them a taste of the lash to keep them in line, but no mercenary worth his pay would stand for that.

''But now, you see, if I can spread it around that someone picking fights would have to disgrace himself fighting with a slave . . .'' Garan stared grimly at Gault, who tried very hard to look abashed.

Roldan chuckled. ''I see your point, Garan. Well . . . I suppose if you can keep it from getting back up to their lordships, go ahead.''

''You know as well as I do they won't be back until spring. Wintering at the Royal Court is more to their taste than wintering here at the edge of nowhere.'' Garan stretched himself out comfortably in his chair and grinned companionably at Roldan. ''Personally, I find nowhere without their presence much more to my liking. You know how they swagger about, looking down on all the rest of us like they're the gods themselves.''

''And mercenaries never swagger? Let's get back to the

point. When and where do you want him so you can administer this punishment?''

''Send him over to our arms-practice about midafternoons. That will give you a good morning's work out of him before he gets his punishment for the day.''

8

DISCIPLINE

Farris approached the big open room with resignation, trying to quiet the gnawing quiver in his belly. This wasn't Roldan's idea, he knew. It was not his way to punish a slave repeatedly for a single offense.

The echoing clash of wooden swords on shields hit his ears with almost the force of a physical blow. They were practicing melee fighting, group against group. A few fighters, already "dead," stood out of their way watching the contest, Captain Garan among them.

No point in putting it off, Farris thought bitterly. Carefully skirting the battling fighters, he moved to kneel in front of the mercenary captain. "Sir, Master Roldan ordered me to report to you for discipline."

Garan looked him over thoroughly before replying. Yes, he could see what Gault meant. "Discipline" was not the word for what this young man needed. The slave had his face and body under the tightest control he had ever seen. If Farris had no real idea of Gault's scheme, he had to be dreading the possibility of being beaten bloody every day for weeks. If so, only the tension in his body betrayed him. The eyes that didn't quite meet Garan's were rock-steady and held no trace of fear or submission, only a rebellious acknowledgment of what must be.

The captain kept his voice harsh as he answered. "I might have used another word than 'discipline.' On your feet, boy. Gault, you get over here, too! Joss, call a hold. I want everybody to witness this." He waited until Gault moved up to stand beside Farris and the melee halted.

Garan fixed the raffish crew of mercenaries with a steely eye, although his voice was mild enough. "You lads are slipping. You're not the fighters you ought to be. Pretty soon you'll be little blackbirds instead of Garan's Ravens."

At their outraged looks and protests, he continued, "There Gault is, one of the best fighters we have, and he lets a *slave* give him a broken arm. Well, if it takes a slave to put a challenge in you brawlers, then that's what I'll use. Farris!"

"Command me, sir." The slave's voice was carefully controlled, too, but not quite unemotional. It held an edge of . . . anticipation?

"Gault says you know which end of a sword is sharp. Roldan's turned your punishment for fighting over to me. I can't let you have a real sword, so we're going to see if you and Gault can't give each other a good set of stick-bruises. Sound good to you?"

Farris met Garan's eyes squarely, a savage smile spreading slowly over his face. "Yes, *sir!*"

"Good. Minimum protection for both of you. I told Roldan we'd try to leave your bones whole, but I didn't promise him anything. Get ready, you two. Now, any of you bastards who takes a notion that picking a drunken fight with a slave is an entertaining way to pass an evening may find out differently."

"Minimum protection" meant a belted loin-guard and an arm bracer, both of heavy leather, and a helm. The practice swords were made of leather-wrapped wood that duplicated the weight and balance of a real sword, but they were whippier. Blows to unprotected areas would leave bruises and welts, but would not do much more damage than that. Since Gault couldn't manage a shield with his splinted arm, they would be fighting with swords alone.

As Farris advanced to the middle of the floor, "sword" in hand, eight years fell away. Garan's voice became that of his first swordmaster, reciting the familiar rules of combat.

"Two blows to an arm or one blow to a leg causes shock and sends you to your knees. Another blow to a limb kills you. A blow to the body or head causes immediate death. Best three rounds out of five. When you are ready, fight!"

Farris dropped without thinking into one of the basic defensive stances, alertly studying Gault as the shouts of the watching mercenaries receded into a blur of background noise.

"Watch his eyes and his body, boy," Rykard's voice whispered from his memory. *"His face, his arm, even his sword can lie, but not his eyes or body. Watch them and they will always tell you what he is going to do."*

He hadn't completely understood it all those years ago; he had been too young, too impulsive. Now he did understand. Gault's body said the sword was going to move *there,* and it did. Farris blocked the blow, somewhat to his own surprise. It was true—the body remembers what the mind forgets.

The observers broke into ragged cheers or jeers, depending on whether or not they supported Gault. "Come on, Gault, give it to him! You can do better than that!" "You gonna let a slave beat you, Gault?" "Stick it to him, slave!"

Gault pressed to the attack with a flurry of blows intended to catch Farris off balance. The slave's sword moved, it seemed, almost of its own volition to parry as he gave ground slightly. The mercenary was better than Farris, but the fine edge of his fighting was blunted; he was too accustomed to fighting with his own right hand and facing a right-handed opponent. Farris spotted a hole in Gault's patterned attack that left him undefended for a heartbeat; his sword whipped into it and caught him a solid whack on the helm, just an instant before Gault's own sword swept in to hit him across the ribs.

"Hold!" Garan yelled, and both fighters dropped back a step. "One point each, both dead. Fight!"

Farris "killed" Gault once more and "died" twice himself in the next quarter-hour, both times as he pressed in to attack rather than trying merely to defend his own precious hide. He didn't care that he could have prolonged the fight indefinitely that way; all he had learned as a fighter, all his instincts, said to hit his opponent and hit hard. His blood sang in his ears and through his body; it was sheer joy in the fighting itself that twisted his face into a grimace that was half smile, half snarl.

He didn't know that the watching mercenaries had fallen silent as they observed the combat, didn't see the thoughtful look on Garan's face as he nodded his head in some private satisfaction. When the last cry of "Hold!" rang out, he remained poised and ready, his breathing steady and even, not relaxing his stance until Gault dropped his own sword and pulled awkwardly at his helm.

"Someone help me get this off, I can't do it one-handed," Gault growled. "You *lied* to me, man! It can't have been eight years since you held a sword. You should have forgotten everything in that time."

Farris pulled his own helm off and gratefully accepted the waterskin that someone held out to him. "What year is it? You lose track in my kind of life." He threw back his head and squirted water down his throat.

"It just turned 418," someone said.

"Sorry, Gault," Farris said as he wiped his arm across his mouth. "I guess I did lie to you. It's been seven and a half years. You going to lash me for it?" His eyes glinted with laughter, although his face was solemn.

"Bloody hell, no. I'm going to teach you how to attack without getting yourself killed. You'll wish I had lashed you and gotten it over with."

Captain Garan said quietly, "Gault's right, Farris. You apply the body control and concentration that I think you have to your swordplay and you'll be a damned good fighter."

"That's right, we can teach you . . ." Gault began eagerly. Then his face clouded and he muttered a quiet curse. "What good will it do? You'll still be a slave, you poor bastard." He glared at the other mercenaries and added fiercely, "What the hell are you six-fathered sons-of-sheep all staring at? Get on back to your own practice!''

Farris retreated behind his impassive slave-face as the crowd of men around him reluctantly dispersed. He stared at nothing as he said quietly, ''Gault, a slave learns quickly to take what pleasures he can when they're offered, and not to worry about what might happen afterward.''

''Even if it will make it harder or more dangerous for you afterward?'' asked Garan sharply.

''Even then, sir.'' For the first time since Gault had known him, Farris' unemotional mask cracked. Naked hunger stared out of his eyes and his voice shook as he said almost inaudibly, ''Captain, in seven and a half years I've never begged a free man for anything . . . but I'm begging you now. I *want* this, any crumb of training you are willing to give me . . . *please,* sir.''

Garan caught his eyes and held them in his own fierce blue stare. ''And if I say no?''

Farris stared back at him, despair rolling across his face. He closed his eyes and dropped his head. He took a deep breath, then another, squared his shoulders, and brought his face and voice under firm control. ''Then I submit to your will, master. Are you finished with me, sir?''

''No,'' Garan said sternly. ''Pick up that sword so Gault can teach you proper offense.''

''*Sir?*'' Disbelief flickered in his eyes as his head snapped up.

''You heard me. Farris, self-discipline, both of body and of mind, are necessary to be a good fighter. I knew you had the body-discipline, and you just showed me that you have the mental one as well. I'm going to give you the chance to fight that you say you want. Now quit wasting time and pick up that sword!''

Gault worked with Farris for another two hours, demonstrating the finer points of attack and defense using a sword alone, rather than the sword-and-shield training that Farris had concentrated on as a boy. They worked unhurriedly as

Gault sometimes had to go slowly and think through a move to demonstrate it left-handed.

Running slowly through the moves reminded Farris of his fighting exercises; it did not give him the same kind of satisfying elation as facing another swordsman, but he could see the reason behind it. Only when Gault was satisfied with his form was he allowed to practice a move at normal speed against an imaginary opponent, while Gault watched him with a critical eye and yelled at him for his mistakes.

After a time, the captain drifted over and watched while he toweled off the sweat from his own practice. "Gault, he doesn't have enough bruises yet. Put your helm on and go after him with your sword instead of your voice. I'll evaluate him."

Farris collected more than a few bruises that afternoon as he tried to put the teaching to work instead of relying on memory and instinct. Nevertheless, Garan pronounced himself satisfied with his initial progress.

As they watched the captain walk away, Gault crowed, "We'll make a fighter of you yet, boy," and raised a hand to give him a friendly slap on the back. Farris flinched reflexively and jerked away.

The mercenary stared at him, suddenly serious. "That bad, is it, Farris?" he asked quietly.

Farris sighed and rubbed his hand across his sweating forehead. "Sorry, Gault. But yeah, it can be that bad. There's a lot of men who'll beat up a slave for no more reason than that he *is* a slave who happens to get in their way. Sometimes a flinch like that, a sign of submission, will let me off easy with just a cuff and no more."

"I couldn't do it. Submit, I mean. I think I would kill myself first."

"And let your masters win?" asked Farris fiercely, finally and completely trusting Gault as a friend. "Let them know that they've finally broken you? They can force me to kneel, to flinch, they can lash me till my back's in ribbons and my blood soaks the ground, but they can't break me unless *I* let them, unless *I* admit that I'm broken. And they haven't. What

I do, I do to stay alive. Every day I live is my victory over them.''

His voice became quieter at the unhappy look on Gault's face. ''Don't look like that because of me, Gault. I could be a lot worse off.''

''How?'' Gault asked bluntly.

''I could be Lordling Torkild's body-slave. Now there's a slave even I feel sorry for. He's been broken, and he knows it.'' Farris shivered and then shook himself like a dog. ''But thanks for reminding me. I can't go out of here grinning like a cat. You brutal mercenaries have been beating me up all afternoon.'' He indicated the bruises already starting to color his ribs and the welts across his arms, and flashed Gault a conspiratorial grin. ''Watch this.''

He covered his face with his hands and took a deep breath. As he took them away his body seemed to shrink into itself. His face took on a hunted, sullen look as he dropped his head, and he refused to meet Gault's eyes. ''Is my punishment finished, master?'' he asked dully.

The mercenary gaped at him. ''You little faker. Do all of you put on an act like that?''

''No. Only the unbroken ones. See you later.''

9

BARAK

Just as he was leaving for arms-practice, Farris heard a great noise of horses. A large group of riders trotted into the forecourt, and all the stable and yard servants and slaves were summoned to deal with the new arrivals. To his dismay Farris recognized both the leading horse and his rider. It was Lord Torkild, and the other riders were his friends. They were back, two weeks or more before they were expected.

Roldan took charge, welcoming his lord and issuing rapid orders to the people under his command. To Farris, he said, "When you've finished with those horses, I need you to take a message to Captain Garan, of the mercenary guard. Tell him I need the item returned that he borrowed just after Yearsend."

"Yes, master. I understand," Farris murmured in the proper submissive tones. Oh, yes, he understood. He had hoped for another two weeks, but the end of his arms-practice had just ridden into the yard.

As he tended to the horses, the familiar work left his mind free to roam. Could he sneak in some practice with Gault now and then? Not likely, as Garan would have to tighten down, too. He resigned himself to the loss with only a little bitterness; he had known it would end eventually.

When he ran the message to Garan, he found out that the mercenary captain already knew. "Yes, I'll get it back to him. Tell him I'm sorry I can't use it anymore."

As he left the arms-practice area, a hand grabbed his collar and stopped him in his tracks. A harsh voice growled, "Hold it right there, slave."

Farris froze. The voice was that of Barak, the only mercenary who actually disliked him. He seemed to take it as a personal affront that Farris dared to exist in the same room as a Free Mercenary.

"You think you're special, slave-boy, because the captain likes you?"

"No, master." Farris kept his head down, not turning to face the big mercenary. Barak had not ordered him to do so.

The fingers in his collar tightened. "You think you can keep looking free men in the face like you've been doing and get away with it? Well, I've got my eye on you, slave, so don't try that kind of insolence with me." He pushed Farris away with enough force that he staggered. Farris didn't see Barak's fist coming at him, but the blow to his head was not unexpected. It knocked him up against the wall; he scrabbled at the rough stone for support and managed to remain on his feet.

Hatred for this man welled up inside him. He wanted to retaliate, to go after him not with a sword, but bare-handed. It would be pure pleasure to have that thick neck in his hands, to feel the bones snap and watch Barak's head loll sideways. His breath came short and he quivered, caught between that intense desire and the knowledge that if he did so, he was a dead man. No slave could attack a free man and live, not even one provoked into it. Only a direct order to fight could excuse such actions.

And Barak had no intentions of doing that. "On your knees, slave-boy," he ordered.

Farris forced himself down as Barak circled him like a

hungry ice leopard. "That's where you belong, slave-boy, crawling and shivering with fear at a free man's feet. And you've got the balls to think you can take on a Free Mercenary. So you think you're a fighter, do you?"

Farris hesitated only a moment. Barak's hostility was not appeased by his submission. It was growing, and he knew he was going to take a beating from the free man. It might as well be for something.

He raised his head to look Barak in the face. "Yes. I am."

This time he saw Barak's fist coming. He managed to dodge enough to take it on his cheek instead of his nose, but he couldn't evade the next one. Sharp pain exploded in his head as he was struck to the floor. He curled himself into a ball, trying desperately to protect his belly from Barak's booted feet. Ribs splintered as one kick caught him a sharp smash over the kidney, forcing the first gasp of pain from him.

Barak did not allow him to protect himself that way for very long; he grabbed him from behind by his collar and pulled him up to his knees. The mercenary's grip was merciless as he caught Farris' right arm and twisted it up behind his back. He did not stop at the control position but forced the arm even higher, until one last vicious jerk wrenched the shoulder joint apart.

Farris' face twisted in silent agony as Barak shifted his grip to drag him by arm and collar to his feet, forced him back against the wall, and used that same arm to pin him there. He then proceeded to beat his captive savagely with his free hand.

"Beg, little horseboy. Beg me to put you out of your misery, you crawling little coward! I can stand here and backhand you all day until you do." Barak emphasized his words with another twist to Farris' arm and two more blows to the face.

He had nothing more to lose. This man was going to kill him, for no more reason than that he was a slave who was not allowed to fight back. Farris forced the words past the pain and out of his bloody, swollen mouth. "Eat shit, Barak."

Barak's face changed from red to purple as he realized what Farris had said. Farris stared at him defiantly and waited for his chance to retaliate, watching as Barak's arm drew slowly back and his big fist clenched.

There was a thud of booted feet and another man's hands appeared just above Barak's wrist. "I wouldn't do that if I were you," Gault said coldly.

Barak released Farris' arm; the sudden easing of the pain made the slave's head swim, and he slid slowly down the wall. Through the red haze that clouded his vision he heard Barak sneer, "What's the matter, Gault? Afraid I'll break your little playtoy? I didn't know you liked slave-boys instead of women. Do you and Garan take turns swiving him, or—"

Gault's growl of rage followed by Gault's fist in his mouth interrupted him. Barak wiped his hand across his cut lip and looked at the smear of blood it left behind. The dagger at his belt was suddenly in his hand, hanging glittering and sharp just in front of Farris' eyes. Gault saw it, too, jerking back just in time to avoid the vicious slice that would have split his belly open like a gutted pig. The tip of the dagger ripped his shirt and dragged across his upper abdomen. He caught Barak's wrist in his left hand, digging his fingers into the tendons to try to make him drop the dagger while he pawed clumsily for his own. It was not there.

Farris forced himself to move through his pain, not out of the way of the battling mercenaries, but directly into their path. He braced his feet against the wall and pushed off hard. His uninjured shoulder crashed into the back of Barak's knees and sent the big mercenary sprawling onto his back, the knife flying from his hand.

Pulled off balance with him, Gault felt his foot punch into something soft. He bounced up to his knees, straddling Barak's belly, and hit him on the point of the jaw with all the weight of his body behind the impact. Barak jerked and lay still; for a moment there was no sound but Farris' agonized gasps.

Gault turned to him and pushed Barak's legs away. "Where are you hurt?"

Farris couldn't answer. The jolt of his own body landing on the dislocated shoulder had been grinding agony; before he could scream Gault's boot in his belly had knocked the wind out of him. He was dimly aware of fabric ripping as Gault cut his tunic off and ran rough hands over his body, looking for obvious injuries. When he came to the damaged shoulder, Farris heard someone moan.

"Shoulder's out of joint, from the looks of it," another voice said. "Where's Brody? He knows about these things."

"Don't move him, Gault. There may be other injuries, like his spine. Farris!" said Garan's voice in unmistakable command-tones. "Farris, can you move everything? Can you feel your arms and legs?"

Command-voice; he had to obey. Legs, yes. Left arm works. "Can't move . . . right arm . . . sir," he gasped out.

"We'll tend to that. Brody?"

Again hands felt his shoulder; even Brody's light touch left behind spears of torment, and he bit his tongue to keep from screaming. "That's got to be fixed now, sir, before it swells any more," Brody said, and his voice seemed far away and then suddenly loud. "It can't wait, even for the healer. I've done it before."

"Then do it now," ordered the captain.

"Gault, you hold his body, yes, like that. Farris, I need you to go absolutely limp. Don't fight us. I have to pull your arm out and twist it back into the socket."

"Understood." Farris was finally able to pull in a deep breath. As he let it out, he tried to push all the tension of his body with it.

Gault's arms around him tightened; more wrenching pain swept from his shoulder to his head, and a spinning wave of blackness swept over him, sucking away his last rags of consciousness.

Brody, kneeling with Gault over his suddenly limp body, grunted, "Good. Now he can't fight us. Ahh, there." There was an audible *pop* as the bone snapped back into its socket. Brody took his elbow and carefully rotated the arm. "Yes, it's in. He should have that arm strapped to his side to immobilize it for a while, to let those muscles and tendons heal.''

Captain Garan said curtly, "All right, Gault, tell me what happened. I saw Barak draw steel on you. What led up to it?''

"He was beating up Farris. I tried to stop him and he tried to knife me.''

"I said I saw that. What had Farris done?''

"I don't know, sir, maybe nothing. You know how Barak hates slaves. But whatever it was, Barak didn't have the right to try to kill him.''

Some time later, Farris knelt in front of Garan, Roldan, and Lord Torkild in the stablemaster's office. His right arm was in a sling and fastened firmly to his body by the same bandages that strapped his broken ribs. Bruises on his face and body gave their mute evidence of the beating he had taken. The castle's healer had stitched his split lip, but she could do little for the swollen, blackened eye or the bruised kidney that was making him urinate blood.

He kept his eyes fixed determinedly on the floor in front of his master's feet. None of the free men could see anything more than the carefully blank mask, or read the seething resentment that was barely controlled.

"All right, boy," said Lord Torkild. "I can't let this go. If it were a matter of Captain Garan's fighters alone, any discipline would be his concern. But when one of my slaves is involved, it becomes my affair. What were you doing in that area where you didn't belong?''

"Carrying a message, master." *Message: No more swordplay for you, slave.*

"And that message was?''

"Master Roldan asked for the return of an item borrowed by Captain Garan." *An item. A slave. Nothing.*

"What was this item?''

"They did not tell me, master." *That's the truth. Nothing I needed to be told.*

"It was a private matter between the two of us, Lord Torkild,'' interposed Garan smoothly. "Not the concern of a slave."

Torkild grunted, "I see." He seemed willing to let that matter drop but continued relentlessly, "Then what happened, boy?"

Boy. I'm two years older than you, lordling. "I delivered the message and was returning when Barak stopped me."

Torkild leaned forward from his chair and slapped him. "Master Barak to you, slave."

Farris took a deep breath and by sheer force of will kept his hands from curling into fists. The words were bitter in his mouth as he repeated, *"Master* Barak stopped me. I don't remember his exact words, but he accused me of insolence and cuffed me. He ordered me to kneel and then he hit me again, hard enough to knock me down. He kicked at me, and then pulled me back to my feet by my arm."

"Was that when your shoulder was dislocated?"

"Yes, master." *Because I'm not allowed to protect myself.*

"Did you resist him at any time?"

"No, master." *Not much of a choice. His fists or your lash.*

"Go on."

"Master Barak hit me again. Then he told me to beg for him to kill me, that he would beat me until I did."

"Did you?"

Farris hesitated. Barak had probably told them his side of the story already. If they caught him in a lie, they would punish him further. "Not in those words, master. I wanted to make him angry enough to kill me quickly."

"Exactly what did you say, boy?" Torkild asked coldly.

"I said, 'Eat shit, Barak.' "

Roldan coughed; was he hiding a laugh? Garan broke in quickly, "Lord Torkild, it certainly seems that the man was obeying orders. A response like that to one of my men *is* asking to get killed."

"Captain Garan, I am conducting this interrogation," the lordling said stiffly. "I will ask for your information at the proper time."

"As you wish, my lord, but that is the point where my

information comes in. My man Gault stopped Barak from killing your valuable slave. Barak drew a dagger on him, and they fought. This man is responsible for saving Gault's life. He tripped Barak so that Gault could take him out.

"Farris, I am officially placing my thanks to you on record. Barak has been discharged for drawing steel on an unarmed comrade. It is due to you that Gault is still alive."

Farris risked looking up at the captain. "Gault just saved my life, sir. I couldn't let Barak kill him for it."

Torkild snorted. "This is all very touching, Captain Garan, but it agrees with other reports I've had that this slave is a troublemaker. Isn't he the one I had to lash last autumn? Roldan, if you say he is too valuable to you to sell, then find some other way to tame him. Cut his rations. One meal a day for a few weeks ought to do it."

"My lord, the man can't do his work without adequate food. We're coming into our busiest season and I need him," protested Roldan.

"Oh? Do I need *you*, stablemaster? I have other poor relations who would be happy to have your job. Who is master here, Roldan, you or I?" Lord Torkild's voice was cruel and his expression smug.

The stablemaster's jaws clenched tight and his face took on a pinched look. "You are, my lord Torkild. I will see to your orders. Sir."

"*I* will see to my orders. Don't think you can get away with ignoring me, *cousin*. Captain Garan, attend me." The arrogant lordling swept away with the mercenary at his heels.

Farris held his breath and wished fervently to be any place other than where he was. Master Roldan had always been a fair and dispassionate man, but he had never before been humiliated in front of a slave by having his poor-relation status thrown in his face.

"Get out, slave," the stablemaster ordered harshly, and Farris scrambled hastily to obey.

They allowed Farris to eat his evening meal that day, but the next morning at breakfast Roldan roughly shoved him out of line.

"Nothing for you this morning, slave, or at noon," the stablemaster growled. "One meal a day from now on. During the other meals you'll stand over there where I can keep an eye on you."

From these orders there was no appeal, no possibility that he could convince Roldan to ignore Torkild's instructions. Farris quietly took his place against the wall, keeping his eyes resolutely down so that he did not have to meet the faces of his friends or watch them eat. It did little good. While the meal was only the porridge and fruit of their usual breakfast, the smells were still enticing to a young man with a normal healthy appetite. He could control his face and body, but not his stomach. It growled loudly in protest at being denied its usual fare.

After watching him for a short while, Kiam took the matter into his own hands. Farris saw him leave his place and make a quiet request of Master Roldan. The stablemaster scowled but gave a grudging nod of assent. Shortly after that, a food-server brought Farris a mug of water. It was better than nothing, he supposed. At least it quieted his stomach rumblings for a time.

In the weeks that followed, his punishment continued. Even after his injuries healed, he was kept to the single evening meal. No extra helpings were allotted to him, although the servers tried to give him as large an amount as they dared. He had always been lean, but now he grew even thinner. Before his bruises had faded, his ribs were showing plainly and his face had grown gaunt. He was endlessly gut-aching hungry. Even the evening meal seemed to fill his belly for only a few heartbeats; he was hungry again before lock-up time.

Gault would have helped him, but Captain Garan had forbidden any more contact between the two, feeling that it would make things worse for Farris, not better. His slave friends tried to smuggle food out to him until Kiam was betrayed, caught, and lashed for it.

On his knees, his arm twisted behind him by a smirking guardsman, Farris was forced to watch the whip draw blood

from Kiam's back. It was worse than the lash on his own
back a few moments later.

He refused to allow anybody to smuggle food to him after
that, and when they persisted, refused to accept it. The slaves
lived under harsh enough conditions as it was without in-
curring the anger of either Lord Torkild or Master Roldan.

As the mud of Springthaw dried and gave way to the new
growth that gave the month of Treebloom its name, Farris
grew even more short-tempered and embittered. Under the
onslaught of his fierce hunger, the control he maintained to
show an emotionless mask to his masters began to crumble.
The sullen expression he had faked during the time of his
''discipline'' by the mercenaries became all too real. This
did not please Lord Torkild; as a result, he cut Farris' evening rations by another quarter.

He began to steal anything edible to fill his empty belly.
The other slaves soon learned to know when he had succeeded; his temper was somewhat less savage. In the barracks at night, nobody came near him, fearing it would
provoke him into a vicious fight. At last even Kiam started
to avoid him.

Only to the mares and foals under his charge did he show
any gentleness, and even that was for purposes of his own.
He found it was possible to steal a few swallows of mare's
milk without depriving the foal or upsetting the mare. Milk
and somewhat more easily stolen but rarer raw eggs became
the uncertain mainstays of his diet.

He was not, then, in the best of moods when the Lady Viveka
rode back into his life.

10

RAPE

Year 418 D.S.: Third day of the month of Greenleaves

Viveka took up where she had left off the autumn before, with petty, malicious complaints about Farris' work and his attitude. Twice in less than two weeks Lord Torkild gave him five lashes with the twoblade on the strength of those complaints, leaving him smoldering with hatred and bitterness that grew daily.

One morning she came early to the stables on the pretext of scolding Farris for allowing another horse to kick her mare. She watched him as he worked, alone because the other stable workers always disappeared whenever Viveka came around. She did not remark at the other slaves' absence; her intended prey was right here.

"Look at me, boy. That's an order." She preened in front of him, brushing back her silky hair with her fingers and running her hands slowly down the outline of her body. "Do you think I'm pretty, slave? Wouldn't you like to bed me?"

Instead of answering, Farris stripped off his tunic with a quick violent motion and knelt in front of her, head down.

"What are you doing? Answer me, slave-boy," she demanded.

"Waiting for my beating, mistress," he said sullenly. "If I say 'no,' you'll beat me for insulting you. If I say 'yes,' you'll beat me for daring to think such a thing. Just go ahead and beat me. You don't need any excuse."

"No, I don't, do I?" She struck out viciously with her riding whip, striking his bare back repeatedly. The blows raised welts and stung, but the riding whip was not designed to cut the skin and she did not have the strength to hurt him badly. He refused to flinch, refused to give her even that small satisfaction. He merely endured it in hardened defiant silence, waiting for her to get tired and stop.

At last the blows ceased. "How *dare* you defy a beating from me?" Viveka shrieked. "I *will* hurt you, slave. *I will!*" She whirled and ran out of the stables.

Farris remained on his knees, burning with rage and hatred; the tapping of her feet on the stones was long silent before he moved. He fully expected that she would complain to Torkild and he would receive a real lashing, but nothing more happened to him . . . that day.

The next day was cold and rainy, one of those days that push the season from late spring back into early spring. Farris wished he had his heavier wool winter tunic even though it would irritate his still-raw back, but it had been taken away the week before and replaced by the thin summer tunic. He was going about his assigned task of feeding the stalled horses when he heard Viveka irritably calling his name.

She smiled spitefully when she saw him. "I want to see your body, slave-boy. Take that tunic off." Although he was already cold enough to be uncomfortable and had no wish to go about half-naked in front of her, he had no choice and no way to protest. He peeled it off and laid it aside.

As was her habit during these past few days, she was eating something. This time it was a small flaky pastry stuffed with spiced apples. A half-forgotten memory said his mother used to make them for holidays. The scent alone was enough to drive him nearly insane with gut-cramping hunger.

"Lord Torkild does not wish to go riding with me today. You will accompany me instead." She licked the last crumbs of pastry off her fingers and smiled in a way that he did not like. He knew she was up to something, but what? If she wanted to beat him again, all she had to do was order him to his knees.

Farris sent a quick prayer for help to Ydona. "Please, mistress, I can't. I have orders from Master Roldan to watch a mare that is due to foal very soon." This was not exactly an untruth; watch was being kept on the mare, but not the close watch that would be needed in a day or two.

"I think you're lying, slave. Show me this mare," Viveka demanded.

Silently he led the way to the small foaling barn, not realizing that she was observing with pleasure its outlying location. In the barn she barely glanced at the mare, then stepped aside as Farris entered the big loosebox and checked the horse with careful, gentle hands, all the time talking to her in the soothing voice that she needed.

He painstakingly closed and latched the box; not only was this little mare one of his favorites, but the last to foal this year, and he was determined that nothing should go wrong. So intent was he on the mare that he didn't see or hear the girl padding on silent cat-feet to stand right behind him.

As Farris turned away, he nearly stepped on her, so close had she come. He froze, still wary of her unpredictable anger. She looked decidedly strange, the blue of her eyes only a thin rim around dilated pupils, her breathing harsh and ragged.

Viveka put her hands on his bare chest and ran her nails down to his navel, scratching hard enough to leave trails of bright beads of blood. She dabbed one up with her fingertip, delicately licking it off as she spoke, her voice oddly husky. "So you were telling the truth, slave. Were you there when the stallion did it to her? I saw horses mating once, even though they told us girls not to look and hurried us off. She squealed when he shoved it into her, he was so big. I've heard the slave-girls talking about you. Are you that big?" Her hand trailed down to his crotch, squeezing and fondling.

One corner of his mind screamed to him that he was in deadly danger, even as his body responded to her touch. She smiled ruthlessly as his arousal became obvious under her seeking hand. "What would you do if I said to take me in your arms, slave? If I ordered you to kiss me?"

"I . . ." His own breathing grew uneven, and he could feel his heart begin to pound. As her erotic fondling increased, the anger began to build, began to war with the warnings of danger and the conditioning of years of submission to those who owned him and used him. "I would obey, mistress," he said flatly.

"Then I do so order you."

Slowly he complied, his arms sliding around her to pull her closer as her head tipped back and her mouth hungrily sought his. She tasted of apples.

Abruptly she pulled back and slapped him with all her strength. "What kind of stupid, respectful, *slave* kiss was that, you—you . . ." Her voice died and it was her turn to freeze. She had never seen unrestrained rage on a slave's face before.

The unexpected blow had snapped his last threads of sanity and control. A venomous flood of anger and hatred swept over him as he yanked her into an embrace so crushing that she feared her ribs would break. One hand brutally pinched her jaws open and his tongue invaded her mouth. Breathless with excitement tinged with fear, she thought she would faint before he stopped.

He broke it finally, pulling her away from him by a handful of her hair tangled in his clenched fist. "Is that what you want, bitch?" he rasped. "A stud instead of a slave?"

"Yes!" she cried, and caught his free hand in both of hers to pull it to her breast.

The demon of violent rage that had taken control of him would not let him stop, would not let him think beyond this instant. This bitch, this little slut, was all the masters who had tormented him, lashed him, starved him. He would have his revenge on them all—through *her*.

Her small breast was soft in his hand as he squeezed hard, digging in his fingers and pinching her viciously. In return, she bit him on the shoulder as she began to unlace her blouse. Then in a fit of impatience she caught the neckline in both hands and ripped from throat to waist.

He never remembered, afterward, which of them pulled the other down on a pile of fresh straw, which of them tore off her riding skirt. But he did remember, to the end of his life, how eagerly she fumbled for the drawstring on his breeches. He remembered how he pinned her squirming body beneath his as she willingly spread her legs for him, remembered the overwhelming rage that drove him to hurt her as he had been hurt, remembered his savage anticipation of her screams.

Viveka did not scream; she met him eagerly, biting him again and again and ripping at his back with her nails.

Deep in the grip of insane rage and approaching climax, he never heard running footsteps and shouts behind him, but Viveka did.

She screamed suddenly and began to struggle, clawing at his chest and shoulders as if to throw him off. As he reared up on one hand to slap her hard with the other, she lashed out at his face, her nails tearing deep gashes along his cheek from ear to mouth. He growled and caught at her hair again to force his mouth over hers. Before he could succeed, something hit him hard on the back of his head.

In a daze he felt rough, hard hands pulling him off her. Someone held him on each side, and a rain of blows fell on him, on his face and belly and groin. He barely felt them. He felt nothing but a remote icy knot of fear in his guts, and the knowledge that he was a dead man.

Viveka was crying hysterically, turning frustrated arousal into a very convincing display of maidenly terror and relief. "You're too l-late!" she sobbed. "He—he t-tore my clothes off and—and he threw me d-down, and he—he r-ruh-*raped* meee. . . ." She became too distraught to continue as she tried unsuccessfully to cover herself with her ripped blouse.

Her rescuers, Torkild and some of his friends, politely averted their eyes from her nakedness and one of them stripped off his own shirt for her to wear.

Torkild helped her to her feet and cuddled her close, patting her back and murmuring the meaningless ritual, "There, there, it's all right now. Hush, hush, my darling." His face became hard and cold as he stared at Farris, still hanging dazed and numb between his captors. "Lock him in that storage closet over there, before I kill him now. That would be too quick, too easy a death. Nothing quick and easy for *him*, my little love, I promise you."

And as the lordling soothed the still-sobbing Viveka, she buried her face in his chest so that he would not see the look of cruel satisfaction on it.

11

———◆———

ESCAPE

They moved him, later, from the storage closet to a cell in the keep itself. He came out fighting, trying to make them kill him right then so that he could go down like a warrior. And although these were men who owed their lives to their fighting skills, they did not take him easily. At least two were disabled with broken bones before they managed to shackle his hands behind his back.

Even so, he did not give up. He fell more than once on the rain-slick cobbles of the stableyard, lashing out with booted feet, cursing and trying to anger them enough to make a mistake. Finally four of them held him down while a fifth forced poppy syrup down his throat.

It was the drugged nightmare of his enslavement again when they finally dragged him into the keep, only half-conscious but still struggling feebly. He was barely aware that they took the shackles off before shoving him into one of the lower-level cells.

It was the next morning before Farris came truly awake. He had time only for a moment of disorientation before he doubled over in a spasm of retching. There was nothing in his stomach to come up; the dry heaves left him sick and shaking.

A sympathetic voice from the other side of the heavy door said, "Here, lad," and someone shoved a waterskin through the feeding slot. He eyed it warily at first, suspecting that they were trying to drug him again, then picked it up with a shrug. What difference would it make now? Soon *(Tomorrow, dear gods? Today?)* he would die a very unpleasant death; maybe drugging him would be a kindness on their part.

The water was cold and clear and sweet; he held it in his dry mouth and let it trickle in tiny drops down his throat. It stayed down, but he didn't try to push his luck.

Maybe he shouldn't drink it. If he refused food and water, he would die in a few days. No, that wouldn't work. They could force water down him as easily as poppy syrup, and would probably leave him shackled to boot for causing them so much trouble. He took another small mouthful and corked the skin.

"Hey, out there," he called. "Thanks. You want your waterskin back?"

"Keep it for now, lad. I've got better out here."

Farris laughed, a dry-throated chuckle. "Impossible. This is sweeter than a virgin's first kiss. That you, Brody?"

"Yeah. Farris, you have really kicked over a beehive. Is a bit of bed-sport really worth what's coming to you?"

"That wasn't bed-sport. That was revenge."

"You'd make a good mercenary with that viewpoint. Too bad you won't get the chance."

That day crawled on endlessly as the knot of fear in his guts grew tighter.

They fed him when the evening guard-shift came on. By then he was so hungry his belly felt plastered to his backbone. The slab of dry bread that they shoved under the door was topped with some gluey substance that might be gruel. From the little he could see of it, it looked like someone had already eaten it and tossed it back up.

It didn't taste any better than it looked, but he ate it anyway. Compared with this, the food they fed to the slaves was a feast.

He knew it was evening because the guard complained about having his own supper delayed, and he allowed himself to relax a little. They'd not drag him out of his cell to his death now. No, it would be the bright daylight in the exercise yard for him again. And this time his punishment would be much worse than a simple lashing, so that it would be an even better lesson.

The guard changed again, and this time he knew the voice of the relief. It was Gault.

The sound of the other's boots died away on the stones before Gault spoke. Farris had been lashed many times, but never before verbally. Gault angrily informed him of his misbegotten ancestry, sordid personal habits, eventual unpleasant destination, and general lack of intelligence in minute detail and increasingly colorful invective.

When he had run out of words, Farris was silent while he mulled over possible replies. Then he said plaintively, "Hey, Gault? I'm not a smart mercenary like you, just a dumb slave, remember? I didn't understand all those big words. Could you make it simpler?"

Gault leaned his head back against the wall and shook with nearly silent if somewhat hysterical laughter. His respect and grief for Farris leaped higher when he realized that it was being echoed on the other side of the door. A man who could laugh like that in the face of death was no slave. The warrior had stopped hiding behind the slave-mask; this man would go down fighting, would go to his death cursing and swaggering. He was truly sorry that the man in the cell would never fight by his side.

The ring of boot-heels on the stones chopped their laughter off short and brought them both to silent, wary attention. Not the captain making his rounds; there were too many. Who, then, at this time of night?

It was Captain Garan, trailing after Lord Torkild and a bull of a man with the grizzled look of a wolf and the wide gold rings of a duke in his ears. His personal bodyguard strode at his heels.

Duke Launart scowled impartially at Gault and the captain and demanded irritably, "Well, let's have the bastard out, then. I want to see the slave that would try to rape my niece."

Gault threw a stiff, exaggerated salute halfway between the duke and his son and turned to unlock the door, snarling, "Get back, you mangy cur," as he entered the cell. There were sounds of a struggle, and Gault finally appeared pushing Farris ahead of him, the slave's arm twisted firmly behind his back. Farris' battered head was held defiantly high and he met the eyes of the man who owned him in a level, challenging stare.

The torchlight flickered on this silent tableau for perhaps the space of five heartbeats before one bodyguard ordered, as he might a dog, "Down, slave. On your knees before your masters."

Farris' eyes never wavered, and the ghost of a smile played over his mouth. "What masters?"

Torkild hit him across the face. He staggered, and felt Gault's supporting hand at the small of his back. The broken scabs on his clawed cheek oozed fresh blood to drip down off his jaw, but the reckless light still danced in his eyes.

Launart broke the eye contact to motion to Gault. "Put him back in the cell." As Gault tightened his grip, the duke added, "The evidence on his body is clear proof of how hard the poor girl struggled against him. I agree, Torkild, no other trial will be necessary. I'd not shame her further. Do you still plan to geld him?"

"Oh, yes, Father." Torkild watched to see the results of his statement, and was disappointed. Farris did not react before Gault pushed him back into the cell and slammed the door shut.

"In the morning then, before you geld him, start his punishment by cutting out that brash tongue. Don't take his eyes just yet, or his ears. Let him know when we're coming for him."

Launart, Torkild, and the bodyguard marched away.

Captain Garan pulled a cloth from his pocket and used it to wipe his sweaty forehead as he dropped onto Gault's vacated bench.

"Mangy cur, Gault?" asked Farris with all the bravado he could manage. "You didn't use that one before."

"I didn't think of it," Gault answered flatly. "Captain's still here, Farris."

"Oh. Sir?"

"Why 'sir' to me and not 'master' to the lord duke, son?" Garan asked gently.

"I'll give respect when it's due, sir, but I will *never* call any man 'master' again. There are two things I want to ask of you, Captain. When they come for me tomorrow, please sir, don't come yourself, or assign Gault. I won't go meekly. I'll fight every step of the way, and I'll fight to kill."

"I expected that, Farris. Any warrior would."

"Thank you, sir. D'you think you could get Barak back?"

That drew a chuckle from Gault and a brief grin from Garan before the captain asked, "And the second thing, Farris?"

"I wanted to ask, sir—while I still can—did they tell you . . ." He stopped and swallowed hard, fighting to keep his voice under control. "What else do they have planned for me?"

"I don't know for certain, Farris. But I talked to one of the men who rode up here as Lady Viveka's escort last week, and he gave me some idea.

"It seems this is the second time a slave has tried to rape the poor girl. Last spring her brother's body-slave attacked her, she said. He was all scratched and bitten, just like you are.

"They beat that poor bastard to death, and not just a simple fourblade thrashing until he bled dry. He was a long time dying. They used the kurbasch on him."

There was a short pause before Farris said in a flat, emotionless voice, "I don't know that word, Captain."

"It's a snake whip, son. It's studded with pieces of lead, and I've seen it rip out chunks . . . well, never mind. They used this whip on the other slave and gave him a couple of

lashes every hour until he died. The man said—dammit, I'm
sorry, Farris, but you should know so you can prepare yourself for it. He said that by the time they finished, you could
see every bone in his back.''

A soft gasp came from the cell; inaudible whispered words
that had the urgency of a plea followed.

Garan watched Gault's face turn white and then greenish.
He swallowed convulsively, and again. In the silence that
followed, both of them could clearly hear Farris vomiting.

Under cover of the noise, the captain said quietly, ''I
wouldn't bed that scrawny little rat-faced wench if you paid
me, and here two different slaves lust after her so much they
try to rape her, even knowing that they'll die for it. Funny,
isn't it?''

''Yeah,'' muttered Gault, still trying to keep his own stomach mastered. *He's my* friend. *I never thought I could be
friends with a slave and they won't even give him a decent,
clean death.*

''That's a good man in there. Knows when to swagger and
when to be scared,'' Garan said.

After there was silence in the cell, Gault called out, ''You
all right in there, Farris?''

''Yeah. For a while. Any water out there?''

''Here.'' He shoved a waterskin through the feeding slot.

The captain said loudly, ''That's right, Gault, take good
care of him. Remember the duke wants him kept alive, at
least for now. My cousin got in big trouble last year that
way.''

''Yeah, what?'' Gault asked inattentively.

Garan elbowed him in the ribs and glared at him. ''Seems
he was stupid enough to feel sorry for a valuable prisoner
and gave him an apple just like one of these I just brought
you. The prisoner pretended to choke on it, and when my
cousin went in to check on him, the bastard knocked him
out and escaped.''

''Oh. Tough luck.''

''Yeah. Well, I've got rounds to make. I won't be back
this way, so you've got about four hours here *all alone* until
Malik relieves you. Think you can handle it?''

"Yes, sir." Gault saluted as the captain left.

He looked after him with a puzzled scowl. *Huh? Garan doesn't have any family at all, much less a cousin. There wasn't any point to that story . . . except . . . gods, he couldn't have meant it like it sounded, could he? Let him escape? He's a slave. If he really raped her, he deserves to die. Even the little bitch, can't let a slave get away with that. But still, the kurbasch, brrrr. Not even a slave deserves that. A slave. He's not a slave anymore. He never was. They locked a collar on him, but they never broke the man inside. And he's my friend.*

Two different slaves. And I wouldn't bed that little bitch, either. Could she have set them up somehow? Damn right, she could have. What was she doing down there alone with him? Just who was being raped in that barn?

The captain's right, he's a good man, be good to have at your back in a fight. Even good men die. I've killed some of them myself. But they were decent clean deaths in battle, with a sword. They had an equal chance to kill me. I've never chained a man down and ripped chunks out of his back like that. Nor will I. I'll resign first. They can do their own dirty work. But dearest gods, can I let them do it to a friend and still live with myself? He saved my life when Barak drew steel on me. I owe him a life.

What could they do to me? I'm a free man. They can't use that kurbasch on me, not like that. Was that the point of Garan's story? If it looks like he tricked me, they won't think I let him escape. Might get an ordinary flogging for care-lessness. What's the matter, Gault? Can't take a lashing for a friend? Farris has guts enough to take one. Likely they'd just dock my pay. My pay. Blood money, torn out of a friend's back. At worst I could only get turned out.

He looked at the cell door and tried to imagine how he would feel locked inside, waiting helplessly for mutilation and savagely vindictive death. *What the hell. It's only money, and there are other warbands that need good men.*

Inside the cell, Farris sat with his back to the wall, curled into a tight ball, his arms wrapped around the legs pulled up to his chest, his forehead resting on his bent knees. He felt

drained, empty, purged of all emotion, not only the fear that
had spewed out with his food. Even his goddess had abandoned him, and his masters had won. Whether they had broken him or not, it made no difference. He could look at his
own death dispassionately now; he had known all along it
would be something as painful and horrifyingly prolonged
as that.

Idly he wondered if he should kill himself first, if he could
bite through his own wrists to cheat his owners of their prey.
As if from a distance of years, he remembered telling Gault
that suicide would let them win; was it still true now?

He ran his tongue speculatively over his teeth. No. That
was what Ydona had meant by "Help yourself." Taking his
death into his own hands would give him the final victory.
When Gault went off duty, he would do it. It would be a
betrayal of his friend if he did it now.

Gault's footsteps, pacing back and forth in front of the
cell, suddenly stopped.

"Hey, Farris! You hear what the captain was telling me
just before he left? About his cousin?"

"Yeah."

"You want an apple?"

Farris moved quickly through the darkness. He knew these
pastures as well as he knew the inside of the barracks, and
he knew how far he could get in the hours remaining to him.
With luck, he might have even more time. Malik was stupid.
When he came to relieve Gault at the cell, he might not even
wonder where Gault was.

He'd hated to crack his friend over the head like that, but
Gault had insisted. "If I don't have a lump on my skull to
prove this story that you knocked me out, *I'll* wind up in
this cell. And you have to tie me up and gag me and strip
me bare. If it was Barak or Malik that you knocked on the
head, would you leave his clothes, his weapons? Or risk him
yelling for help when he came to?"

"No."

"All right, then. Besides, this sword isn't my Vessa. Garan
told me not to wear her tonight. It's one of Launart's issue

meatchoppers. Good enough for a new recruit.''

"Will a mercenary warband take an ex-slave?" Not that
it mattered to him now whether he was mercenary or outlaw,
so long as he was free and alive.

"Don't tell anyone and nobody is likely to ask. We mercenaries don't ask each other what you were or did before.
I have seen a few other men with backs scarred like yours."
Gault had paused momentarily, as if uncertain whether he
should reveal what he said next. "Captain Garan is one of
them. Now, if you can, try to find Bayard's Wolves or Storran's Stallions. They're both like Garan, good captains with
decent warbands, not the half-bandit scum that some of them
are. Tell them I sent you."

When Farris was ready to go, Gault had held out his hand.
"Luck ride with you, *sabro.*"

Sabro. Swordbrother. The name they used for each other.
Farris slapped his hand into Gault's and the two clasped fore-
arms hard. Then Gault turned his head away and waited for
the blow that would knock him out.

Gault's shirt was much too big for him, even with strips torn
from it for binding and gagging, and the sword was rigged
to hang on the wrong side, but those were minor problems.
He had been lucky that Gault had worn his short riding cloak
for warmth while standing guard. The hood, pulled low as
if to shield his face from the cold rain, had done an excellent
job of hiding his collar, shaved head, and battered face. He
had swaggered past the inattentive sentry and out through the
main gate, just another mercenary coming off duty and heading out for a night on the town.

Now he needed to steal a horse, and he knew just the one
he wanted.

At his whistle the horses drowsing under the dubious shelter of the trees raised their heads. He whistled again. Yes,
there he was. The full moon broke through the clouds momentarily, although the rain still poured down. That fitful
light showed Farris the white forefoot and the blaze running
down the gelding's face. Whitefoot was not much to look at,
just an ordinary brown horse; nothing showed the care that

had gone into his breeding. He had heart and intelligence and stamina instead of good looks, and Farris felt that he was one of the best horses he had seen in his five years here. They had gelded Whitefoot because he wasn't the pretty satin-hided palfrey they were breeding for, and kept him as a general working horse.

Lady Viveka had insisted that he should be destroyed for kicking her mare, but Roldan had moved him to these far pastures with the rest of the culled stock awaiting sale; nobody would miss him for days.

Farris coaxed the horse to him with the core of Gault's apple. He wished momentarily for a real bridle and saddle instead of the piece of rope he was rigging into an Avakir war-bridle, no more than a loop over Whitefoot's lower jaw. A wild image, himself walking into Roldan's quarters and asking for the key to the tack room, came into his head and he laughed as he made a running leap onto the horse's back. Might as well ask Duke Launart for the key to his collar!

Collar key. That was the other thing he needed. He trotted Whitefoot over to one of the trees and reached up into a hole in the trunk. This was the hiding place he and Kiam had established years ago, when they had started making wild imaginary plans to escape. Though most of them hinged on some fantastically improbable situation, none of them had been as preposterous as this reality.

He lifted out a small leather bag and carefully poured the contents into his hand. Most of it was small coins they had found on the ground. He intended to leave all of them; Gault's pouch had contained much more. The item he wanted was longer and thicker, easily distinguishable even in the dark. Farris had risked a lashing to slide it into his boot on a long-ago visit to the blacksmith, but the smith hadn't even noticed that the piece of broken file had disappeared.

Now he sat momentarily weighing it in his hand, wishing he could get Kiam out of the barracks somehow so that they could escape together. It was impossible, he knew, and he couldn't waste time wishing. Quickly he slid the file into the belt-pouch and poured the coins back into the leather bag. He carefully replaced it in its hiding spot. That was all he could do to help Kiam now; he would have to escape either on his own or not at all.

He let himself and the horse out of the gate and headed east into the forest, vanishing into the rainy night.

12

FLIGHT

Farris had been on the edges of this forest often. Loarn sat at its western edge, and the far pastures were just out of bowshot of its cover. It had an evil reputation. Local legend said it was fai-haunted, and that humans who ventured in were taken by the fai and kept for a hundred years. Well, if they did, that would certainly be enough to throw any pursuit off his track!

He held Whitefoot to a walk, although he wanted to urge him to his fastest gallop. That would be sheer stupidity; although the horse's night vision was better than a human's, it would still be all too easy for him to put a foot wrong in this gloom and break a leg.

He doubted that they would set tracking dogs on him before dawn, but a night search was not impossible. The rain, alternating between downpour and drizzle, would wash out any scent and most signs of his passage. They knew that as well as he did, and might have dogs on his trail already. It took an effort to stop in the gray dawn to let Whitefoot graze and rest.

Food for himself was only a little harder. As a caravan slave he had often been sent into the woods to forage for part of his master's meals, and Gault's stories had given him other ideas. A woodsrat had the bad luck to flash down its hole when he was looking; he dragged it out with its fur tangled in a forked branch. The hole itself yielded the remains of its winter stash. Raw woodsrat and wormy hazelnuts were no feast, but more breakfast than he had been getting.

Farris tried to keep Whitefoot to either grassy or rocky places during the day that followed. He had little experience with tracking, but common sense told him that hoofprints would show up better in mud.

Once he thought he heard hounds, very faint and far away. He stopped and listened carefully, but the sound was not repeated. His hand went almost unconsciously to the weapons at his side. They would not take him alive—and he would take a warrior's honorguard with him.

The rain continued the rest of that day. By the time the light started to dim he was near to collapse, hungry again, wet and cold except for his clawed cheek. That was hot, and sometime soon he would take the time to worry that it was becoming infected.

When Whitefoot started up a grouse off her nest, Farris ignored her broken-wing act to hunt for the nest itself. Eleven eggs sat there waiting to be eaten. How close they might have been to hatching he didn't know or care. He wolfed them down without tasting them.

First food, now shelter. He couldn't hope for a cave, or an abandoned peasant's hut, not here. The only shelter that presented itself was a downed tree. Its hollow trunk drifted with leaves proved to be more or less dry. He had just enough strength left to tether Whitefoot where he could graze; the grass was wet enough so that the horse wouldn't suffer from lack of water. He crawled into the hollow, curled up under his cloak, and fell asleep.

The next day had barely dawned when he snapped awake. Were those voices he had heard, or had he only dreamed them? He must have. "*. . . Mine now, Ydona,*" an oddly familiar male voice had said. Hand on sword, he listened carefully for a long time.

It was still raining when he finally crawled out of his shelter and resumed riding. His face felt better, cooler than it had been, but when he saw healall growing, he took enough time to pull it and chew it into a poultice. He had no way to apply it, but merely holding it to his face helped him to feel he was doing something.

During one of the breaks to let Whitefoot graze, he dug the bit of file out of his pouch. It was awkward trying to cut something by feel, but at last he succeeded in scraping out a shallow groove in his collar, as close to the lock as possible. The piece was small and missing several teeth; it caught on almost every stroke. He persisted until the groove was half the depth of the collar, and the cramping and burning of his fingers forced him to stop.

He had better luck with his foraging, tickling a trout from a stream and raiding a cattail patch, but found no shelter that night. His sleep was not the deep one of exhaustion, but the light doze of a hunted wild thing. More than once he woke when Whitefoot snorted or stamped, although tense listening did not reveal any sound of danger.

Farris was on the move before dawn the next morning, too uneasy to sleep any longer. The rain had stopped, and although he knew the clouds had not hidden him in any way, he had the feeling now that he was being watched. The cattail roots he ate as he rode, and he only stopped briefly to let Whitefoot snatch a few mouthfuls of grass.

During these short breaks, he continued to gnaw away at the collar, nerves on edge in case he should have to drop the file and snatch at his sword. Even foraging for food became secondary to getting that collar off his neck. It was noon when he scraped through the last bit of iron and scratched himself. The collar did not fall off his neck; the hinge was stiff and probably rusty. He had to use both hands to force it open.

Pain and pleasure are relative things. The burning of his hands was lost in the wave of relief from the bite of the collar as he dropped it. For the first time in nearly eight years he was free of cold iron on his throat, free of that which marked him as a slave. It was sheer ecstasy; he felt bigger and stronger and somehow more aware of things around him. The forest looked brighter and more . . . *alive*, somehow.

Let them try to recapture him now. *Nobody* would put a collar on his neck again; he would kill the next man who tried! Sheer elation drove him to his feet, sword in hand. He slashed and thrust at an invisible enemy, blocked and countered imaginary blows before the foe went down before his onslaught. He dropped into an exercise Gault had taught him, his blade flickering as he wove a pattern that ripped the air.

In the midst of his play another feeling struck him like a blow in the back: *Someone was watching him.* He whipped around to face the unknown, a snarl twisting his face into an ugly mask of defiance.

No one was there. Whitefoot continued to graze undisturbed, and the feeling ebbed as quickly as it had come, as if the unseen watcher had retreated.

Farris did not waste any more time in play. He leaped for Whitefoot's back, kicking him into a gallop through the trees. Whoever or whatever watched him was not friendly; the feeling of enmity was as real as a shout of hatred.

Two days passed before he stopped again for any length of time. He grabbed sleep in brief uneasy naps while Whitefoot grazed and rested, and only the worsening condition of his horse and the bite of hunger in his own belly forced him to stop running. Neither of them could go much farther without a day or two of rest, and the mouthfuls of food that they snatched on the run were not enough; Whitefoot was starting to look as gaunt as Farris himself.

When he topped a rise and looked down into an inviting green valley, he was almost too tired and hungry to worry about danger. His belly growled loudly, reminding him that he had not eaten since robbing another bird's nest that morning.

He raided another cattail patch for roots and shoots, and took note of a rabbit warren and the animals' network of trails. A few hairs from Whitefoot's tail gave him the makings of snares; he set two of them where he thought they were most likely to catch his breakfast, and moved on in search of a place to camp. These hills should be riddled with caves.

They were not. A few promising holes turned out to be only cracks in the rock, small enough to curl up in for a night's sleep, but no larger. He wanted a place big enough for both of them, a place he could defend if need be.

A place where he could hide out for the next few months, he realized as he thought about it. He had to stop running eventually. There was no sign of pursuit from Loarn; there hadn't been since that first day. Maybe Ydona had sent him some luck at last. Either the rain had washed away his trail, or they were afraid to come into these hills after him. Perhaps both. And whoever or whatever had watched him with such hatred seemed not to have pursued him at all.

If he kept going, he would be in D'Alriaun before long. If anybody saw him, his stubble of hair and the untanned band of skin around his throat would mark him as a former slave if not a runaway. He couldn't risk that, not when any runaway slave could be turned over to the local provost for the standing reward. And who knew how much more reward Launart was offering? He had to hide until his hair grew to a decent length and his tan covered the area where the collar had been.

This valley might be a good place to hide. *And if it isn't . . . ?* He turned in a full circle and looked at the emerald meadows and the jade-and-gold dapple of the trees. *If it isn't, then this is a good place to die.*

The valley was a good place. There was no sign that humans had ever come here. Slopes and river bottoms that looked arable (at least to his untrained eye) had never felt the plow, and there were no buildings, not even ruined ones.

Farris spent the night curled up in one of those cracks in the rock face, with Whitefoot grazing nearby, and checked his snares the next morning. Only one still held a rabbit. The other had been gnawed through, by what animal he could not tell.

He hobbled Whitefoot to graze his fill while he continued his search for a suitable cave, and found one farther down the valley. It was big enough to hold both himself and his horse, with a jagged ceiling high enough to let smoke collect and dissipate before it made its way out. The floor was rocky rather than the hard-packed dirt he had imagined caves should have, but that couldn't be helped. He could bring in pine needles or something to make a bed.

In his search for bedding materials, he startled a deer and her fawns. They slipped away from him so silently that at first he thought they were spirit animals. Spirits, however, did not leave droppings or beds of compressed vegetation where they had rested.

Food, his belly reminded him insistently. *Venison.* Venison hadn't come his way often, only leftover scraps from a few feasts, but the memory of the flavorful meat made his mouth water at the prospect. But how did one hunt deer alone? He knew how the nobles hunted, with dogs to track the deer, beaters to flush them out, and spears or archery gear to bring them down. He had none of those.

And yet there was this network of game trails. He looked speculatively at the trees. How often would deer pass this way, to make trails like this? Every day?

Well before evening he settled himself in his chosen tree. The Hunter God Vorndal might have put the branches overhanging the trail there just for his purpose. A bath in the creek had washed away most of his human scent, he hoped, and he had taken the further precaution of rubbing some smelly weeds on his body. He had only to wait for a deer now. He seemed to remember that they preferred to feed at dusk and dawn.

The sun was only two fingers from the horizon when he saw the first deer. He blinked but did not move, except for the hairs rising in a chill down his back and arms. It was a white doe.

Everyone knew that white animals were sacred. Deer belonged to . . . the Goddess of Wild Things. He couldn't remember Her name. *Ydona, please, help me. Tell Her I do not commit sacrilege. I must take this deer.*

The doe moved closer and closer, suspiciously testing the air and looking about. He could see her nostrils twitch as she paused. Three more steps and he would leap, white doe or not. He grasped the hilt of his dagger tightly, already rehearsing in his mind the leap that would take him to her back, the slice of the blade across her throat.

He heard it an instant before he saw it, a soft *thnnng* and then a *thwack!* The doe stood motionless for a few heartbeats longer, then collapsed where she stood with a green-fletched arrow in her side.

Farris froze as he crouched, for who would hunt in these woods? A lord, kin to those he had fled? A peasant, who would turn him in for the reward?

She was neither of those; she was small and slim with white-blonde hair, a silver-white moon in contrast to his own wheat-blond and sun-bronze. Both fair and fai she was, and as she bent over her kill he slid out of the tree with a rush. She stared at him as if she were a frozen maid, one of those formed of snow in the beginning of the world, and as he spoke and reached toward her, she turned and fled, swift as the white doe herself.

"No, please, wait!" he cried. "I need help, and I'm one of you, I claim kin-right!"

She flitted before him, not fleeing now, for now and then she turned and sent coy glances his way. He did not know how long he chased her, nor where she was leading him; he only knew that he must follow her. At last she passed between two trees, and the last shaft of the setting sun caught her and turned her to palest gold; then she vanished as the sun did.

A cold wind blew about him as he stared in bewilderment, and a deep voice said, "You have no place here, half-kin."

In place of the girl was a man, no taller than Farris himself. He could not tell if the man was young or old; his hair might have been white or the same pale blond as the girl's, but his eyes were ageless. The fai held a staff of red oak, darkened with age and carved with figures that Farris could not make out; whether it was the gathering dusk or that the figures curved and twisted and changed, he did not know.

"Go back, half-kin. Our lands are not for you."

"I claim kin-right. My father was of the fai." Farris said stubbornly.

"Your father. His name, his Lineage?"

"I don't know. He did not wed my mother, but only lay with her, in the moonlight on a winter hill green as springtime, she said. If he told her his name, she did not tell it to me."

"Many of us lie with humans, man and maid, on a green hill in the moonlight. You have the Heritage and the Powers, but there are none here who will claim you as son, half-kin. You stink of cold iron, you carry it in your hand, and we have seen that you wore it around your neck."

"That was not my choice. It was done to me by those I flee." *Where are these words coming from? This is no bard's tale, it is the world I live in, the world of cold and hunger and pain.*

"So you flee, do you? Not to us. One of our own would have died by his own hand before cold iron was locked on his throat. You have no kin-right here, no place. Be you gone!" He raised the staff in his hand.

Against his will Farris followed the movement of the staff. His legs felt turned to stone, and a deep wave of dizziness washed over him. He fought to remain on his feet and closed his eyes, leaning his hand against the bark of the tree next to him. It shivered like a live thing, like a horse that twitches flies off its skin, and he jerked his hand away. It was the wrong move. He fell, down and down, but whether it was years or miles he fell, again he did not know.

When he awoke, it was to the half light of the deep woods, but it was the half-light of dawn, not dusk. He stood, stiff and shaking and cramped with hunger, and turned to go as he had been ordered.

In front of him were the butchered remains of a white doe. Seated cross-legged on the ground behind her kill was the fai girl, studying him with a sorrowful look in her amber-brown eyes.

13

FAI

"I'm leaving," Farris growled. "You don't have to watch to make sure of it."

"No, wait, half-kin. Wrong they are."

He gave her no answer, but turned away to look for White-foot.

"Help you I will—help you I *must*," she insisted, catching at his arm. "Kin we are. Human speech I have not much. Word is what? *Please.*"

"Didn't you hear him? 'You have no place here, *half-kin.*'" There was savage mockery on his last word.

"'Here' valley is not. 'Here' S'Eyrr rra Irrnan—Land between Worlds—is. Valley you may stay, in safety. I, Ylorath, swear on Ancestors of us both, is true!"

A spark of hope flared. If he understood her, he was not forbidden the valley, only the "Land between Worlds"—the land of the fai?

"Why?" he asked suspiciously. "Why does he say 'get out' and you say 'stay'?"

"*Kin* we are," she repeated, as if exasperated at his denseness. "S'Eyrr rra Irrnan you may not go. Twinborn you are. This we know, from your birth. Legend is, twinborn half-kin disaster will bring upon us. Scrying I did, you it is not. But law remains. If born you were among us, destroyed you would have been.

"Powers you have, you know not. Teach you I will, I must, how to use." She tugged at his arm again. "Come. Eat together we will."

Those last words made his decision for him. His belly gave a mighty growl and cramped tight from hunger. Farris let her lead him to a clearing only a few yards away, where firewood was waiting for a spark to give it life.

Ylorath did not use magic to light it, as he half expected, but an ordinary spark-striker. Strips of meat lay ready on a platter of enormous leaves; she did not wait for the fire to die down to coals, but skewered the meat on sharpened sticks and held it over the flames.

To keep his mind off the gnawing ache on his belly he asked, "How are we kin?"

"Lineage name I may not tell. To me, brother's son you are." Sorrow crept back into her eyes, and into her voice. "Dead he is. Much like him you look."

Farris could not grieve for a father he had always hated. "Human legend says fai are immortal."

She shook her head. "Many lives of humans we live, but old we grow, in time. And killed we can be. My brother, warrior he was, of much courage. From him, warrior courage, warrior skill, you have. To honor my brother, you I will help."

Farris pondered her offer even as he ate her meat. (Barely seared, it was but after nothing but raw food for so long, it was heavenly.) Could he trust her? All the legends of fai said they were devious beings, that their aid could be either help or disaster, depending on nothing more than their whim. What sort of "powers" could she mean? And how could he have them without knowing about them?

He did not much like the answers that followed that meal. As he had suspected, his eyes, his face, his size all said "fai." But it seemed that he owed strength and speed and sword-skill to his father also.

"Warrior you are," Ylorath said firmly. "Brother's son could not be less. Like him you fight. I watch, I see. Other warrior skills I will teach. The Unseeing, the Guiding, better to use Beast-Voice."

Unseeing? Guiding? Those sounded like the vague mystic prattle of a wandering priest he had heard during his boyhood. But the other, now . . .

"Beast-Voice?" he asked.

"Talk you to horses, no? And you they obey, willingly? All beasts will do so, if you wish. Watch." Ylorath made a soft noise deep in her throat.

A rabbit hopped out of the bushes and put its front paws up on her leg. It quivered in fear; she put her hand out and stroked it, crooning softly. "To you they will come. Wild ones afraid, tame ones friendly.

"There are rules. To hunt this way you may *not*, ever. Your . . . goddess, She of wild things, angered will be. Destroy you She will."

Farris reached out a cautious hand and touched the rabbit.

"Yes," Ylorath said. "This one is your key. Yourself open to it; it is you and you are it. Its fear feel, and banish. To all creatures you are kin; *feel* that kinship."

"But . . ." he began. The rest of the words he meant to say vanished in a dizzying swirl of colors in front of his eyes, akin to the odd brilliance that he had noticed when the iron of the slave-collar left his neck. He squeezed them shut; when he opened them again, he was seeing through two pairs of eyes. He could see his own hand on the rabbit's back, feel the texture of its soft fur with his fingers—and look up at the human above him, feel its hand on his own back, trembling with the terrified drumming of his heart.

She put it—him—into the human body's hands. The fingers scratched gently; a soothing wave of comfort flowed from them. He would not die, not this time.

The trembling of the furry little body eased. Farris opened his hands and the rabbit sat there unafraid, content for a moment before it hopped down to investigate an edible-looking plant.

Whitefoot wandered over, stretching out his neck to sniff at the creature that was taking his rider's attention. Rabbit eyes saw the horse as a huge creature. For a moment he was afraid that it would step on him, and he scrambled back into the safety of the human lap.

"Contact you must break," Ylorath said softly. "Eyes you will close."

Reluctantly he obeyed. When he opened them again, the double vision had vanished, along with the rabbit.

"Touch you must, to be one with beast," Ylorath continued briskly. "To call them, speak softly. Of things they would like, think."

"But—*you* did something, to join us. How do I do it alone? Is there a spell, or something?"

"Spell? No. High Magic this is not. Inborn, this is, from my brother who sired you. Most simple it is—so." She reached out and took his hands, touching him for the first and only time.

There were no words. There could not be, not for this. As if her touch had triggered it, a flood of knowledge swelled from some indefinable part of him and lodged itself in his consciousness. He *knew* now what she meant, and what she had done.

Whether he could bear to do it again or not, he did not know. It would be a long time before he could eat rabbit again. "But—you said warrior skills. How will this help me?"

"To slaughter needlessly you wish, unheeding other's pain?" Ylorath snapped. "Too much time we have wasted. Return I must, soon, or the Council will know. You would know the Guiding, the Unseeing also?"

"What are those?" He was still wary of her gifts. Would all of them change him as he had just been changed?

"Guiding is to know where you are, where you must go. Lost you cannot be."

"That I have already. I've never been lost."

Ylorath's face twitched in a brief smile. "Good. The Unseeing, then. Watch.'' Her body blurred suddenly—and vanished.

"Still here I am. See me you cannot, yes?'' said her voice from the empty air.

"No. What sort of trickery is that?''

"Trickery it is not. Thinking it is. I think you cannot see me, so you cannot.''

That learning was more difficult, for her command of Sharrese was not sufficient to explain herself fully. As near as Farris could make out, thinking was all that was involved. If he could concentrate hard enough on the idea that he was not there, no one could see him. It sounded too simple to be believable.

Perhaps that was why Ylorath frowned at him. "See you I still can, half-kin. Think harder!''

"I *am* thinking,'' he grated through clenched teeth. *I'm not here, I'm not here, I'mnothere.*

"Better,'' she said with a tight smile. She glanced at the sun overhead in the midmorning sky, stood and stretched like a cat. "I must go, brother's son. Ancestors keep watch over you.'' Again her form blurred and vanished.

"Wait! At least let me say thank you!'' Farris cried.

There was no answer from her, then or ever.

14

HUNTING

Date—unknown

Farris scowled at the marks on the wall of the cave and counted them again. He had scratched one every day, first thing in the morning before he started the fire. There was no way he could have marked a day twice, and very little chance that he had forgotten to mark more than one or two days. There were four rows of them, thirty marks in each row. That was one hundred and twenty days, by his count, four months that he had been living in this valley, and yet nothing added up.

There had been wild strawberries flowering here when he had arrived. Four months later they were still bearing, long past their season. Blackberries had bloomed and ripened, were still blooming and ripening, heavy with flower and fruit at once as he had never seen them.

If he was right, it was the first week of Harvestend, and the first leaves should be starting to turn. Kingsgold should be blooming to herald the end of summer. Instead the grasshoppers still buzzed and the birds still sang their mating calls as they did in spring. It looked like late spring or early summer; it felt like that, too, and every day he spent here sent greater trickles of uneasiness down his spine and a restless unnameable longing.

You're giving yourself the creeps, Farris, he told himself firmly. *Maybe it's the fai's doing. If they can make a single night stretch for a hundred years, why shouldn't they keep their own valley always summer? Quit fretting about it, get your arse moving and take Whitefoot down for some water.*

At the quiet spring he preferred for his own drinking water he stopped for a moment to study his reflection. The man who looked back at him was very different from the runaway slave of four months ago. Shaggy blond hair, no shorter than the way peasants wore it, covered the once-shaved head, and the scars that had formed on his clawed face pulled one corner of his mouth into a permanent half-smile. Both beard and mustache were well grown—too well, in fact, for the mustache was ragged where he had trimmed it with his dagger to keep it out of his food. He was well-fed and rested; the band of white around his neck was gone, tanned the same warm brown as the rest of him.

The almost physical tugging that made him want to jump onto Whitefoot's back and *ride* grew stronger. It was time to move on. Though the cave was warm and dry and White-foot's presence was comfort and company of a sort, he missed other humans, especially Kiam. Never before in his life had he been so completely alone; other people had always been at least within earshot. Even Haral or Roldan would have been preferable to these months of solitude.

It was this aching loneliness that was driving him as much as anything. Loneliness, and a need to get on with his life. If he wanted to hire on with a mercenary warband, it should be soon. The fighting season ended with the onset of winter; none of the lords who hired such warbands wanted to conduct cold uncomfortable winter campaigns.

He had no doubts now of his own skill with a sword. Feeding himself took less time than he had imagined; the rest of the hours of daylight he put to practicing with his weapons. He ran through innumerable drills for strength and speed and agility, drills that Gault had taught him and ones that he remembered from his boyhood.

Even that had left him with time on his hands. He turned to hunting, and found that even when he didn't make a kill, there was satisfaction in perfecting the skills of silent unseen approach; more than once he had crept close enough to touch an animal.

He had made no more attempts to contact the fai. Twice he had seen them ride past in procession, gloriously beautiful men and women in shimmering garb even more splendid than that of King Tiorbran and his family, mounted on horses barded with silken draperies.

Just yesterday they had swept past not twenty feet from him, ignoring him as if he were a rock or tree in their path. They laughed and chattered among themselves, as if they were the only living creatures in the whole valley. Ylorath had been among them; she, too, had pretended that he was not there.

Damn them, then! Rejection could work both ways. From now on, he would think of himself as human, not half-breed.

And he would leave this eerie summerland to them. He whistled for Whitefoot, swung up onto his back, and rode away without looking back.

Two days' ride later he was no longer sure if he was still in Dur Sharrukhan or had crossed over the border into D'Alriaun. The eastern kingdom was somewhat larger but poorer than its neighbor, and the two had been at war off and on for centuries. An uneasy peace had held between the two kingdoms for the last few years, ever since they had allied to repulse an invasion of Avakir barbarians from the northeast. Songs and stories still circulated about that invasion, for the rumor had it that the God of Evil had prodded the Avakirs into the war Himself.

Farris didn't know the truth of it or particularly care. All he did care was that he would be safer in a neighboring kingdom than in his home one.

He traveled through the woods for three more days before he finally trusted to the roads. He knew now that he was into

D'Alriaun, for the wolfbirds he had heard last night did not
live in Dur Sharrukhan. Their eerie wailing cries made him
laugh now at the scared city boy he had been seven years
ago; he had been certain then that they were real wolves that
would just love to make supper of a young slave.

This road now was familiar, too, from his years in the
caravans. The next town was Wolfdale. The guardsman at
the gates of the wooden palisade that protected it looked
rather askance at him, but accepted his story of being a freesword looking for work.

The noise of the open market made him want to bolt back
for the woods, but the scent of baking bread was enough to
draw him like a magic spell. Farris hadn't realized his crav-
ing for something besides meat and foraged plants until he
wolfed down the first hot breadroll the bakerwoman sold
him. The second was rolled around slices of cheese, and the
melted tang of it made his face curl into an expression of
pure bliss. The small copper coin he spent was well worth
it.

Even if he hadn't known this was a different kingdom, the
change in language would have told him. It was not much,
mainly a difference in the vowel sounds. The D'Alriaun
word was eorl rather than earl, for instance, and his own
goddess was changed from Ydona to Edana. Still, their language was pleasant to the ear and not too hard to understand
or speak. He listened with dubious enjoyment to the sound
of human voices as he made his way to the blacksmith's
shop.

Along the way he noticed girls chattering and giggling as
they hung bright banners over windowsills and draped garlands of flowers everywhere they could reach. One of them,
a plump, pretty red-haired lass, caught his eye as she leaned
out of an upper window to fasten an especially long garland
across the narrow street. Her blouse had slipped down far
enough to expose the enticing valley between her breasts.
She saw him looking, and where, and giggled again. The
garland "accidentally" slipped from her fingers and draped
itself across Whitefoot's neck.

"Whoa, boy! Fair maiden, I believe this is yours," he called with a grin.

"Indeed, stranger. Would you please hand it back to me?" she answered with a dimpled smile.

"I don't think I can reach, but wait." He guided Whitefoot directly under the window and gave him the signal to stand firm. With utmost care he put both hands on the horse's withers and gathered his feet under him, then stood up on Whitefoot's back. The maiden blushed and dimpled again as he gave her the garland.

"What are you celebrating, my lady?" Farris asked.

"Why, sir, I think from your speech you come from Dur Sharrukhan. Do they not celebrate the Summerlord's Day there with flowers and feasting?"

"Summerlord's Day? Indeed we do, and with other pleasant customs as well. When a young man gives a pretty young girl flowers on Summerlord's Day, he claims a kiss for his reward."

"Not from *my* wife you don't!" roared a male voice from inside the house.

"Uh-oh. Some other time, sweetheart." He dropped down onto Whitefoot's back and nudged him into a trot. The girl's laughter followed him down the street.

So, Summerlord's Day. The first day of Yellowgrain, more than a month earlier than his reckoning. Again the chills crawled down his spine and he wondered just how long he had been in the fai valley. Four months—or a hundred years?

The smith clucked over the state of Whitefoot's hooves. "A fighting man like you ought to take better care of his animal. What have you been using on his feet, that sword? This horse should have been reshod weeks ago."

"I know. But bad luck and little money . . ." Farris let the statement trail off with a shrug. "I've got his old shoes here in trade. You know of anyplace I could pick up a job?"

"Thought you were one of those mercenaries that're camped outside of town," the smith said gruffly.

"No, I'm a freesword. An unemployed freesword. Mercenaries, you say? Did you talk to them?"

"Yeah, but not that I wanted to. Scruffy-looking lot. Wolves, one of them said they were, and they look it. Bared's Wolves, Bayard's Wolves, something like that. Said they were hiring and wanted to get the news out."

Farris knew when he swaggered into the mercenary camp that he didn't look much like a mercenary; most of them followed the tradition of long hair, flamboyant mustache, and short-clipped beard. His own hair was still too short, although he had spent one of his hoarded coins to have his mustache and beard neatly trimmed.

He headed straight for the meanest-looking man there and asked to see the captain.

"You found him," the mercenary said, eyeing him distastefully. "Looking to hire on, are you?"

"Yes. Had a recommendation for you from a friend."

"Who?"

"Only name I know for him is Gault."

"Red Gault? Did he tell you I was the man that broke his thumb for him?"

"Black Gault, I'd call him. Straight black hair, thinning on top, badger-striped beard, black eyes, and a Riazan accent you could cut with a knife. Old scar running through one eyebrow and down his cheek, and a dozen different stories about how he got it. And he said he broke *your* thumb."

The mercenary grunted. "Maybe he recommended us to you, but he didn't recommend you to me. How's your sword-work?"

"Not bad."

"Not bad isn't good enough. Can't use you."

"Can't use me, huh? You don't think you can use one of the nastiest unarmed combat men you'll ever see, a man who can slide past any sentry and not be seen? You can't use a man who can ride any horse ever foaled? Or a man who can always tell when he's being lied to?"

"Prove it."

"Well, for one, you're not the captain—*he* is." He kept the smile off his face; the man's body language had said all along that he was lying, nor did he match the description Gault had given Farris.

The mercenaries who had drifted in closer, eager for anything to break up the monotony of a day stuck in camp, broke into loud laughter and comments of "He's got you there, Serlan!"

Farris raised a quizzical eyebrow at them, gave a twitch to his mouth that was not quite a half-grin, and shrugged. "Shall I go on, Captain Bayard?"

The captain, a blocky, bearlike man who looked like Gault but shorter, snorted and motioned for him to continue.

"Next, call in your north lookout man; big bald guy, wearing a streaky green shirt and lying up in a big oak tree with a broken branch. Ask him if he passed me through."

"I'll do that," the captain said. "Perrin, go fetch Conal and take his place. And you, what's your name?"

"Faron." Necessity dictated the name change. Surely Duke Launart had reward notices out for him all over Dur Sharrukhan; he didn't think they had come over the border here into D'Alriaun, but it wasn't impossible, nor were bounty hunters.

"All right, Faron, you see that big ugly roan over there? Ride him."

"Now, sir?"

"No, next week. Of course now."

Farris shrugged again and trotted toward the horse. It shifted uneasily and its ears swiveled back flat to its skull. "Now, lad, you don't want to do that, do you?" he said softly. "Easy, now." For the first time since Ylorath had given him the knowledge, he tried to use that skill she had called Beast-Voice.

The roan stamped a foot at him and shook its head. He continued to talk softly until the flattened ears pricked up to listen to him. "That's it, lad, that's it. Come on now; we'll show them a thing or two, won't we?" He was close enough now to extend a hand to the horse and stroke its neck. Again the world spun and resolved itself into the view from two pairs of eyes. This time, though, there were vague thoughts to go with the vision.

Stranger. Not-master. Must bite, kick . . . no. Not this one.

The horse made no move, even after he broke the contact, to bite or kick him as he released its tether line. It shivered when he swung onto its bare back, but did not move otherwise. Farris could feel the tenseness of the sleek muscles as its desire to obey him warred with its training to allow only one rider. *"Now* we show them."

The horse reared at his signal, then kicked out as it dropped back down. War moves, those were, intended to crush an enemy beneath its battering hooves. A quick pivot ended with another rear-and-kick. He rode the roan in a mincing trot toward its master (watching with hidden amusement as mercenaries scrambled out of its way) and ended with one of the bows that he had trained into so many nobles' palfreys.

As he dismounted he said to the captain, "A bit skittish, isn't he, sir?"

Captain Bayard stared at him a moment, then broke into loud gusty laughter. "Whether we take you in or not, that show was worth supper at least. Got a horse of your own?"

Farris whistled loudly, a shrill rising two-note summons. There was a startled shout from a man just entering the camp center, the lookout that the captain had identified as Conal, as Whitefoot cantered easily up to Farris and stood with pricked ears and an air of expectant waiting.

The captain looked at him closely. "Nice animal. Not a warhorse, though."

"Yeah. Culled palfrey. Got him cheap because he wasn't pretty enough for a lady or heavy enough for a plowhorse or warhorse. But for someone my size, he's fine."

"Conal, did you pass this man through?" the mercenary captain asked.

"No sir. I haven't passed anyone through since Bors got back from market."

"Well, he's here somehow. Claims to be an unarmed combat expert. Take him."

Conal whipped around at the command and lunged for Farris, but the smaller man was not where he had been, nor was he so easily taken. Twice the larger mercenary thought he had him in his grasp, and was surprised to find that he was the one tossed aside. The third time Conal managed to hang on to him and throw him, only to find himself pulled off his feet, his neck twisted, and his arm slammed across the other's knee.

Farris flipped to his feet and faced him warily. "You didn't tell me whether you wanted him disabled or dead, Captain. A little more pressure, and I could have broken either his arm or his neck."

Conal sat up, rubbing his neck. "Yes sir, he could have. I can feel it. Damn, you fight *mean* for a little man. Again, sir?"

"Not yet, Con. I get him now." The captain drew his sword.

Farris lunged for his. The world narrowed to the man and the blade in front of him. This was real, now. This sword would not leave a bruise or welt behind, but raw red pain, and his life running out with his blood.

The swords rang repeatedly as he concentrated on defense. A tiny corner of his mind hysterically insisted that he should kill this man facing him, while another one rebuked sensibly, *How can he give you a job if he's dead?*

But defense won't give me the proof that I know how to fight, a third part of his mind said. He began to watch for holes in the captain's own defense, and at the next opportunity slid his blade in to tap the other on the helm. And the arm. And the ribs.

"Hold!" someone roared after an endless time. Farris dropped back a step, his chest heaving, but remained ready and waiting. The captain grinned crookedly at him and sheathed his sword.

"You'll do for now. Bors, get him some water. Serlan?"

The two mercenaries went aside to talk quietly. Evidently Serlan was the second-in-command. Farris tried to hear what they were saying as a boy about twelve years old brought him a cup of water, but caught only murmurs, not words.

"Well, what do you think, Serlan?"

"As he says, sir, not bad with the sword. Damn good in fact, but a little rusty. Like he's been working out alone instead of with a partner. I think with practice he can do a lot better. But look at his hair, sir, and the way he holds himself. Ex-slave, I'd say, not been free for more than a few months. And did you see the way he starts at every unexpected noise?''

''Runaway, maybe? If he is, he's got guts, coming here. But I agree, I think we can use him. Wargames coming up soon.'' The captain turned and beckoned to Farris. ''Faron!''

''Yessir?''

''All right, man, you say you can ride, sneak, and fight. Our testing says you have some skills, at least. What sort of job do you think you can do with those skills that we might need?''

Farris didn't hesitate. Long hours of solitude had caused him to ask himself the same questions. ''I can think of two, sir. Scout and courier. I can get through and take cover in brush where a bigger man can't, and I ride light. A horse can carry me faster and farther than it can almost any of you.''

Captain Bayard nodded as if he agreed. ''Provisional acceptance. Half-pay through the end of Eorl Lyulf's wargames, then we either sign you or kick you out.''

''Three-quarters pay, sir. Yes, I'm green, but either I earn it or I don't. Hold the other quarter until you decide if I'm worth it. If you give me the boot, then you keep it.'' He kept his eyes steady on the captain. This was easy; he couldn't lose either way.

''Done. Bring in your gear. You'll share a tent for now with Jehan.''

''Well, there's a slight problem, Captain. The only gear I have is what I'm standing in right now.''

''Thought it looked like you've been living rough. What happened?'' The mild-sounding request had the force of an order.

Farris rubbed the fresh scars on his face ruefully. ''I tried to bed the wrong wench. Got out with breeches and boots and a more-or-less whole skin, and was thankful for it.''

Bayard laughed again at his sheepish expression. ''Don't

you know the first rule of wenching, man? 'Always know where her husband is!' "

"Ah! That was my problem. She didn't have a husband."

"That other quarter pay goes to the warchest then, to outfit you. Welcome to the Wolves."

13

※

WARGAMES

Farris received extensive training over the next two weeks, not only to hone his own fighting skills but to fit him into the team that was Bayard's Wolves. They outfitted him with such spare armor as was available and would fit him, which was very little. Helm and mail coif and shield were easy; body-armor was not. He finally had to settle for plain boiled leather rather than the brigandine he yearned for.

His new comrades were casually friendly, especially Balian, the warband's cook and healer, and his helper Bors, the boy who had brought Farris his water on the first day. The others waited somewhat before offering him their friendship, but he did not blame them. A green recruit had to make his own place in a warband like this.

Wargames turned out to be fun, even though their ultimate purpose was not. Eorl Lyulf and several of his neighbors hosted the games to keep their own fighting forces in training and to evaluate the mercenary warbands that participated. Bayard's Wolves were regarded as good but not outstanding; the captain was determined to change that at these games.

The participating forces were divided into two teams, Golds and Blues, and issued armbands to identify them. Bayard's Wolves drew Gold, under the command of Eorl Lyulf himself, who promised his troops "a glorious war to defeat that vile enemy, the Blue forces of Baron Lovarn."

The next two weeks, if not exactly glorious, were challenging enough for a new recruit. Open field battles alternated with guerrilla warfare in forest battles and cottage-to-cottage village battles.

Farris held his own in the field battles, "dying" only once, when a pikeman pulled him off his horse and another "stabbed" him with a mock dagger. The other forms of fighting, however, gave him his chance to prove himself.

As a green recruit, he was partnered with two more experienced scouts, one his tentmate Jehan, and another from the warband Fadrean's Foxes. Both of them laughed at his surprise when the Fox introduced herself as Anya.

"I didn't think you were that much of a greenie, Faron," Jehan chuckled. "Or hasn't news of the Foxes leaked over the border into Dur Sharrukhan? About a quarter of Fadrean's warband is female. They're specialists, not sword-swingers like us. Scouts, couriers, saboteurs—almost anything that takes wits instead of muscle."

"And that's why we're the highest-ranked warband, Jehan. But thanks for the compliment anyway. I didn't think you even noticed females had wits. You Wolves don't look any higher than a woman's tits," Anya grinned back at him. "Just you remember, I'm a Fox, not a vixen."

The forest battle was set up as Gault had described it. Five banners were posted in the forest; the side that controlled three or more of them by the time the bells rang to end the battle would win.

Jehan, Anya, and Farris worked well together as a team. Anya was a tracker; it was she who picked up traces of concealed passage where they knew no troops should have been, and showed Farris how to read the subtle signs that led them to the banner. The rules of the wargames did not allow them to hide it, or move it until it had been fought for. Someone must return to their main unit and bring them back here.

"Good," whispered Jehan as they nodded to the marshal

and grabbed drinks from the watergirls. "Faron, think you can get back to the warband from here and lead them in?"

"No problem. The way we came, or straight in?"

Jehan twisted his head to look at his new partner, a skeptical look on his face. "You don't know these woods. How can you tell where we are without going back the way we came?"

"Can't everybody?" Farris asked with a grin. "They're . . . that way, about three-quarters of a mile if I go straight, twice that if I retrace our path."

Anya shrugged. "Let him try it his way, Jehan. We were all hotsword greenies once. I'll go back by the original path as backup."

"All right. Go." Jehan settled into a place of concealment to keep watch.

Farris slipped silently through the woods, on as straight a line as possible. The fai skill that Ylorath called the "Guiding" was working, as it always had. He knew exactly where he was in relation to both banner and unit; his ignorance of the local terrain didn't make any difference, unless he should fall into a ravine or river.

Bayard's Wolves had been augmented by a troop of Eorl Lyulf's household Swordguard, under command of Lyulf's nephew (although the young lord might have thought it was the other way around). Farris found them with no trouble and reported to both leaders. He kept his mouth shut while Bayard wrangled with the lordling over his report, as that young worthy wanted to wait for his own scouts. When Anya trotted in a bit later, her confirmation decided it.

She raised an eyebrow at Farris and grinned at him. "Making Jehan eat his words, huh? We'll go back your way."

They reached the banner in time to see a unit of the Blues heading for it as well. The lordling made a sound of dismay. "Damn! That's Lovarn and his personal guard. We don't stand a chance." Nevertheless he trotted forward, drawing his sword. "Hold! My Swordguard and I challenge you to one-on-one combat!"

The leader of the Blues grinned and drew his sword as

well, eyeing the young men of the Swordguard hungrily.
"Done! Lay on!"

Farris followed Jehan's lead and swarmed up a tree to
watch the fight. "Why aren't we fighting?" he asked.

"Challenge of honor. It's a nobility thing. Us mudslogger
hired swords aren't supposed to interfere."

"Oh." Farris watched for a time and then climbed higher
up in the tree. *Might as well do part of my job, at least.* He
slid down much faster than he went up. "Captain! More
Blues headed this way, mercenaries!"

Bayard cursed and then grinned as the last of the Swordguard fell "dead." "Time for us to play, lads! Take 'em!"
The Wolves charged howling into battle and the captain
grabbed Farris' arm. "Faron, where are those Blues?"

"Coming up from the south, sir, about twenty of 'em."

"Grab that banner. You three try to get it to the Foxes.
We'll hold them off as long as we can."

It felt like running away from the fight, but orders were
orders. He scrambled after Jehan and Anya.

Farris remembered boasting about his skills getting
through brush, but he had never attempted to do it with a
large blue-and-gold banner in his arms before. With all the
deliberate perversity of an inanimate thing, it caught on tree
limbs, wrapped around his arm and hindered him, and insisted on flapping loose as if waving and calling for help.

And all too soon, he was alone.

Anya "died" first. An archer, concealed in a tree, got her
with a blunt round-tipped arrow as she set a trip-line. Farris
and Jehan could not help her; all they could do was escape
before the archer summoned more Blues.

Both of them were hot and tired and thirsty a long time
later. They had avoided two troops of Blues and were sneaking very carefully through the undergrowth when they spotted the black-and-white-checked banner that marked the
neutral area of a marshal's site. Farris could almost taste the
cold sweet water when a shout burst out on their right. They
took to their heels again.

"How many . . . damned Blues . . . are there?" he panted.

"Too many." Jehan turned his head to look behind them

and failed to see the same sort of trip-line that Anya had set up earlier. He fell headlong and rolled down a low bank. Farris leaped it and skidded to a stop almost on top of him.

"You all right?"

"No. My ankle!"

"Get your boot off. How bad is it?" Farris dropped to his knees and reached for Jehan's foot.

"No! It's either sprained bad or broken. Move that banner out of here!"

Farris moved, but not quickly enough. The chase was on. There was no time to try to lay a false trail or set a trap, no time even to hide. He could only run ahead of the baying pack of Blues.

His direction-finding skills did not help him avoid the ravine that opened suddenly in front of him. He teetered on the brink and recovered only by throwing himself backwards, losing precious heartbeats of time before he rolled to his feet and ran along its edge.

It must have been the capricious malice of some god that caused another ravine to open suddenly at his feet, running into the first one at a sharp angle. He was trapped. Farris dropped the banner and drew his sword. He would sell his life dearly.

The Blues' leader grinned wolfishly at him. "Give up, mercenary, and save yourself some bruises. You know we'll cut you down eventually."

Farris grinned back. "My captain will have my hide for a hearth-rug if he finds out I surrendered. Better to let you kill me."

BONNG. The note of a great bell sang through the woods. *BONNG, BONNG, BONNNG.* Farris had not believed them when they'd said the big bronze bell of the castle could be heard for five miles. He did now. The battle was over.

At the marshal's site he found Jehan with his ankle strapped, using two branches as crutches. He let out a whoop when Farris flourished the banner. "I thought for sure you'd be caught, man!"

There were cheers and howls in plenty when at last they made their way to the staging point where Eorl Lyulf and

Baron Lovarn waited to discover the outcome of the battle. The Blues controlled two banners and the Golds the other two. Farris' prize gave Lyulf's Golds the win, and earned him the backslapping praise of his warband.

No matter what had happened during the day, the evenings were for revelry. Free-flowing ale and wine contributed to the bragging contests and wagering that erupted between the mercenaries and the nobles' household troops, and between rival mercenary warbands themselves. Farris found himself in the middle of one such wager when Conal started to tell how he had slid past him to hire on.

The second-in-command of Storran's Stallions laughed at Conal through a mouthful of ale, snorting it up his nose and choking in the process. "Yeah, I'll believe even a greenie could get by *you*, Conal," he sputtered. "I'll wager he couldn't get past any of our men, even our recruits."

Jehan and Anya, sitting with Farris at the Stallions' fire, looked at each other, waggled their eyebrows in some obscure signal, and chorused, "Wager taken. How much?"

"So ho, the Foxes want to get in on this, too?" a Stallion said. "Terms first. He has to get into the heart of our camp, take something that belongs to one of us, and get out again without being caught."

"That's easy," Farris grinned. "What do I take? Your ale barrel?"

Shouts and jeers greeted this, as he had intended. Their ale barrel was considerably larger than the barrel of wine he and Kiam had smuggled into the barracks.

"Anything you can carry, Wolf. But it has to be something we can identify as ours, so we know you've been here."

Farris slid carefully, handspan by handspan, through the little cover left in a campsite full of armed men. No time had been specified for his accomplishment, and while Jehan and Anya had given him advice, they had left the decisions up to him.

It was dark, with no moon, and he could hear the shouts and laughter going on at the fire only a few dozen yards away. It must be an hour or so till midnight, and the evening

revels would not die down until then. This was his chosen
time; there were more people around, but most of them were
not on watch. At any other time, the sentries would be more
alert, especially since they knew he was going to make the
attempt.

Yes, there was the sentry, and he was no green recruit.
Farris had chosen to make his attack here for just that reason.
He knew how tight-strung his own nerves were; surely any
other greenie would be as wary, giving alarm at the slightest
unusual noise.

Farris came up silently behind him and sliced the edge of
his dagger-scabbard across the man's throat. Following all
the rules of the game, the sentry fell "dead." The only sound
he was allowed to make, a strangled gurgle, did not carry
far enough. He tried to make up for it by falling as heavily
as possible into the bushes, but that did not work, either.

Careful listening did not reveal any noise from the area of
his chosen target. Farris dropped to his belly and wormed
under the wall of the big tent. There was the item he had
chosen to lift. Challenge one of Bayard's Wolves, would
they? He knew they expected him to go after a small item—a
mug or gauntlet or something of the sort. *This* was small
enough, too, and nobody would expect a greenie to make a
hit like this!

A sharp noise outside the tent gave him scarce heartbeats
to scramble into the shadows. Storran himself entered the
tent and glanced around. It didn't seem possible that Storran
would not see him.

Well, this would be the perfect opportunity to see if Ylorath's "Unseeing" worked. *I'm not here. You can't see me,
there isn't anything to see,* Farris concentrated fiercely. *I'm
not here, I'm not here I'mnothereyoucan'tseeme.*

Storran looked straight at him, yawned, and scratched his
crotch. He turned away to rummage in a nearby chest, finally
unearthing a leather bottle. A grin spread over his face at the
heavy sloshing sound it made. As he turned to leave, his
eyes slid again over the shadows where Farris crouched. He
left the tent without looking back.

Farris remained where he was for a hundred-count before

emerging, expecting every instant to hear the shout of alarm
that told him they had discovered the "dead" sentry. Hastily
he detached his target from its mounting, rolled it up, and
stuffed it under his jerkin.

Even more careful listening told him that his way was
clear to leave as he had come. As he slid out through the
bushes and past the sentry, the Stallion lifted his head to
watch him go by. Farris gave him a salute and faded back
into the camp.

The next morning Captain Bayard snorted with vast
amusement when Farris told his story and exhibited his prize.
All the Wolves formed into marching order to descend on
the Stallion camp. Many of them dressed up in their finery,
and all but Farris sported some fancy flourish or other. Bayard even wore the helm crest that he saved for field-battles,
a tanned wolfhide that was complete right down to the nose
and ears. The head pulled down over his helm like a mask,
the front paws draped over his shoulders, and the rest of the
hide flowed like a cloak down his back.

Storran himself met them at the Stallion's fire. "Come to
pay off your bets, Bayard?" he smirked. "Nobody's missing
anything, even if your man did make it to the edges of our
camp. He didn't get any farther than killing the sentry."

Bayard and Serlan, facing him shoulder-to-shoulder,
grinned back. "You haven't been in your command tent yet
this morning, have you, Storran?" Bayard asked with a smirk
of his own. "Faron!" Both of the Wolf leaders stepped away
to either side, revealing Farris between them.

He unfastened the clasp of his cloak and let it fall to the
ground as he pushed the hood back. The white stallion-mane
crest mounted on his helm caught a stray beam of sunlight
and gleamed as if it shone with its own light. "Is your command tent not the heart of your camp, sir?" he asked quietly.

Storran stared at his own crest decorating the recruit's
helm, shook his head, and made a noise halfway between a
groan and a reluctant laugh. "Likarion, Bayard, where do
you find them? Recruits like this, I mean," he said over the
whoops of laughter from the Wolves and the groans of the
other Stallions.

"Conal told you. He wandered in out of the woods."

"All right, Wolf, you win," Storran said ruefully, and held out his hand. "I'll take my crest back now."

Farris pulled his helm off and looked at it thoughtfully. "I was thinking of keeping it, sir. I've been feeling downright naked wandering around without one."

More howls of laughter and derisive noises greeted this pronouncement. "Ransom it, Storran!" one Stallion shouted, as Bayard shook his head at his recruit.

"Aye, lad, you've been looking naked, too, without even a hat, but helm crests are for captains only. But ransom sounds like a good idea. Stick it to him!"

"Damn, but you're in a ornery mood this morning, Bayard," Storran complained. "I don't know whether to be glad or sorry that we're on the same side this time. Here, Daran, go to my tent and fetch me that hat I won off that Dagger last week, the one with the rooster feathers. Does headgear for headgear sound like a fair ransom, greenie?"

"Yes, sir!" For years Farris had wanted the kind of hat worn by most mercenaries. Low-crowned and wide-brimmed to keep the sun out of one's eyes and the rain off one's neck, it was invented to be a practical item of clothing. But in the hands of a mercenary, the hat became the most gaudy and dashing part of his distinctive garb. The brooch that fastened up the brim on one side and the sweep of feathers that decorated it were limited only by the owner's funds and imagination.

The saffron-gold hat that Daran handed to Captain Storran had a crowing rooster pin in bright enamel colors, and an entire rooster's tail of iridescent green-black feathers. Farris happily exchanged the helm crest for it, and tugged it down into place.

"Gods above!" Jehan crowed. "It's a bantam gamecock!"

Farris laughed and took up a fighting stance. "Anybody my size has gotta be a bantam!"

Even Serlan had a grin on his normally grim face. "Come on then, Bantam. Time for everybody to get back to work."

The nickname "Bantam" might soon have been forgotten,

but the Wolves' minstrel Daveth made a song of the recruit's
exploits that spread like wildfire through the wargames. Farris had more than one opportunity to prove his fighting prow-
ess, and found that the bets few mercenaries could resist were
an easy way to pick up extra money. The approving cheers
of "Bantam!" when he stepped up to fight kindled a fierce,
hot glow of pride and confidence in his heart, and he was
soon as swaggering and cocky as any other Wolf.

So Bantam became his name, and not only among Bayard's
Wolves. Soon he found he was thinking of himself by that
name. Everyone, from Captain Bayard down to Bors, seemed
to forget the name Faron, as did Bantam himself. In some
corner of his mind, he was grateful to let both former names
slide into oblivion. "Faron" had never truly been his, and
Farris had been a boy and a slave. Bantam, now—*Bantam*
was a mercenary!

16

———•❈•———

MERCENARY

Year 418 D.S.: Month of Tallgrass

Bantam spent a good bit of time during the wargames finding out the limits of the "Unseeing." Judicious tests with Jehan and Captain Bayard taught him that it was not foolproof. If someone was looking at him, he could not vanish before their eyes as Ylorath could. Nor could he move about. Quick movements exposed his presence; only very slow, almost imperceptible moves kept him concealed. Practice did not change that, and he was forced to conclude that he was limited because he was only a half-breed. For his job of scout, though, it was perfect. If ordinary concealment was insufficient or he had reason to think that he would be discovered, concentrating on "I'm not here" caused a man's eyes to slide right over him.

Serlan, paymaster as well as second, handed him his pay at the end of the wargames. He stared almost dubiously at the handful of copper and silver until Bors pushed him out of the way. "So they're nice and shiny, Bantam. Let me get mine, willya?" The silver pieces in his hand gleamed mockingly back at him. It had been eight years since he had held a silver piece, and then only one of them had seemed like riches. Abruptly he clenched them in his fist and stuffed them into his belt pouch.

Bayard looked up from cleaning his sword when Bantam asked to speak to him. "Now don't come complaining to me, lad. I told you the other quarter-pay was going into the warchest."

"This is half-pay, sir?"

"Half less a silver for room and board, since we're not under contract, plus a small bonus from Eorl Lyulf. I won't take any of that. You helped the Wolves earn it. We're rated number three now, up four places."

"I see. Am I being kept on, sir, or booted?"

The captain frowned down the blade of his sword as he sighted along it for dents. "Now why would I give a scout like yourself the boot? Jehan says you've quieter feet than he does, and Fadrean was trying to steal you away for his Foxes last night. I guess we can put up with you fading in and out like a fai at solstice. Was there anything else on your mind?"

A weight Bantam hadn't known was there flowed off his shoulders. "One thing, sir. If it's possible, I'd like you to continue to hold back a quarter of my pay, even after I've paid off the warchest, so I can get it in one lump sum later." *Somehow I've got to find Amethyst, and that will let me save money to buy her free. And someday when I get back to Ardesana, you're a dead man, Jared.*

A smile split briefly through the captain's whiskers. "Thinking of retiring already? I can't do that myself, hold your money I mean, not for more than a couple of months, but you can look into that new Mercenaries' Guild that they're starting here. I hear that's one of the things they want to do."

"A guild, sir, for *mercenaries?*"

"Why not? If they can do what they want to do, it's a good thing for all of us. They'll save your money for retirement or when you're injured, help you sign on somewhere else if you leave the warband, and pick up jobs for all of us. A lord could go to the guild and hire a warranted warband

or some freeswords and be sure they wouldn't go rogue on
him, because then they'd lose their guild standing, see?''

"I guess so, but . . ."

"But what?"

Bantam swallowed the question he'd meant to ask. Guilds
didn't usually accept freedmen. "But they surely won't do
that for free, sir. What will it cost me?"

"I don't know. It's being set up through the Free Traders
at first, and you're right, they're honest but they never give
you anything. Let's both of us go take a look. I'm thinking
of warranting the Wolves as a warband, anyway."

When they returned to camp, Captain Bayard was determined to put guild membership to a vote, and a bronze guild
token hung warmly against Bantam's chest on its cord
around his neck. Guild membership was worth the monthly
dues; they had two of his silver pieces in keeping now, and
would get more regularly, both wages, winnings, and loot.

The Wolves were in possession of the swimming hole
when he came to cross the creek, and everyone was soaking
contentedly or roughhousing like boys. Bantam paused on
the footbridge, and gazed wistfully at the inviting water. He
could swim, more or less, and the day was already so hot
that he had opened his shirt collar and cuffs. He couldn't
swim in his clothes, however, and he was still wary of allowing anyone to see the scars on his back. The Wolves were
friendlier now, but would they change their minds about him
if they knew he was an ex-slave?

He found out. A voice said in his ear, "Hey, can bantams
swim?" and someone grabbed his shoulders just as another
seal-sleek figure erupted from the water and pulled his feet
out from under him. He flew into the pool with a startled
yelp, hat, boots, sword, and all. The water was only waist-
deep, so he thrashed back to the surface and stood up, unsure
whether to laugh or curse at his fellow mercenaries.

They had no such uncertainties. Laughter rang around him,
and someone said, "Hey, what's that around your neck?
Let's see." He tried to fend them off, laughing himself a
little now, until they tripped him and his head went under
again. His mouth and nose filled with water. Someone

grabbed his shirt and stripped it off as he struggled, his head finally breaking water as they pulled him up.

He stood gasping and panting, surrounded now by the Wolves. The ones facing him still laughed, but the mercenaries behind him fell into silence, unbroken except for a soft "Good *gods*, look at that," in Jehan's voice. Bantam whipped around to face him, unmindful now that this would let everyone see his back.

"Yeah, Jehan," he snarled. "I was a slave. Got anything to say to me about it?"

Jehan stared back at him, his face sober. "Just one thing, *sabro*. When you catch up to the bastard who did that to you, let me know. I'll help you kill him."

"Me too," piped up Bors.

"You're at the end of the line, boy. I'm right after Jehan," Balian put in as he picked Bors up and tossed him further out into the water. "Hey, don't kill the son-of-a-sheep, Bantam. Tie him to a tree and let me use him for a pell."

"Is that before or after I rub him with honey and stake him to an anthill?" Conal asked. Other offers were drowned out as several men tried to talk at once.

Bantam twisted his head from one mercenary to another as the suggestions became more painful, ludicrous, or obscene, wanting more and more to laugh with relief. The Ravens had ignored him, but these Wolves accepted him for the fighter he was, slave-scars and all.

"Bantam!" bellowed Bayard's voice from the bridge.

He turned and looked up at him in the sudden silence, his laughter gone. If this man, the captain that he already respected and admired and all but worshiped, gave him the boot for what he had been, no amount of approval from the others mattered. "Sir?" And he waited as he had waited for the lash.

Bayard looked expressionlessly down at him for a heartbeat, then grinned suddenly. "Your hat's floating away, *sabro*."

Only two weeks passed between the end of the wargames and the start of real war. Eorl Lyulf, whose family had been involved in a generations-old feud with his nearest neighbor in Dur Sharrukhan, hired Bayard's Wolves and two other warbands before they could leave the area. Bantam stood with the others and listened to the eorl explain who and why they were fighting. It didn't make much sense to him, but he knew that border skirmishes like this broke out all the time. As long as they provided a living for men like him, why should he worry about *why?* He didn't much like their initial orders, however. They were ordered to burn a peasant settlement founded by Baron Koit on land that Lyulf claimed. The peasants themselves were to be driven back over the border.

Now Bantam sat tight on Whitefoot's back in the early morning chill and loosened his sword in its scabbard. Gault had told him once that waiting was the hardest part; now he believed it. His hand strayed again to the hilt of his sword, although he was unlikely to need it against peasants. His own scouting foray earlier had turned up no weapons of war, only farm tools.

Balian, on his own horse next to him, showed white teeth in a brief grin. "Your first real fight maybe, is it, lad?"

"No. I fought off bandits once, unarmed, when I was with a caravan. But there wasn't this waiting."

"So you're a blade-virgin? Bors is, too. Ahh, there's the captain's signal."

Bantam hoped he didn't look as young and scared as Bors. They rode into the central square of the village, rounding up stray villagers as they went, then sat there and looked menacing while Bayard gave the elders orders to collect what the people could carry and be on their way.

Children cried, women looked frightened and men sullen as they hitched up oxcarts and threw household possessions into them. There was no overt resistance, however, until the mercenaries lit torches and began to fire the thatched roofs.

There was a cry of fury from one of the young men of the village. He grabbed up a pitchfork and ran at Bantam. Other men followed his lead and snatched up farm tools to try to defend their homes.

The peasant's clumsy attempt to stab him was not successful; Bantam dodged the pitchfork easily and skewered

him through the heart. Screams rang around him and he saw
Bors take the head off another man with a forceful swipe of
his blade; he saw, too, in an oddly disjointed way Balian's
face split in a mad grin and heard him yell, "That's it, lads,
virgin no more!" Other mercenaries fought their own
clashes; when the dust cleared, four peasant men lay dead
and several were wounded. One Wolf clutched at a slash that
furrowed down his thigh, but no other fighter was injured.

They were not gentle with the displaced peasants after that,
but harried them roughly over the border.

When it was all over and they were back in their camp,
Bantam found himself wishing for the tranquil solitude of
his valley. He retreated to a stand of trees by the river as the
next best thing, to have a chance for a little quiet and time
to take out his soul and look at it. When he got there, he
found that Bors had beaten him to the spot.

"You want some company?" Bantam asked quietly.

Bors shrugged and looked away over the river. Bantam
took that to mean the boy didn't mind. They sat together in
companionable silence for a time, with the only sounds the
buzzing of grasshoppers and the burbling of the water.

"Bantam?" Bors said after a long while. "D'you think
it . . . gets any easier?"

Bantam sighed. Guilt had been nagging at him, too. He
had killed out of reflex, and in the bloodfire of battle had
felt only a fierce orgasmic jolt at first. But now the realization
that he had killed a man was twisting uncomfortably in his
conscience. Some woman was weeping now for his victim.
"If what you mean is did I want to spew my guts up afterward, the answer is yes."

"I never knew a man had that much blood in him. I was
just standing there holding the horses, and then he came at
me with that ax . . . and I took his head off, and it spurted
all over . . . and then I saw his head try to scream, and . . ."
Bors rolled over onto his belly and hid his face in the crook
of his arm. "It ain't that way in the songs."

"No. It's not," Bantam agreed. There was another long
silence while he sorted out his own feelings, then he added
with another sigh, "I don't like killing, but what it comes

to, I guess, is who would I rather Sumrakh send the ravens for, him or me? And the answer is always 'him.' '' Belatedly he remembered to spit through his fingers, as one always should when speaking the name of the Lord of Death. ''I've looked That One in the face once already and cheated Him. I don't really want to do it again.''

''What did you do? Spit in His eye?'' asked Bors with a quavery grin.

''Mother of Mares, no!'' Bantam grinned back. ''I puked all over Him and escaped while He was trying to wipe it off!''

Other fighting followed that first skirmish, and their opponents were not always peasants. The other baron also hired mercenaries to augment his own fighters, and at times true battle conditions prevailed. Bantam never found any words to describe them, even to himself. The nerve-tingling elation of fighting, keeping himself alive through wits, sword-skill, and luck in the midst of chaos only partially controlled by the bugled signals of the warleaders, was both excitement and terror.

Between battles, however, boredom threatened to kill the whole warband, and during lulls in the fighting Bayard gave some of them off-duty time to hit the taverns.

The taverns that catered to fighting men, mercenaries and regular troops alike, were as far from the quiet respectable inn of his childhood as a warsteed is from a placid milking cow. These taverns nearly burst at the seams with noise and excitement, for some of the fighting came here as well. If no brawl was going on, somebody would be happy to start one.

Bantam was still too new at being a mercenary to feel comfortable leaping up onto a table and shouting, ''I can take on any man here!'' even if that was the normal method of announcing one's willingness for a match-fight.

His *sabros* had no such reticence. More than once they provoked some other warband into putting up their best fighter against him. The few fights he lost were irritating, but only added spice to the wagering.

Tonight he had won easily, for the big man pitted against

him was strong but slow. Now he was enjoying the entertainment, both the pretty girls who sang or danced, and the
outrageous boasts of his friends.

After a particularly bawdy song about a mercenary who
kept getting into trouble by sheathing his sword in pretty
scabbards that didn't belong to him, the boasting broke out
again, this time with wenching as the subject. Balian claimed
he could entertain three girls at once, one in the usual way
and one with each hand.

Serlan countered with a claim of six, provoking jeers of
disbelief.

"Come on, Serlan, *six*? How?" Balian challenged.

"One on top of me, one with each hand makes three, one
with each foot makes five, and one with my mouth. Six,"
he leered.

More jeers greeted this statement. Conal turned to the
serving-slave in his lap and asked, "What about it, sweetling? Should we collect five more of your collar-sisters and
try it out?"

"Can I be the one on top, please?" she replied pertly. "I
think any man would be too distracted to give the other five
proper attention."

Howls of laughter and shouts of agreement caused both
the taverner and his bouncer to look their way, and the table
of mercenaries quieted somewhat.

"What about you, Bantam?" Jehan asked. "You're being
awful quiet over there."

Bantam took a swallow of his mead, enjoying the taste
even if he couldn't get drunk. "I don't need to boast about
the girls I've had," he said loftily. "The ones who boast are
the girls who've had *me.*"

Bayard's Wolves roared with laughter. "How many at
once, Bantam?" someone said facetiously.

"Mmm, just one. I like to give her proper attention." He
grinned at Conal's girl, for her dark-eyed beauty attracted
him greatly. She giggled and winked at him.

"Hey, little one," Conal rebuked her. "You're s'posed to
be flirtin' with me, not eyein' Bantam."

She snaked one arm around his neck and kissed him. "Oh,

but master, I thought you wanted six of us. I'm just one little wench.''

Conal started as a finger traced a line up his back. One of the other serving-girls stood behind him with a pitcher of wine. "I'll take you on, master, if you want to try six. I can be three all by myself."

Conal looked from the tiny dark-haired girl in his lap to the tall blonde one who continued to caress his face, then over at Bantam. An enormous grin spread across his face, and he stood up with the smaller girl in his arms.

"Here, *sabro,* this one's more your size than mine!" He dropped her into Bantam's lap.

Bantam's mead went flying as he barely caught her, and her weight nearly knocked him out of his chair. He settled her more firmly in his arms before he heaved himself to his feet. "You're better off with me, sweetheart," he told her. "The biggest thing about Conal is his mouth. Which way to the bedrooms?"

He marched off to the howls and whistles of his friends, with the girl squealing and giggling but very carefully not kicking. This was the man she had had her eye on all along. It didn't happen very often that she got the one she wanted. Tavern-wenches like her didn't choose; they were chosen.

"What's your name, my dove?" Bantam asked as he put her down inside her tiny room. He felt vaguely guilty over his desire for her, since she could not refuse him, but what other women were available to him? And she didn't seem to mind.

"Daina," she said softly. "Or whatever name you like, my lord."

" 'Daina' is very pretty. And you know I'm no lord. Just Bantam."

"Do you want me to use your name, master? Some men don't like us to. They say we have better things to do with our mouths." She reached up to him, pulled his head down, and kissed him deeply, her tongue brushing warmly against his and then retreating, coaxing him into tasting her sweet welcoming mouth.

He buried his face in her hair and kissed the angle of her

jaw just under her ear. "Use my name, use anything you want to, but don't call me master. I don't want us to be master and slave, just a man and a woman. . . ."

She laughed up at him. "Will I be able to boast, too, that I've had you?"

His face twisted into a smile. "Prepare yourself, my sweet Daina. Neither of us may live through the night."

17

---❖---

WAR

Bantam watched the armies assembling with veteran eyes. The last two years had made a warrior of him through innumerable battles and skirmishes. He could assess the worth of other seasoned troops with an experienced glance, and felt entirely justified in sneering with lordly condescension at the ragged groups of peasant levies that were forming before him.

"Sword-fodder," he remarked to Bors as they rode slowly through the assembly area toward their own camp.

The other mercenary made his own horse swerve and dance just to scatter the conscripts in his way. "At least Her High-and-Mightiness has sense enough to hire *real* swordsmen." Bors too had grown into a warrior; the boy who had grieved for the loss of his own innocence was gone, buried deep in the cocky cynical shell of a man who depends on his sword for his living and his life.

"Aye that, packmate!" Bantam grinned back. "Hey you, you're not plowing now! Outta my way!"

"Her High-and-Mightiness," their new employer, was

more properly titled Her Gracious Highness the Princess
Ashlana of D'Alriaun. She was the only living legitimate
child and heir of the late King Corleon. The kingdom had
not fallen into her royal lap at her father's death, however.
Corleon had asserted the royal privilege of mistresses, and
he was hardly cold in his grave before his eldest son from
one of those unions also claimed the crown.

This man had his own supporters, for Princess Ashlana
had been betrothed since childhood to Alnikhias, King of
Dur Sharrukhan. Some D'Alriaun nobles preferred an unen-
cumbered king, albeit a bastard, to a queen who would tie
them to their traditional enemies. Even the King's Shields,
the D'Alriaun equivalent of the King's Elite, had deserted to
the Bastard. Full-scale war was inevitable.

War, of course, made work for mercenaries. The Free Mercenary Warband of Bayard's Wolves had ridden into this
staging area yesterday, singing at the tops of their lungs (and
only slightly off-key). Since their new employer was a female, the song was in her honor and only mildly bawdy,
about a warrior princess whose armor was so well endowed
with true breastplates that she distracted all her opponents.

"Ah, now there's some fighters," Bantam pointed out.
"Leopard's Garders, from their banner. That must be Baron
Varian. They said he was liaison from Alnikhias." He pulled
aside respectfully to watch the lord go by. Even in caravan
and slave barracks he had heard the songs about this man,
how he and his lady had gone alone to the Dread Keep and
there had slain the wizard that hosted in his own body the
God of Evil.

"I suppose he's not bad, for a Sharrese," Bors said grudgingly. "Is that his swordbrother there, then?"

"I guess so." The minstrels sang of this man Corven, too.
Once a slave, he was a warrior second only to his lord, and
had turned the tide of battle against the Avakir invasion that
had united the two kingdoms. Bantam turned in his saddle
to watch them ride out of sight.

It was the last time Bantam had for a leisurely ride through
a war-camp in the next few months. The fighting of this war

was scattered, but hot and heavy. He rode courier more often
than he scouted or fought, although there was more than
enough of the latter to satisfy even the most battle-hungry.

In between fighting each other, the two sides battled unsuccessfully against a common enemy—the weather.
Corleon had not picked a good time of year to die and leave
his kingdom in turmoil. Early spring campaigns like this always had more than their fair share of mud, and this year
the rains and the war kept on going well into the summer.
Fields that should have been growing crops were now bat-
tlegrounds, trampled deep into soggy wastelands. More than
one battle left both winners and losers so covered in mud
that telling the sides apart was impossible.

Worse, there were few dry places to set up camp, and
Bayard's Wolves were only marginally more comfortable on
those occasions when they invaded a peasant village and
forcibly claimed shelter in their huts. The debates over such
invasions were long, loud, and fruitless; it was never settled
to anyone's satisfaction which was worse—mud or fleas. Often Bantam wished for a dull, boring job in a nice dry castle
somewhere, even at the price of dull boring guard-duty.

And as the wet weeks dragged on, still no consistent victor
appeared. The forces of Princess Ashlana and her half-
brother were so equally balanced that it seemed the war
might go on for years. The month of Sunheat was nearly
over when King Alnikhias finally committed forces to the
field to help defend the rights of his betrothed.

The fighting spread now to the borderlands, and with the
support of this new ally Princess Ashlana's side began at last
to see signs of victory. King Alnikhias even seemed to bring
the summer with him, for the clouds scudded away to rain
on somebody else.

Bayard's Wolves fought late that month in the siege and
battle that took the city of Blackmere, a major supporter of
the Bastard. Afterward they were rather disgruntled, for as a
new policy the princess prohibited looting, feeling that it
caused resentment that would only turn support of the locals
to her brother. Her generals supported her, and passed the
orders down to the troops, royal and mercenary alike.

Nobody, however, tried to keep them from hitting the taverns, and hit them they did. There was a small altercation in which some royal soldiers were forcibly ejected by some mercenaries from a tavern that the latter contended ought to be for them; if it wasn't, why then was it called the Crossed Swords?

A particular lone mercenary thought so, too, for he only glanced at the sign in passing as he came in. He paused a moment at the door, surveying the situation and listening with only half an ear to the slave-entertainer singing, for she was nearly finished.

Her audience was banging on the tables and demanding more when one group in particular noticed the newcomer. "Hey, Balian!" one man yelled. "Are we dreaming, or did old Black Gault just wander in the door?"

"I usually have prettier dreams, but yeah. Gault, you old bugger, come sit down with old *sabros* and celebrate!"

Their welcome was loud and tipsy but so insistent and enthusiastic that Gault didn't feel like refusing. He wouldn't have refused anyway, for this was the company he had been seeking. "Hey yourself, Balian," he growled back as his face crinkled into a grin. "Tell me why I should sit down with you and Conal when last time we went carousing we just made it out of town ahead of the City Guard?"

" 'Cause we was all younger and dumber then," Balian said cheerfully. "Grab that chair and sit down, man! Where have you been hiding yourself? Oh, yeah, you don't know anybody else." His introductions were rather sketchy, for he rattled off names as he pointed to people. "You guys ought to know Gault. Likarion knows we've told you enough about when him and the captain and us was freeswords together."

Gault had barely sat down when the very young man who had been pointed out as Bors scowled at Conal.

"Hey, that's Bantam's chair. When he gets back from the latrine, he ain't gonna be happy," Bors warned.

"Yeah," grinned Conal. "That's the whole idea."

"Bantam, huh?" Gault said coolly. "Sounds like he's a fighter with that name. He'll have to be some fighter, then, to get me out of this chair. It seems right comfortable." He reached out a long arm and snared the hem of the table-slave's tunic. "Bring us a good bottle of wine, sweetling."

Conal and Balian looked at each other, somewhat puzzled. "You don't know him, Gault?" Balian asked. "He said you recommended the Wolves to him. Little blond Ardesanan, and one of the best damned fighters we've got."

"Bantam's what we named him, remember?" put in Bors. "Hey, here he comes now."

But the man who came toward them was nobody that Gault remembered meeting before. Surely he would have remembered a blond mercenary so much shorter than himself; most men were smaller, true, but not as much as this man.

Bantam, however, had no problem at all. His face lit up and he bellowed happily, "Gault, you potbellied, baggy-eyed old badger, get your decrepit carcass outta my chair!"

He advanced on the table, then realized from the puzzled scowl on Gault's face that the older mercenary didn't recognize him, and realized also from the gleeful faces of his *sabros* that they expected him to challenge Gault.

Instead, Bantam pulled his face into a doleful grimace and heaved an enormous sigh, shaking his head sadly. "It's a *pitiful* thing, *sabros*, when a warrior gets old and senile. Here I broke his arm for him a couple of Yearsends ago, and he doesn't remember me!"

Gault slowly rose from the disputed chair as recognition dawned on him. "You, is it? I still owe you for that broken arm! And the bloody nose!" He advanced slowly, circling Bantam, who backed away just as slowly. The table of mercenaries waited with bated breath; those who knew both Gault and Bantam expected to see one of the finest brawls in years.

Both lunged suddenly, grabbing each other in a bear hug, and Gault lifted Bantam off his feet. Instead of the quick and deadly retaliatory move the waiting mercenaries expected, Bantam only pounded on the bigger man's back with one clenched fist. "You're squashing my ribs, you big bastard," he said happily.

Gault set him down with a thump that rattled his teeth. "Bantam, is it now? It suits you, lad. You've changed more

than a mite; I didn't know you at first.'' He snagged a chair
from another table as Bantam took his own back.

"I know. But when you think about how I looked the last
time you saw me, I'm not surprised. And I thought the name
change was a good idea. But you, Gault, what are you doing
out here in the rain with us mudsloggers instead of staying
dry at Loarn?''

"The Ravens' contract with Torkild ended the last day of
Springthaw and he wasn't amenable to the captain's sugges-
tion that we'd need better pay to re-up.'' Gault shook his
head at the thought of such folly and took a few swallows
of the wine he'd ordered. "So with this war going on, Garan
didn't have any trouble signing us on with Alnikhias'
forces.''

"Hold on, Gault,'' Conal broke in. "Alnikhias' forces are
still a good bit further west.''

"Yeah, I know.'' He looked down at the mug in his hand
and turned it thoughtfully as if examining it for flaws. "But
I'm a freesword now.''

"You left the Ravens?'' Bantam asked. "I thought you
liked working with Garan.''

"I did.'' Gault looked up finally at his friend's concerned
face. "There's no easy way to say this, Bantam, and I know
you thought of him as a friend, too. Garan's dead.''

He watched Bantam's face fall into the familiar blankness
as he took in this painful news, and gave himself a moment
to grieve for his captain as well. "It was quick and clean,
Banty, the warrior's death we all hope for, in the fighting at
Wolfdale last month.''

There was silence for a moment at the table, for even those
who did not know Garan were chivalrous enough to let their
sabro recover from his bad news.

Even so, Bantam's voice was still tight when he said,
"Thanks for telling me, Gault. I know the telling isn't any
easier than the hearing. So that's why you left?''

"Yeah. Joss and I never got on too good, so when he took
over the warband I decided to look around for another. Is
Bayard hiring?''

"Not only is he hiring,'' Conal broke in, "but he's been

looking for a second-in-command for a couple of weeks, ever since Serlan died. Everyone in the warband but Bantam and Bors have been angling for it and he doesn't want to make a choice and get everyone's feathers ruffled. I think we might be better off if he brought in someone like you."

There were mutters of assent from the table, although some of them were somewhat reluctant.

"Don't you think Bayard ought to be the one to decide?" Gault parried.

"What, and give him the notion that he gives the orders?" Bantam said with a forced grin. "I'll take you back to camp if you want and put it to him. Are we agreed then, gentlemen, that we have a new packmate?"

At the camp, Bayard was entirely agreeable to the thought of Gault as his new second. He and Gault were distant cousins, and had known each other from boyhood. The captain knew the quality of fighter he was getting; there was no need for provisional acceptance of Gault as there had been for Bantam.

After it was settled, they sat around the fire, staring into its heart while Gault told Bantam the details of Garan's death. Bantam was silent for a while when he finished, trying to think how to phrase what he must ask without giving it away to Bayard that he was an escaped slave under sentence of death.

"I owe him my life, Gault, as much as I owe you. In more ways than one, I think. It was your idea to get me more sword-training, but he had to approve. They wouldn't have accepted me here without it. And I've always wanted to know—would you have helped me leave if he hadn't told you that story about his cousin?"

"I don't know, Banty. I couldn't figure out how to help you without putting myself in your place. The best I could come up with was to give you my mercy-dagger, in case you wanted it.

"When Garan came and told that story, it took me a lot of soul-searching, before and after. But then I thought, I owed it to you, too, after Barak drew steel on me."

"Are we even then, *sabro?*" Bantam asked. One of his rare true smiles spread slowly over his face as Gault nodded and held out his hand.

"Aye, *sabro*, we are," he said huskily. Their handclasp was brief, but both firm and heartfelt.

"So we two are even then, but Garan and I are not. How do I repay a debt to a dead man?" Bantam's own voice was husky.

Gault pondered for a moment, wondering how much Bayard knew of Bantam's history, and how much to tell. "Bayard, what has Bantam told you of his past? I don't want to give away things I think he'd like to keep quiet."

"Not much," Bayard answered. "We know he used to be a slave; a man doesn't get a back like his any other way. But he doesn't talk about it."

Bantam was silent for a while, too. He trusted Bayard with his life; should he trust him with his secret, as well? Finally he said quietly, "This is for your ears only, sir. I was a stable slave at Loarn. Gault and Captain Garan worked out a scheme to give me sword training and later helped me get free."

"I thought from the first you might be a fugitive, Bantam. But it takes guts to swagger into a mercenary camp the way you did, so I gave you a chance."

"I told you once Garan's back looked something like yours, Banty," Gault said. "After you left, he told me someone helped him gain his freedom, and he couldn't repay that person, either. So he passed it on to you. If you feel you still owe him a debt, the best thing you can do is pass that freedom to someone else."

"I will do that, then. Life for life, and freedom for freedom. Warrior's Oath on it." Bantam stroked his fingertips across Ydona's brand on his upper arm, his face very solemn in the flickering light of the fire. "This I vow by my brand." He pulled his sword from its scabbard, and clasped both hands on the hilt. "This I vow by my blade." Finally he drew his right palm down the sharp edge of the sword, and held the bleeding slash out to them. "This I vow by my own

blood. I call upon Likarion and Ydona to witness, and you
as well.''

"It is witnessed, Bantam," Bayard said quietly, echoed by
Gault; then both watched in silence as Bantam held his hand
over the fire and let his blood fall sizzling into the flames.

Her Royal Highness, of course, had no knowledge of the
happenings among her hirelings, but to Bantam this marked
the turning point of the war. The Bastard lost one of his most
skilled warleaders the next week, a duke of the royal line,
and with that noble's death much of the rebels' support
melted away like mist at sunrise. The Bastard was a brave
man, but not a strategist to match the likes of King Alnikhias,
and his next two battles were crushing defeats. Repeatedly
he turned and fled, until at last Alnikhias brought him to bay
right up against the border between the two kingdoms.

That last battle was long and bloody; three days of hit-
and-run guerrilla tactics finally culminated in pitched battle.
The Bastard died bravely, as a warrior would wish, with a
sword in his hand.

Not until later did Bantam realize that he was back in his
home kingdom. Four days of heavy fighting had left all par-
ticipants drained and exhausted. He wanted only to curl up
somewhere out of the way and sleep for the next three days
or so.

No soldier of any kind is ever too tired, however, to keep
from listening to and spreading rumors. The rumors that began to circulate over the next few days were particularly
juicy. Rumor said that King Alnikhias was on his way to
welcome Her Gracious Highness to the kingdom that he
would share with her when they were married. Rumor said
that the nobleman who governed this duchy of Draksgard,
one Duke Launart, had offered his royal cousin Princess Ashlana comfort and shelter in his own luxurious tents in honor
of their distant kinship. And rumor said that once in his keeping, the princess had vanished as if by magic, and the duke
as well.

18

———

PLANS

Alnikhias of Dur Sharrukhan, King by Grace of the Gods and Right of Arms, did not need to rely on rumor. How he got his information was a matter of great speculation; some said magic, some said a very cleverly concealed network of spies, some merely shrugged in bafflement. Whatever his source, however, all assembled here in this council of war knew that his information was reliable.

The protocol that would have controlled such an assemblage during times of peace had been dispensed with, and his own nobles and warleaders sat around the tables crowded elbow to elbow with D'Alriaun nobles and officers of the army of Princess Ashlana. Even the mercenary captains and their seconds were in attendance, for Alnikhias did not discount skill and knowledge in favor of rank.

The king rose and looked out over all of them. "I have news of Her Highness," he said quietly, and his words fell into a silence so complete that the tent might have been empty. "She is being held in Draksgard Keep. I have in my hands a letter purporting to come from her, saying that now that she will be a queen in her own right, she chooses to ally herself in marriage with her kinsman Duke Launart, rather than honoring her betrothal to me.''

The silence vanished in a roaring wave of noise as old enemies that were only precariously allies shouted that they knew D'Alriauns were untrustworthy, all of them, and that it was a lie, Her Highness would never break her word and besides, didn't this *prove* that Sharrese were the sneaky bastards that everybody always knew them to be?

Alnikhias twitched his fingers in signal, and the brassy squawk of heralds' trumpets rose above the din. All eyes turned back to him, and he quelled the noise with a sharp gesture. ''I did *not* say that Her Highness sent this letter. On the contrary, I have in my possession genuine letters from her, and I am satisfied that this one did not come from her hand. The treachery here is by one man, regretfully one of my own nobles. Launart has always been manipulative, but before now not to the point of disloyalty. I will deal with him as a traitor, doubt it not. You yourselves are here because I have personal knowledge of and trust in all of you, Sharrese and D'Alriaun alike.

''But for now, my concern must be with Princess Ashlana. I am requesting your comments and ideas at this time, so that we can make plans to rescue her. If we cannot get her out, that traitor Launart will marry her and claim the kingdom through her. None of us can allow that to happen.''

One of Alnikhias' most trusted nobles, Baron Varian of Leopard's Gard, rose and was recognized. ''Your Majesty, this all works down in the end to a matter of time. She can hold them off for a while, claiming to need the goddess' blessing and preparation time and so forth, but all it will buy her is time, and precious little of that. If we besiege the castle or make any other show of force, they'll ignore her demands and marry her off immediately. Somehow, very soon, we must get in and get her out unseen. Our best plan might be to smuggle someone in and have him try to get her out.''

Varian's swordbrother Corven looked up at him, his brow wrinkled in thought. ''Unseen,'' he mused. ''Varian, who is more unseen than a slave?''

"Where will you find a slave who has both the courage and the loyalty to do that?" Alnikhias asked.

"Someone who could pass for a slave, then," Corven persisted. "I *know,* sir, how most people will just look right past a slave if he doesn't do anything out of the ordinary to attract their attention. The right man could walk in under their noses and nobody would ever notice him."

"Who? None of us could pass as a slave. Not even you, Corven, not after all these years."

Alnikhias noticed one of the mercenary seconds nudge his captain and speak quietly and rapidly to him. The captain cleared his throat, and the nobles looked at him in surprise. "Sirs, I believe I have just the man you are looking for. It's not personal loyalty to you that you want. It's revenge against Launart."

"If you have any kind of idea with a chance of success, explain it, Captain."

"What would you say, sir, to a man who was once one of Launart's slaves, an unarmed combat expert, and one of the most . . . inconspicuous scouts I've ever seen?"

Bantam trotted up to the royal encampment, half suspecting someone was pulling a practical joke. It might be—might be, bloody hell, *would* be—hysterically funny to his *sabros* that he was that cocky, to think the king himself had summoned him. But to his surprise, Gault was there in the door-flap of the big tent, beckoning urgently for him to enter. He reluctantly handed over his sword and dagger to the door-sentry and ducked inside.

His eyes swept the small cluster of nobles in the nearly empty tent, checking for danger, for any other exits, for anything that felt wrong. Then his gaze came back to Captain Bayard, sitting at the table with several other men. Three of them he recognized immediately: Baron Varian, that they called the Ice Leopard; his swordbrother Corven; and at the head of the table, the king. He threw them all an impartial salute and said, "Sirs, I was ordered to report here?"

Bayard said, "Bantam, I think we have a job here that only you can do. Have a seat."

As they explained, he was at first disbelieving, then angry. "Let me get this straight. You want me to go into that muckin' big castle as a slave, find your princess, knock her guard on the head, and get her out like I was lifting an apple off a market stall?"

"That's a rather simplistic way of putting it, but yes." The king sounded distinctly annoyed to have his plans questioned.

"Your Majesty, I think the man is right to be cynical. We all know what mercenaries are like. How in the world can this—this cocky little bastard pass himself off as a slave?" said one of the more distinguished-looking nobles.

Bantam felt the taunt like a blow to his belly, and then, incredibly, the high sweet euphoria singing in his blood and through his head, the euphoria Ydona always sent to tell him he was riding his luck. A feral and rather unpleasant grin snaked across his face. " 'Cocky little bastard,' yer lordship? Guilty on all charges. But as for 'passing myself off' as a slave, look you."

The chair tipped over backwards as he abruptly stood and stripped off his shirt, turning to give them all a good look at his whip-scarred back. He spun back to face them and included his captain in his hard-eyed stare. "I was a slave for eight years and I swore I would never call any man 'master' again." His eyes shifted to the king. "But you, King Alnikhias, you give me what I want and I'll fetch your princess out for you." *And take my revenge against Torkild and Launart at the same time.*

Some of the nobles exchanged disgusted glances and the unspoken opinion was clear. *What else can one expect from a mercenary?*

Alnikhias said quietly, "We can negotiate terms. How much do you want?"

A slave set the chair back up just as Bantam dropped into it. "How much is your princess worth to you, Your Majesty? As much as she'd bring on the block? Fifty golds? A hundred?

"But I'm not that greedy. Let's start with a year's pay, guild rates. That's less that it would cost you to buy a real slave. You're not looking for just another hired sword here. When I hit a battlefield, I know death is the worst thing that could happen to me. This scheme, who knows? And it's sure as hell not in my current contract!''

"You said to start with. What else?" asked Alnikhias contemptuously, as if he thought Bantam might demand his firstborn child.

"Something that won't cost you a copper." Bantam resisted the temptation to lick suddenly his dry lips. This was it, the last roll of the dice that would decide whether he was legally free or slave. "Amnesty. I'm a runaway, a renegade. I want my legal manumission and a pardon, free and clear, before I even go in there."

"A pardon for what crimes?"

"The usual crimes a slave commits when he escapes. Assault, theft, use of weapons. And rape. They said I raped a noblewoman."

"And you didn't?" the king asked sarcastically.

He gave a short bark of derisive laughter. "M'lord, I was a slave, not a fool! She knew what she wanted, and all but ripped my clothes off to get it. Torkild interrupted us, and she screamed rape."

The king looked down at something in his hands, caressing whatever it was with his fingertips, then back up at Bantam. "And with that attitude, if I said 'no' to amnesty?"

The mercenary did not move, but more than one man sensed the sudden tension in his body. "Then, my lord king, we'll find out how many nobles a mercenary can take with him before he dies."

Alnikhias made a brushing motion with one hand as if to dismiss Bantam's distrust. "Nobody said anything about attempting to arrest you. If we cannot come to an agreement, you are free to go. Am I correct in assuming Duke Launart was your master?"

"*He* thought so."

"As anything that is or was his property is now forfeit to the crown, manumitting you is no problem, nor is pardoning you for escaping. How likely is it that he would recognize you?"

"Not very. He really looked at me only once, and my own mother wouldn't have recognized me then. These," and Bantam flicked a finger over the scars on his face, "were fresh and I'd just had the shit beaten out of me."

"I see," the king said dryly. "Now, about this rape that you didn't commit, who was the woman?"

"Launart's niece. I don't know who her father is. Her name is Viveka."

"Very well, mercenary, you have your manumission and pardon. We can attend to any legal paperwork in private later. Do you have any other demands, or any ideas that might improve the plans as we've laid them out?"

"My name is Bantam, my lord king," he said softly, with an edge of menace clear in his voice. "And I do. First, you figure out some way for me to carry a blade, a mercy-dagger or something of the sort. I won't go in there completely unarmed. Launart has a very nasty death planned for me, and if I'm captured, I don't intend to participate.

"Second, I need someone to instruct me on being an Inside slave. I was Outside, a stable slave at Loarn. I never got further inside than the arms-practice room there."

"I can handle that," said a voice from the side. It was Corven, Baron Varian's swordbrother. Bantam acknowledged his offer with a slight nod, then returned to his own course.

"Third, Your Majesty, I won't wear a slave-collar I can't get off. I want the key to it."

Alnikhias nodded. "You would have that anyway. To smuggle the princess out as a slave, you would need to transfer the collar to her."

"Also, I need to have a description or see a picture of this princess. I have to be able to recognize her so I don't kidnap the wrong noblewoman."

Alnikhias frowned and looked down at the object in his hands. His eyes momentarily lost their focused, determined look and his face became softer. Abruptly he thrust the object at Bantam. "Look at this, then."

It was a tiny oval painting, no bigger than the palm of his hand. It showed a dark-haired young woman in a blue gown, seated at a window with a kitten on her lap. Bantam held out his own hand, expecting the king to pass it to him, and was surprised when Alnikhias shook his head vehemently. "No. This doesn't leave me. Come closer if you want a better look."

There was no accounting for the whims of the nobility. Bantam had learned that a long time ago.

Pictures were not something he was familiar with; the wealth of detail that an artist could produce in such a small painting was incredible. The little face in the miniature was not beautiful, certainly not in the fragile, blonde, blue-eyed way that was the current standard of beauty. Her face was not the admired oval, but squarish, with level dark eyes and a generous mouth. Her jaw was firm and also squared; if she had been a boy instead of a girl, she might have been called handsome. The longer he studied the picture, the more this princess intrigued him. She looked like a young woman of sense and courage, not the pretty but witless broodmare that the tales made princesses out to be.

"Well? Have you seen enough?" The open hostility in Alnikhias' voice struck harshly on Bantam's ears, and he jerked his gaze away from the picture to the king's face.

So. That's what's gnawing at him. It's eating him alive that he can't ride up on his white horse and heroically sweep her away from their enemies. Time for diplomacy, Bantam.

"She looks to be . . . an exceptional young woman, Your Majesty. Not one who will obediently follow the instructions of just any man who happens along. How can I prove to her that you are sending me to her rescue? For all she'll know I could be kidnapping her for some ruthless scheme of my own."

"How will I know that, as well?" demanded the king. "You have no loyalty to me."

"We mercenaries have our own code of honor, King Alnikhias," Bantam said angrily. "That girl"—he stabbed a finger at the picture—"is my contracted employer, and I will no more betray her, or you, than I would betray my sword-brothers. If I broke that code by doing so, every mercenary in two kingdoms would hunt me down and kill me themselves, slowly, for bringing dishonor to all of us. Captain Bayard there would lead that hunt.''

''That's true, Niko,'' said Baron Varian. ''We've all hired mercenaries at one time or another. I've never heard of a mercenary betraying his employer if he was paid as promised.''

The king sighed and closed his eyes for a moment. ''All right, Varian, you win. Here, mercenary, this letter is from her; read this. Tell her you've seen this letter and I'll give you the reply I made. That should be enough to confirm to her that you've come from me.'' He pulled out a folded, much-worn piece of paper and indicated a particular line of writing.

''I'm sorry, Your Majesty, but I can't read,'' Bantam confessed. ''Whatever it is, you'll have to tell me.''

The king flushed red. ''Come down here so I can whisper it. For security reasons, I don't want anybody else to know.''

''They won't hear it from me, sir,'' Bantam assured him. What sort of thing would he not want his nobles to hear? He bent his head and listened carefully, biting his tongue to stifle the amusement that welled up in him.

''Most certainly, Your Majesty, nobody but the princess will ever hear that from me.'' Bantam kept his face carefully blank. Who'd have thought that royalty could get that bad? No wonder he didn't want anybody to hear!

They worked well into the evening, going over any possible contingency in the plans to smuggle out the princess. Corven was to pose as a merchant with Bantam as his slave; they would be traveling on ''urgent personal business'' to Draksgard. Bayard's Wolves would also travel east to Draksgard and remain in the area, ostensibly to check out the prospect of hiring on with Duke Launart's forces. It would make sense then, for a merchant to pay them for their protection on his journey.

Once there, Bantam was to infiltrate the castle, confirm the whereabouts of the princess, and carry any messages to or from her until they were ready to smuggle her out. Corven would wait at the house of a trusted merchant for Bantam to deliver her, then ride back toward Dur Sharrukhan with his slave and his "orphaned niece."

Finally Alnikhias dismissed most of the council, asking only Bantam, Captain Bayard, and Duke Govert, one of the older nobles, to remain.

"Captain, Govert, I am asking you to stay for only a few moments, to witness this man's manumission." At their quiet responses of understanding, Alnikhias looked at Bantam and continued, "There is a very short ceremony that accompanies a manumission. Kneel and put your arms out, wrists together."

"Submit again as slave?" he replied angrily. "Not *this* mercenary! You can hire me to fake it, but *nobody* gets submission from me again. They locked a collar around my neck without a ceremony. You can free me without one."

Alnikhias gave a weary sigh, as if too tired to cope with Bantam's stubbornness. "Captain, are all your men this insubordinate and pigheaded?"

Bayard chuckled. "No, sir, most of them are worse. No mercenary's a good little boy, but Bantam's usually one of the more easygoing ones."

"Gods defend me from an intransigent one, then. Was Bantam your slave name? Somehow I don't think so." He reached for paper and quill, and began to write.

"No. My name then was Farris," Bantam said reluctantly. *Mother of Mares, even the name brings it all back. Can I do this, be a slave again, even in pretense?*

Yes. To be truly free, I'll do anything, even this.

"All right, Govert, Captain Bayard, this man Farris, known as Bantam, is free. Is it witnessed?"

"It is witnessed," affirmed Lord Govert, and Bayard echoed him.

"Sign this as witnesses, then."

The king handed Bantam the paper, the ink still wet and glistening in places in the candlelight. He took it and gazed broodingly at the marks. *Scratches on a paper, and they can do so much. I'll have to trust Bayard on this one. He can read. He wouldn't have signed anything that wasn't right.*

The king was writing on another paper as well. "This is

your pardon. I suggest you keep them where you can get to them in case you're ever recognized as Launart's runaway."

"Will you keep them with the warband's papers, sir? I don't know how to take care of them otherwise," Bantam asked Bayard quietly.

"Sure, Banty. Come on, let's get back to camp. Tomorrow's not going to be any easier. Good night, Your Majesty, my lord."

19

<hr>

SLAVE AGAIN

Corven met Bantam early the next morning. The mercenary was quiet and weaponless, without the swagger and cockiness he had shown the previous day. Instead there was a grim determination in his eyes, and his greeting to Corven was short.

"Let's get this over. What first?"

"Shaving, I think," said Corven sympathetically. "The king's own body-slave, no less. They want to keep the details of this plan as quiet as possible. In here."

Bantam whistled softly as they entered the king's tent and looked at the chairs, chests, and writing table. An open flap revealed another room, this one fitted out as a bedchamber. "Now this, I could get used to real easy. Carpets, a real bed, pretty things I don't even know the names of—all the comforts of home. You s'pose there's any kinging jobs open I could hire into?"

Corven laughed. "I think Duke Launart is fighting for the only vacancy right now."

A young man in the red-and-blue tunic and enameled blue collar that marked the royal slaves burst through the outside flap. When he saw the two men, he fell to his knees with a gasp. "Please, masters, forgive me that I was not here when you arrived."

Corven said kindly, "Easy, lad. No one's angry with you. It won't get back to the king from us, will it, Bantam?"

Bantam didn't answer. Had he appeared like this to free men? He didn't remember ever showing fear like this: caution, yes, but not this appalling fearfulness. Was this how it was to be an Inside slave? A terrified little rabbit? No, it couldn't be. Corven didn't show any signs of having been like this.

"I think it's you, Bantam," Corven said softly. "He's scared to death of you."

Bantam sighed gustily with exasperation. "Mother of Mares, is that story still going around, that we mercenaries eat slaves for breakfast? Look, Corven, I'm not letting him near my throat with a razor, not with the way he's shaking." When he spoke to the slave, however, he tried to sound more kindly. "I need your help, lad. What's your name?"

"Idal, master," he whispered.

Irrationally, Bantam wanted to shout at him, to tell him that fright like that would just make things worse. Clearly, the slave was still afraid. Or was he? Bantam looked closer; Idal's body was shaking, but there wasn't the strain in his voice and the anxiety in his eyes that there should be.

He forced himself to speak calmly and quietly, although now he wanted to laugh. "Look at me, Idal. I won't cuff you or tell on you or do anything else to you. Neither of us will. We were both slaves, we know what it's like. That includes faking fear to appease a threat. You're overdoing it."

Idal looked up at him with a wry grimace. "It works on other mercenaries, sir." He rose to his feet and waited in tense alertness to see what this atypical mercenary would do next.

"Not on me, it doesn't. Have a chair. I meant it when I said I need your help. Corven's going to work with me on what an Inside slave's life is like, but he's been free a long time. Maybe things have changed or maybe they're not the same in different places. I want your information as well as his. Corven, you start.'' He ignored the slave's uneasiness, genuine this time, at sitting with free men.

"One reason we have for trying to put someone into Draksgard Keep as a slave, rather than an upper servant or a guardsman, is because there are so many slaves in one of the really big castles like that. Not many people will know if a stranger is an intruder or just someone from another area. You can wander around all day if you just look busy,'' Corven said. "Most Inside slaves don't live under the strict conditions that Outside ones do. I was Varian's body-slave, and we spent two years in Lord Duer's household, in one big Sundaran castle or another. I had a fair amount of free time, once I had attended to Varian's orders and needs for the day, and nobody ever challenged me about what I was doing.''

Bantam snorted softly, but his voice was amused as he said, "I always suspected most of you Insiders had it easy.''

Corven grinned at him in complete understanding. From the look of his back it was clear that this man hadn't ever had it easy. "Well, I was lucky, too. I never got beaten, except the usual spankings most small boys get for their mischief. Usually Varian got spanked too for instigating whatever it was. Varian thought of himself as my friend and swordbrother, not my master.''

"Swordbrother? While you were still a slave?''

"Yeah, well . . . we kind of bent the law there. When it first started, we were both about seven years old, and I was just another little kid for him to practice on, and with the training swords it didn't really matter, you know?'' Corven said sheepishly.

"Oh yes, I know,'' Bantam agreed softly. "But this isn't getting the instruction that I need.'' He turned relentlessly to specific questions, occasionally asking Idal directly, since the royal slave seemed reluctant to volunteer anything or contradict Corven.

Bantam was running through the information in his mind when Idal's soft voice interrupted his thoughts. "Your pardon, masters, but I must do this shaving now. I won't cut your throat, sir, I promise.''

"Yeah, I know you have to do the job, Idal." Bantam rubbed his hand ruefully over his beard and mustache. "But bloody hell, you know it will take me close to a year to grow back enough hair to look like a mercenary?"

"Is that why you asked for a year's pay, Bantam?" Corven grinned.

"Damn right it is. Have at it, Idal."

He forced himself to sit quietly while Idal cut his hair short with scissors first. The only thing that made it bearable was that he was sitting, like a free man, not kneeling like a slave. Bantam found that he hadn't forgotten the sting of the razor, or how shaving his head made him itch all down his back. For a moment he missed Kiam sharply. They had always scratched each other's backs and brushed away any loose hairs. He stripped off his shirt, and Idal gingerly brushed him down, staring wide-eyed at the scars on his back.

Corven swore softly when he caught sight of another scar, one on Bantam's right arm a handspan below the shoulder. "Gods, we forgot about your warrior's brand!"

Bantam twisted his head to look himself. "Nothing to worry about. It's not the War God's mark. It's Ydona's. They choose who They want, remember?" He pondered telling Corven the whole story—how Ydona had come to him and how She had said Likarion wanted him, too. Had it been Likarion watching over him, since he became a warrior?

Idal brought out a cloth bag and placed its contents on the table. Bantam wondered where they had gotten one of Launart's rust-brown slave-tunics. The collar was no problem, of course. Launart had always used the standard black iron collars.

His belly was quivering again, as it did before battle. This would be nothing like his enslavement, but it made the hair stand up on the back of his neck nonetheless. He stood staring for what seemed like a long time at the slave-tunic and collar. At last he closed his eyes and let his shoulders slump.

Not a slave. Not a slave. A free man. I have the papers to prove it now. Just pick up the collar and put it on, Farris. No! Not Farris. Bantam. But I have to bring Farris back or I can't do the job.

Abruptly he grabbed the collar and snapped it shut around his throat. He shuddered and stood there breathing heavily, as if he had just been lashed. His head dropped and he forced himself to relax, willing away the well-remembered pain from the touch of cold iron on his bare skin.

Corven had his own problems. He had been born a slave, and so had no traumatic memories of his first collaring, but seeing any man change from a proud, self-assured warrior to a subdued slave was unsettling. "Are you all right, Bantam?"

"I will be. Mother of Mares, this is harder than I thought." He lifted his head, his eyes dark with remembered pain. "Who was that bastard that said I was too cocky to pass as a slave?"

"That was Aerdan, Earl of Hawkswood. He's never had a very good opinion of slaves. Or of freedmen."

"Or mercenaries? Damned conceited ass, reminds me of Lord Torkild. I'd like to give him a few good sharp pokes and let some of that condescension leak out of him."

Mischief started to dance in Corven's eyes. "Would you now? Idal, find us one of those royal slave-tunics and we'll put our friend here to the test."

Corven entered the big dining-tent with hardly a glance paid to him. The two slaves in the royal tunics who followed closely on his heels were ignored completely. King Alnikhias and his nobles had turned their noon meal into another council of war. Ideas flew around the table as one plan or another was thoroughly discussed and contested, sometimes with serious discussion, sometimes with heated arguments. The food that appeared in front of them was consumed with very little attention paid to it; most of the lords could not have said what it was that they had just eaten, or how it had gotten there.

A silent, all-but-invisible slave served the fresh fruit that was dessert. Lord Aerdan of Hawkswood, deep in discussion with Varian of Leopard's Gard, reached absently for the last red-gold peach on the tray, only to see a hand flash over his shoulder and snatch it away. He glanced behind himself, star-

tled and indignant, to see a royal slave leaning casually
against a tent post and biting into the peach with a challenging half-smile on his scarred face.

"How *dare* you, boy!" Aerdan sputtered, stood, and lifted
a hand to administer a punishing cuff to the incredibly insolent slave.

The slave took a quick step to meet him. His hand snapped
up to block the blow and shove Aerdan forcefully back. He
said mockingly, "Mercenaries dare damn near anything,
m'lord, for enough pay. Cuff *me* and you'll draw back a
broken arm."

Alnikhias frowned from the head of the table. "This is not
any way to prove you can pass as a slave, mercenary."

Baron Varian gave a shout of laughter. "Oh yes it is, Your
Majesty. I've been watching him ever since Corven tipped
me off. He's been here a good three-quarters of an hour, and
none of you have noticed him at all, not even that his collar's
the wrong color. I think it's damn good proof that this plan
has a good chance of succeeding. Come on, Aerdan, admit
it. You had it coming, saying he couldn't do it."

"I'll do no such thing, Varian," Lord Aerdan said stiffly.
"How was I to know this was the same man? I expected
him to be wearing Launart's colors, not royal ones."

Bantam winked at Corven and mumbled through a mouthful of peach, "Exshactly, m'lord. Just's Launart expects his
slaves to wear his colors." He finished the peach in two bites
before he peeled the tunic off and rolled it into a ball. "Here,
Idal, catch. Throw me my own shirt, please. Thanks." He
dug a key out of his pocket and unlocked the collar, tossing
it on the table before he pulled his own shirt on.

His face sobered as he said, "Your Majesty, no blame is
to go to Idal for this deception. I said 'fetch me a tunic' and
he followed orders. I told him I'd stew him for breakfast if
he didn't, right, Corven?"

"Something like that, I think," Corven grinned.

"Is there any food left, Idal? Even a man my size needs
more than a stolen peach."

"What was left for us slaves, sir. If you don't mind?"

"Bloody hell, I'll eat anything that doesn't bite me first.

I ate slave food for eight years and it didn't kill me.''

Idal smiled slightly. "It's not that bad, sir. What the noble lords left just now.''

"Any of that cheese pie? I wanted to dig into that with both hands.''

"They do allow us spoons, sir," Idal said with a straight face.

Bantam looked at him in surprise and then laughed. "You're all conspiring to civilize me, huh?''

"Don't be too long, Bantam," Corven reminded him. "We're supposed to leave with your Wolves soon.''

"Oh, yeah. Forget the spoon, Idal, and just hand me a chunk of something. Corven, where's my hat? I won't walk into that camp bareheaded. They'll eat me alive.''

Idal found his hat, handed him the bag with the collar and tunic and a pair of slave-breeches, and put a slice of the cheese pie in his other hand. "Good luck, sir," he said quietly.

Bantam did not return to the Wolves' encampment right away. Instead, he took time to detour past the altar to Likarion and ask formally for the blessing of His priest. As he smeared the sacrificial blood from his pricked thumb over the altar, two deities bestirred themselves to look down upon him.

"You see, Ydona? Mine he is, as he has been these last two mortal years. Warrior to the bone, and ready for revenge.''

Ydona smiled sadly at Her brother and shook Her head. *"Only outwardly, Likarion. Warrior I will grant you, but inside there is still the man who can midwife a foal or love a woman, and take joy in it. You will never make a cold-blooded killer out of that one. Give him back to me.''*

"We'll see," the god smirked. *"Is it another wager?''*

Bayard's Wolves did not quite eat their *sabro* alive. Bantam took the harassment he expected over the loss of his hair, but there were no remarks about slaves. They had been briefed on Bantam's mission that morning by Captain Bay-

ard, and more than one man of the warband wondered if he
would have the courage to do the same thing. To go into a
battle with a sword in your hand was something they understood, but to put a slave-collar around your own neck and
sneak unarmed into a castle full of enemies was something
entirely different.

After they were well away from Alnikhias' forces, they
stopped for a few moments. Bantam changed from his mercenary clothes into a plain blue slave-tunic, and put the collar
back on. Bors stalked around him like a cat with a new play-
thing. "He's not Bantam anymore, *sabros*. What was your
name before? Faron, or something like that?"

"Yeah, Faron," he agreed grimly. "And if you give me
too much hassle, Bors, I know a mercenary that just might
find a snake in his bedroll some night."

It was a little easier this time, however, and he even managed a smile at Corven's merchant costume. It was not as
gaudy as a mercenary's dress finery, but still flashier than
the simple jerkin and white shirt of a guardsman. The shirt
was bright blue and the breeches parti-colored green and
blue. His hat was blue and green also, a floppy bag compared
with the low crown and wide brim of a mercenary's hat.
Bantam turned his over to Bors, and warned him that if one
feather were missing from it later, he'd replace it with one
cut from Bors' hide.

They made good time on the road, and camped that night
in a grassy wayfield along with other travelers.

*He crouched in the dark of the tiny cave, shivering in terror.
The masters were coming for him, Torkild and Barak and
Brenen, coming with shackle and whip and gelding-knife.
Jared was leading them, straight to the cave that was no
shelter at all. Piggy grunts echoed through his head as Jared
snuffled outside, and then they laid brutal hands on him to
drag him out. He was helpless as a child in their hands,
helpless to resist as they threw him down and chained him
spread-eagled. Their voices slithered like snakes into his
ears. Torkild was going to geld him. Not quickly and mer-*

*cifully as colts were gelded, but slowly, a little at a time.
And when Torkild was done and he was no more a man,
Brenen would have his turn with his slave's body before they
gave him to Barak and the kurbasch.*

*He heard their laughter ringing, going on and on as the
knives moved up his arms and legs, leaving searing pain in
their wake. They laughed even more mockingly when he
begged for mercy. As the pain and terror overwhelmed him,
he began to scream.*

He was sitting bolt upright in his blankets, with the sound
of his own screams still echoing through his skull. Corven
crouched nearby with wary alertness, a dagger in his hand.

Neither spoke; Bantam was too shaken and Corven not yet
sure that the mercenary was aware enough to know what he
was doing.

Outside there was a thudding of boots on grass and Bayard's voice asking urgently, "What's the matter?"

Bantam managed to gasp, "Nightmare, sir. I'm all right."

Corven sheathed his dagger and reached for his breeches,
whispering, "You've probably roused everybody. I'll cover
for you while you get hold of yourself." He raised his voice
and said, "I'll be right out, Captain."

As Corven left the tent he could hear other voices now,
asking what the problem was. "I apologize, everyone. Faron
sometimes has bad dreams, but he doesn't usually break out
in screams like that. What more can I say? You can't punish
a slave for dreaming."

"You can gag him, if that's what it takes," growled an
angry merchant. "What in bloody hell was he dreaming
about?"

"I haven't asked him."

Bantam appeared at the tent flap at that moment, his face
expressionless.

"Well, Faron?" Corven asked impatiently.

He was recovered enough to remember his mission, and
pretended to flinch. "Master, please, I'm sorry. May I sit by
the fire for a while? If I sleep, I'll dream again." That much
was the truth, at least.

Corven jerked his head in the fire's direction in answer. "Go on. Again—"

"No," interrupted the merchant. "You, boy, what were you dreaming about?"

"My second master was torturing me again, sir. When he got drunk, he would lash me, and rub salt on my back when he finished. And laugh while I screamed. I dreamed he was gelding me."

"Gods! You never told me that was how you got those scars," Corven said. Even in the dim light, he looked sickened.

"No, master. I didn't know then that you wouldn't do the same thing."

"Go on to the fire. Well, merchant, would you have screamed, reliving torture like that?" Corven demanded angrily.

The merchant grunted and walked away.

Bayard and Corven looked after him, then joined Bantam at the fire.

"You never told us about the things that happened when you were a slave, Banty," Bayard said quietly. "Was that true?"

"Yes, once. Not the worst he ever did to me, but bad enough." Bantam shrugged. "What good would whining about it have done, sir? Anybody who sees my back ought to know I didn't enjoy what they did to me."

"You've got money now. You can hire us to hunt the bastard down and kill him, nice and slow. Hell, some of us'll do it for free."

An ironic smile curved over half his mouth. "It'd be a hard hunt, Captain. All the way to hell."

"You killed him already?"

"No. I used to dream about it, though. I still do, sometimes. My fellow slave Teron used bandits to kill him."

Corven's quizzical look urged him to continue, as did the captain's "What? How?"

"Brenen had us both taught unarmed combat so we could protect him against bandits. He called us his 'boot-daggers.' And when bandits did strike, Teron wasn't quite fast enough to stop the one that stabbed Brenen.'' Bantam leaned forward and tossed another log on the fire. "I know, sir, as well as I know I'm a Wolf, that Teron deliberately hesitated just a heartbeat too long before he killed that bandit. He had reason. His back was worse than mine.''

"Tell us if you ever see him, Banty, and we'll try to buy him free. Sounds like he'd make a good mercenary.''

"Yes, sir.'' Bantam turned to look to the east. "Dawn soon, sir. Should I just go about my servile duties, Corven?''

"What duties?''

"You volunteered me to help cook breakfast.''

20

---·•◆•·---

INFILTRATION

Entering Draksgard City was easy, at least for Bantam. He just stood quietly holding Corven's horse, head bowed, while the gate guards questioned his "master" about his business in the city. He was glad enough to have the chance to rest his feet; three days of going barefoot had not toughened his soles very much.

Perhaps that was why the merchant's slave lagged behind, even as they looked through the fruits and vegetables available at the open market. The basket of early apples that Corven eventually bought was hoisted onto Bantam's shoulder, and he resumed his weary plodding. By the time they reached the gates to Draksgard Keep, Corven was nearly out of sight. Nobody noticed when the slave in the faded blue tunic entered a public privy, nor when a slave in the colors of Duke Launart's household emerged.

No slave would use the main gate, unless accompanying his master. It was an even wearier slave who tried to blend in with a crowd of people, both slave and free, at the side gate. He did not, however, make it in unobserved.

"You there, boy. You with the apples. Come here," demanded the guardsman at the gate.

"Me, master?" he managed to squeak, through a mouth gone suddenly dry. *Blessed Ydona, help! I can't get caught this soon!*

"Of course you! Do you see any other slaves with apples?"

Bantam approached, head down and shaking as the tension to fight or run built up. The gate-guard grinned evilly at him. "Well, well, lookee here. Nice new apples. You know how long it's been, slave, since I had a nice fresh apple?"

"No, master," Bantam said meekly. Just one guard, he could kill or disable him easily. If he had to fight free, which way should he run, out or in? Out. They might be able to try again, at a different gate.

But the guard saw only a household slave, fair game to torment. He reached into the basket and pulled out three of the apples to indulge in a bit of juggling. After only a few throws, however, he returned to his game of slave-tormenting.

"What's the matter, boy? Afraid of the kitchenmaster?" An apple crunched as he bit into it.

"Please, master," Bantam begged. "If that basket is short, they'll think I took them. I'll get the lash!"

"So?" The guard cuffed him hard across the ear. "Won't be the first time, will it?" As Bantam tried to pull back, the guardsman hooked a foot around his ankle and shoved. The apples flew out of the basket all around him as he fell.

"Run, boy. Get out of my sight, before I take the lash to you myself."

A thrown apple whizzed past his ear and another hit him in the back as he scuttled away, biting his lip to keep from laughing. He was in, and the possible awkwardness of actually having to do something with the apples was eliminated.

"Bastard," someone whispered in his ear. He jerked his head around to meet the eyes of another slave, looking at him with sympathy. "Here, let me brush the dust off you. No use you getting punished for that, too."

"Thanks." Bantam reached down and scooped up the apple that had missed his ear. "Do you want it? If I get the lash, it might as well be for something."

The other looked startled, then wistful. "I can't. Thanks anyway." He hurried away.

Bantam looked after him, shrugged, then bit into the apple himself as he checked to make sure a tiny slip of paper was still tucked into his waistband. That was his excuse for wandering around. On it, in what he had been told was a feminine hand, was the brief message, "Tonight, in the maze." If anyone stopped and questioned him, he planned to say that he had been ordered to deliver it, but was forbidden to reveal either sender or recipient.

It appeared, however, that the information from Corven and Idal was correct. Nobody seemed to notice a slave who was moving purposefully from place to place. Even when he loitered about to eavesdrop on a possibly significant conversation, the eyes of most of the free people slid over him as if he was thinking himself invisible. This was the easiest scouting job he had ever had.

The purloined apple was only a distant memory to his grumbling stomach when the bell rang to announce the noon meal. He found the servant's hall with no difficulty, and waited patiently with the other slaves for the free servants to be served first.

He was standing in line and had just been handed his bowl of soup when he felt a soft touch on his arm. Familiar brilliant blue eyes looked into his as he turned. It was Kiam. Bantam obediently followed Kiam's "come" gesture and they found seats side by side in a far corner of the hall.

In the soft, almost inaudible tones they had always used to communicate privately, Kiam asked, "How did you get here, Farris? I know you escaped. All of Loarn talked about nothing else for weeks."

Bantam didn't hesitate. He had trusted Kiam with his skin more than once, and still trusted him now. "Long story, but I'm here by choice—Free Mercenary now, on a mission. You?"

"Transferred. Dog handler for the duke now."

"You still get around the way you did?"

"Yes. What's going on?"

"Where is the princess being held?"

Understanding lit Kiam's eyes. "Sooo. Where? Don't know, big secret. But I know someone who does."

"Don't want to get you in trouble. You shouldn't be seen talking to me any longer. Meet me in the slave latrine in the yard in about an hour."

"No. Kennelmaster's office."

Well, if anybody knew a safe place to meet and talk, Kiam would. Bantam nodded, swallowed the last of his soup and left the hall without looking back.

An hour later, he found the kennelmaster's office just as Kiam reached it as well. They left any greetings until they were both safe inside. Once in, Kiam impulsively hugged him and Bantam returned the embrace. Kiam brushed his fingertips over the scars on his friend's face. "What happened?"

"A parting gift from Viveka. Gods, it's good to see you! Are you sure the kennelmaster won't walk in on us?"

"Kennelmaster's dead, died in the war a couple of weeks ago. They haven't replaced him so they stuck me here in his place."

"What, you're an *overseer*?"

Kiam laughed shortly. "Well, I would be if there was anybody here but me! I say, 'slave, go do this,' and then Kiam goes and does it!" He shrugged slightly, and then it seemed to Bantam that his face fell into new lines of unhappiness. He continued, "If anyone walks in on us, they'll just think I've found a new lover."

A new lover? Then . . . "Haral's not here?"

Kiam shook his head. "They didn't have any reason to move him from Loarn, so he's still there." His eyes held more of the pain of that parting than he would say. He didn't need to. The masters who callously separated married couples and sold children wouldn't think twice about splitting up two men.

"Oh gods, Kiam, I'm sorry." While Bantam hadn't been particularly close to Haral, the pain and grief in his friend's eyes struck him to the heart.

Kiam was quiet for a few heartbeats longer, then gave himself a visible shake. "This isn't helping you. What's going on?"

"I told you. I'm a Free Mercenary now. I don't know how much else to tell you. What you don't know you can't be forced to spill."

"It's easy enough to guess from what you've already told me. You have some plan to break Princess Ashlana out."

"Yes, and that's all I'll say. Did you find out where she is?"

"North wing, third floor, probably second room on the left. The masters think it's a big secret that she's here at all, but one of the chambermaids has been boasting about waiting on a lady that she can't talk about. Who else could it be?" Kiam's mouth twitched in a half-smile at the thought of the masters thinking they could keep anything secret from their slaves.

So. As easy as that, half his job done for him. *Yeah, the easy part,* a corner of his mind said. He had a few hours, then; he wanted to get the message to this princess and get out just before sunset.

"Farris? Do you have time to talk?" Kiam asked wistfully.

"I do now. I thought it might take me a day or two to locate her."

They talked for a long time, catching up on each other's lives and reminiscing about good times. Bantam told Kiam as much as he could about life as a mercenary, although he carefully avoided mention of his mercenary name, the name of his warband or his captain, or anything more of their plans. If Kiam noticed the omissions, he did not mention it.

Kiam's own reminiscences came back more than once to Haral and the things they had done and shared. Each time his voice held more pain, until at last he took a deep, ragged breath and looked down at his hands in his lap. "Thanks, Farris. I need to talk sometimes, you know? Nobody here knows Haral, and they don't care how I feel about him."

"I know how you feel, Kiam. And I care," he said awkwardly.

"I know you do, Farris. You can't have changed that much." Kiam reached out a hand and covered the fist on Bantam's knee. "I missed you just as much when you left. I always wished we could be lovers, you know. I didn't always tease you about it just to annoy Haral."

Bantam didn't shake him off as he once would have done. "I know. But you know why I couldn't." He glanced at the light coming through the window. "I've got to go. I'll get you free, Kiam, Warrior's Oath. The king owes me a year's pay for this. I'll either buy you, or get him to free you when we defeat that old bastard Launart."

Kiam smiled shakily. "Sounds good. I don't know how to be free, but I'll try. Can we get Haral free, too?"

"We'll try, but you first. Wish me luck!"

21

---◆━◆---

ABDUCTION

Taking a deep breath, Bantam hefted the basket of logs and walked slowly toward the door of the captive princess. A bored, weary guard saw nothing odd about a slave fetching more firewood, and admitted him without question. The girl of the picture faced the door when he entered, watchful and wary, but relaxed at the sight of a harmless slave and turned back to the closely barred window.

His eyes ran swiftly over the room. There was no other exit then, unless there was one of those legendary secret passages, and he supposed she would have tried all possible methods of exposing one.

He set the basket of logs carefully in place and padded silently across the floor on his bare feet until he was behind her. This was the most ticklish part of the plan. If he spoke to her, she might make enough noise to draw the attention of the guard. If that happened, he was dead; this was the only way. He struck quickly, one hand over her mouth to stifle any noise, the other arm encircling her body to pull it up tightly to his.

He couldn't see her face, but her body told him of her fighting spirit. She tried to elbow him in the belly, stamp down hard on his toes, and bite his hand, all the while squirming like a basket full of snakes.

"Princess!" he hissed urgently. "I'm a messenger from Alnikhias, not a slave. You need to listen to me." She continued to struggle and he repeated himself twice more before she seemed to understand and stopped, standing tensely frozen in his embrace.

"I know you don't have reason to trust me, so I have a proof. The king showed me the picture you sent him, and a little note saying that the kitten in your lap was called Treasure. He says he wrote back that he hoped to give you a better treasure, one that wouldn't hide under the bed and attack your ankles."

The tension went out of her body and she went limp against him. She nodded her head "yes."

"I can uncover your mouth now? You promise not to scream?"

She nodded again.

He slowly let his hand drop and released her, not without some reluctance on his part. She was a sweet armful, and he envied Alnikhias this fiery little bride.

"I don't have time, my lady, for politeness and ceremony. Do you want to get out of here, get to Alnikhias?"

"Of course!" she said in a scornful whisper.

"Good. As I said, I'm not a slave, I'm a mercenary in his hire. My name's Bantam. We have a plan if you can bring yourself to trust me enough."

She looked at him sharply, suddenly struck by the incongruity between his slave appearance and his attitude. Certainly he was no slave, but could she trust a mercenary? Everybody knew what they were like, no respect for authority and rank at all. He was grinning at her, meeting her eyes as no slave had ever done, as if he could read her thoughts.

"What if I don't trust you?"

He shrugged. "Then I go away and tell them you prefer to marry Duke Launart instead of Alnikhias. It's me or Launart, princess," he prodded. "Which of us do you trust the least?"

The princess surveyed him thoughtfully. "Hold still," she

said abruptly and reached out to touch his forehead. An odd warm prickling ran from her fingertips through his scalp, a prickling as if tendrils of some clinging plant burrowed into his head. For a brief disjointed moment he felt naked and exposed. He wanted to jerk away, remembering the whispers he had heard of the D'Alriaun royal line, whispers of magic, but stood his ground stubbornly. Then the prickling eased into a warm soothing wave, as if he stood by a fire on a cold winter's night.

"So," she said with a half-smile. "You are who you say you are—maybe more. I trust you a great deal more than I trust Launart. And my name is 'Ashlana,' not 'Princess.' What is your plan?"

"Quick and easy with not much fancy stuff to go wrong. I carry a message out that tomorrow you'll be ready. I come back, we decoy the guard in here, I kill him, and take his clothes. Can you bring yourself to pretend to be a slave?"

She looked startled and then grinned back at him "I see. A guardsman dragging a slave-girl off to his lair will attract much less attention than one escorting a princess who should be locked up."

"Exactly." Bantam found he liked this girl, even if she had used magic on him. She was no pretty witless poppet fit only to decorate a throne.

The sound of the door unlocking brought both their heads whipping around. Bantam took two swift strides and crouched before the hearth, as if to put more wood on the fire. A woman entered, and he cursed to himself. Of course. Who else would it be but Viveka?

Viveka started to berate Ashlana about something, some political matter that didn't please her. The princess pretended to ignore her, picking up an embroidered napkin as if to examine the needlework.

Bantam didn't understand the politics or recognize any of the names, though he memorized them to pass the information on. He concentrated on *I'mnothere*, hoping to remain unnoticed.

His luck failed him as a burning log broke with a loud crack. He jumped, startled, and Viveka saw him. As she

turned on him, he cringed back like any ordinary slave and
threw his arm up as if to protect his face.

"You stupid fool, can't you even lay a fire—*Farris!*"

With an odd thought of *didn't I just do this?* he threw
himself at her, desperate to stifle the scream he knew she
would make and knowing that he was too far away. But this
time he had an ally. As Viveka drew in a deep breath to
scream for the guard, Ashlana pulled her back by the arm
and stuffed the napkin into her open mouth. An instant later
Bantam knocked both of them over in his attempt to subdue
Viveka. He pinned her to the floor with his body and slapped
his right hand over her mouth to secure the napkin gag.

She lashed out at his face with her nails, trying for his
eyes. This time he knew what she would do and caught her
wrist, squeezing until he felt something crack. A muffled
squeak came through gag and hand and she ceased struggling.

Bantam grinned down at her, his scarred face only inches
from hers. "I thought you liked pain, Lady Viveka. I can
break the other wrist, too, if you'd like. Or are you of a mind
to spread your legs for me again?" He thrust hard against
her and grinned even wider at the fear in her eyes. "Maybe
I'll just break your neck instead. Ashlana, your orders?"

The princess looked unhappy. "Byela knows I've been
angry enough with her in the past, but I can't watch you kill
another woman in cold blood."

"Not cold blood for me, my lady. But if you let her live,
then can you find some cord or strips of cloth to tie our little
friend up? Otherwise, I'll have to kill her to keep her silent."

He heard her quiet assent and then a tiny snipping sound,
followed by a ripping noise as she tore something. The noises
came twice more, and she knelt down at Viveka's head.
"Gag first?" she asked. At his nod she stuffed a wide strip
of fabric that looked like a torn bit of bedsheet under the
other woman's neck, bringing it up to start a knot on the
back of his muffling hand. As he jerked his hand free, she
tightened the knot, aided by his hand moving to fasten in
Viveka's hair. It was a good square knot, he noticed as she
finished, not an old-woman's knot that could work loose.

Viveka tried to break free again when Bantam released her hands. Ashlana pounced on her and slapped her hard across the face, then grabbed her hands herself; Bantam grinned mirthlessly again at her tactics and hit Viveka on the jaw. Her body went limp and the princess hissed furiously, "I told you not to kill her!"

"She's not dead, just knocked out. Do you want her making a lot of racket and alerting that guard?"

"Well, no."

"All right, then." Bantam wondered how it was that the guard was not already in the room to investigate the noises they had made. Was he asleep at his post, or had Viveka dismissed him? Ashlana saw the doubt on his face and his careful listening attitude as he warily approached the door, and beckoned him to return.

"She usually lets him have a little time to go to the privy. Fortuna must have given us luck, but he'll be back any moment," she whispered.

"Then we've got to work fast." He picked Viveka up and dumped her on the bed. They sacrificed more of the bedsheet to tie her hands to the heavy bedposts. Ashlana watched for only a moment before she went to work tying Viveka's feet to the lower posts. When she regained consciousness, she would be able to make very little noise.

There was still no sound from the hallway.

"The plan I was starting to tell you is dead. We have to get you out *now*. Take that dress off. Good thing Launart's got no lady to object to keeping his slave-girls in just tunics. You can use this one." He pulled his slave-tunic off and tossed it on the bed. When she didn't move, he turned his head to find her standing and staring at him with a strange expression on her face. "What are you waiting for?"

"I need help, I can't unlace it myself. But . . . blessed Byela, your back! What happened?"

"Haven't you ever ordered your slaves beaten for displeasing you, Your Highness? That's what the lash does to a stable slave's back." His voice was flat and emotionless, as if the back under discussion belonged to someone else. He didn't look at her as he worked a thin strip of metal out of the drawstring casing of his breeches. A fine wire fastened the strip to a tiny key. "Turn around and I'll get your lacing."

"No. I mean, I've never had a slave beaten, not like that. It makes me sick to think about it." Her voice changed, and even in her whisper he could hear her anger. "Who did that to you?"

"Various people, here and there. A couple of them I even deserved. Turn around, I said. I can't get lacing I can't see." As she followed his instructions he continued, "Ask the little bitch there about one I didn't deserve, a dozen lashes with a fourblade. She ordered it done, and watched with pleasure while Torkild did it. How the hell do these lacing things work?"

"Cut them, if you have to. I won't have any of my subjects tortured like that. Not even slaves!"

"I'm a Free Mercenary now," he said grimly. "Nobody's subject. Not yours, not Alnikhias', nobody's! Hold still."

She felt a knifeblade cold at the back of her neck and a snap as the lacing-cord severed, again and again as his knife made quick work of the intricate decorative lacing that had taken a skilled body-slave a quarter of an hour to do up. The gown slid off her shoulders and arms, settling of its own weight in a shimmering heap around her feet, leaving her standing in nothing more than a plain linen chemise. She moved to pull it off over her head and then abruptly halted. Bantam grinned with amusement as she blushed and looked at him indignantly.

"Turn your back, please. I'm not in the habit of undressing in front of strange men."

He snorted with muffled laughter at her regal tone, but obediently turned away from her. "Princess Ashlana, if you cling to that royal attitude we can't pull off this slave disguise. If a free man wants to watch a slave undress, he does. He can order a slave to strip for his pleasure."

For the first time she sounded uncertain. "I never thought of that. You can turn around now. What do I have to do to pass as a slave?"

The tunic that had come to mid-thigh on Bantam did not

quite reach to her knees. She felt naked with her arms and legs exposed and resisted the urge to try to pull it down farther. He handed her the metal strip and key; she realized for the first time that the strip had a sharp edge and must have been the knife blade she had felt.

"Unlock my collar. The first thing is you never *ever* look a free person in the face, unless you are told to. Keep your eyes down. Ah, Mother of Mares, that feels good." He rubbed the back of his neck as she lifted the collar away and stood uncertainly with it.

"Give it here." He frowned as he tried to put into words things he had never thought about, just done. "Have you ever noticed that people stand at different distances from each other, depending on the situation and the relationship between them? Just now you stepped away from me to put yourself at a more comfortable distance. Slaves do not have that privilege. Free people can come as close to you as this," he moved to stand so near her that their bodies nearly touched and his breath stirred a stray wisp of her hair, "And you would be punished if you moved away, if you even tried. Do you understand?"

Ashlana found her breath catching in her throat. She found it very disturbing and yet somehow exciting to have him so close. Unable to speak, she nodded and felt herself blush again.

"Good. Hold still." He snapped the collar shut about her neck. "Get those shoes off. Launart keeps his Insiders barefoot. I'm sorry, but we'll have to cut your hair. Do you have any scissors?"

"Only these embroidery ones." She handed them to him and reached up to pull the pins out of her hair, freeing the braid that had been wound into a gleaming coronet of dark hair and gold ribbons.

Bantam looked with amusement at the tiny blades, no longer than half the width of his thumbnail. "I thought not. I wouldn't give a prisoner a weapon like that. Don't move. I'll have to use my knife." He lifted the heavy braid lying on the back of her neck and began to saw at it. It reached nearly to her knees; he caught himself wondering what the thick dark-brown mass of it would look like unbound and falling over her body, and gave himself a mental shake. This was a job to do, not an opportunity for bed-sport!

When the braid fell to the floor, Ashlana ran her hands through her hair to pull out the last remnants of braiding and ribbon. Her head felt strangely light and free. The shoulder-length strands of hair tickled her cheeks.

"Now what? You said decoy the guard in?"

"That's the easy part. You stand over there. When I signal, you scream. Not too loud. We don't want the whole castle alerted, just that door-guard."

He went to the fireplace and picked up the log he had mentally marked as the most suitable. It tapered to fit his hands well and was heavy enough for a good club. He swung it a few times to loosen his muscles and get the feel of it, then readjusted his grip slightly.

With his knifeblade in his teeth and the club over his head, he took his position by the door. Ashlana was in the opposite corner. With luck, the guard would look her way first to see what she was screaming about. Bantam hoped that the sight of a slave-girl instead of a princess would distract him even further.

He felt the surging in his blood that was the battlefire building, looked sharply at Ashlana, and nodded. *Now!*

Her scream ripped through his ears and the same fierce joy that he felt flickered in her eyes. She screamed again as they heard the first fumbling at the lock, chopping it off short as the door opened. She stared intensely at the corner behind the door, willing the guard to look that way, away from Bantam.

It worked. Bantam's club came down with a solid *thunk* on the guard's head and he fell without another sound. He was not wearing a helm, only a mail coif not intended to ward off clubs. Ashlana sprang to close the door, leaving it just ajar until Bantam found the key still clutched in the unconscious man's hand.

Quickly they stripped him of everything but his breeches, and tied him as well. His boots were too big for Bantam, but not by much. Ashlana stuffed pieces of cloth in the toes to make them fit better while Bantam pulled on his linen shirt, leather body-armor, and sword-baldric. When he tugged the mail coif on over its soft padded skullcap, it burned for a moment; he willed the pain to go away until it calmed to a manageable prickling along his neck and jaw.

Ashlana stuffed the dress, chemise, shoes, and braid behind the wardrobe, feeling that if the princess disappeared, so should all trace of her. "Bantam, you said your name was? See if you can shove that guard under the bed."

He crouched to look. "Tight fit, but we can try." It was a tight fit, but they managed it eventually. He kept up a running instruction to her as they worked.

"Remember, we want everybody to see a scared, helpless slave. I'm a free man, your master for the night, and I can and will do anything I want to you. It could be pain, or it could be pleasure, but you don't know which. Make yourself feel it gut-deep, not just in your head, if you can. Keep your head down. If I press down on your arm or shoulder, kneel and put your head down farther, so your hair will hide your face."

The battle-surge settled down to its familiar quivering in Bantam's belly. He opened the door to reconnoiter; then they simply walked out and pulled the door shut behind them.

For the first time in his life, Bantam blessed his unknown father for bequeathing him his sense of direction. It would be all too easy to get confused and lost in the maze of corridors, rooms, towers, and tunnels of the sprawling castle. He walked quickly along, almost dragging Ashlana. She took advantage of an empty corridor to protest at his speed.

"We've got to get out of here as quickly as we can. The back gate closes at sunset. If anybody sees us, well, I just can't wait to get you alone and helpless for the night." His head went up sharply. "Someone coming, more than one, wearing boots. Over here."

He dragged her into a dimly lit corner, put his back into it, and pulled her into his arms. "Kiss me," he murmured.

She began to hiss at him that this was no time for his masculine fantasies when she suddenly comprehended his reason. A guardsman and a slave-girl cuddling in a secluded corridor couldn't be such an unusual sight. Shyly she reached up to his mouth with hers.

"You there, guardsman. Are you on duty?" rapped out one of the men who came into view. It was Duke Launart.

Bantam cursed to himself but answered easily, "No, sir! I just came off duty."

"And you have other plans, I see." The duke laughed and Bantam pressed surreptitiously down on Ashlana's arm. She dropped to her knees, her chin tucked down to her chest. Bantam could see her shaking as she fought to control her sudden panic.

So could the duke.

He laughed again. "Well, lad, you'll have to wait a little while for that! I need you to find your captain and tell him I want double patrols tonight. Something is in the wind, and I don't like it."

Bantam saluted and said, "Aye, sir." He gave a resigned sigh and pulled Ashlana to her feet. "Come along, sweetling. What I have planned for you will have to wait." She nestled into the curve of his right arm, hiding her face against his shoulder.

The duke gave them both a malicious grin and his eyes lingered on Ashlana's legs. "I won't deprive one of my fighting men of his well-earned reward. You have my leave to stow her in your quarters until you get back. You'll stay put, won't you, little one?"

She whispered, "Yes, master."

Bantam's answering grin was equally malicious, half-smile, half-leer. "Thank you, sir!" He saluted again and they hurried away down the corridor.

The sun had already set when they reached the gate. They cuddled again in a spot where both could see it. Bantam was dismayed to notice that the guard here was already double that of the morning. Two guards were standing at the gate, one on each side, and nobody was leaving.

"Now what?" Ashlana asked. She reached up and gave him a lingering kiss on the mouth.

"I had hoped to get out the same way I got in this morn-

ing, with a group of people. Either we're too late for exits
at this gate or they make everybody leave through one of the
others for more security." He bent his head and kissed her
again. She was a good height for him; all he had to do was
dip his head a little.

Ashlana leaned trustingly up against him and chewed her
lip as she thought. "Bantam, would a slave-girl be allowed
to get away with teasing a guardsman? Would other guards
stop her, or would they laugh at him and let her go?"

"These guardsmen, I don't know. Most mercenaries
would laugh. The tavern girls flirt and tease all the time."

"Good."

She pulled away from his embrace and ran toward the
gate. Halfway there she whirled back to face him. "Oooh,
nooo, massterrr. You have to catch me firrrst."

Belatedly he understood what she meant and ran after her.
"Dammit, girl, come back here!" he shouted angrily. "You
can't get away that easy!"

Her silvery laugh rang out; they had the eyes of both gate-
guards. Again she turned back to him and he closed the gap
between them. Her teasing tone was straight out of childhood. *"Nyah,* nah-nah *nyah* nah, *you* ca-an't *catch* me!" He
made a grab for her although he knew she was just a bit too
far away, and stumbled slightly. She skipped ahead of him,
staying just out of reach.

Bantam heard the gate-guards' laughter and their crude
comments, and ignored them. "I said come back here!" Ten
more feet, five more feet—they were out!

To the right was the road into the city; to their left was a
wide grassy area that ringed the castle to form part of its
defenses. They must still cross this area before they could
reach the shelter of the forest. Ashlana continued to dance
and tease in the growing dusk just ahead of him, a nerve-
wracking game of tag that slowly brought them closer to
cover.

Shouting broke out in the castle behind them as they
reached the first trees. "No more games! Run!" he gasped.
She hesitated only long enough for him to catch up to her.
Together they plunged deeper into the darkness of the thick

tangle of brush and second growth trees, down a rough trail that opened suddenly before them.

"They'll have dogs out as soon as they can. We need to make it to the river first."

"How far?"

"About a mile, maybe a little more. Can you make it?"

"No—my feet!"

He had forgotten she was barefoot. She was used to wearing shoes. Every rock, every stump, every tangle would hurt her feet worse and slow them down more. And she was too close to his own size for him to carry her any distance.

"Up that tree." He boosted her into the thick branches of a fir. "Go up as high as you can and freeze there. Don't move, don't even breathe heavily." He began to strip off the armor and chainmail he didn't need now. His hand hesitated on the dagger and he looked up at her, then back down the trail. Swiftly he pulled the smaller boot-dagger from its scabbard. "Take this. Use it if you have to, on them or yourself, your choice. I'll go on to the river and try to throw them off our track. Someone is waiting there to carry a message for your escape tomorrow; I'll try to get his horse and come back for you."

"You'll be caught!"

"Not me, sweetling! I'm half fai, and if I can't outfox them nobody can! If I'm unlucky, well, they won't take me alive. If I'm not back by moonrise, try to work your way south, downstream along the river. Someone will be waiting until dawn to try to carry that message. Tell him my name and who you are. He'll help you get to Alnikhias."

"Bantam—may Fortuna be with you."

"Ask for Her help for both of us, Ashlana. Maybe goddesses listen better to princesses." She heard the sounds of his boots thudding off down the narrow trail and then there was silence until the usual night noises began.

He hadn't been gone long when she heard the sound they had both feared. Dogs bayed from the direction of the castle and the shouts of men became louder. They were coming, heading straight for her. Her own heartbeat was so loud in her ears that it seemed impossible that they couldn't hear it.

She did exactly as Bantam had told her, staying as still as possible. She couldn't have moved anyway. Her hands wouldn't let go of the branch.

The pursuers were almost under her when she heard, almost simultaneously, a crack, a heavy thud, and an "oof," as if someone had fallen. Men's voices shouted. "Damn fool slave! He's loosed them!" "Fool yourself, catch them!" The baying of the dogs rushed past her and was swiftly gone down the trail.

There was a moment of silence, then the cracking of a whip and the heavy smack as it connected with flesh. A young man's voice cried out, high-pitched with pain and fear, "No, master, please! I fell. . . ." The whip blows continued unabated, until the unfortunate slave was screaming. Two or three blows followed the sudden cessation of his cries, and then she heard a voice she was certain was Duke Launart's.

"Back, all of you. No use following now. Either they had horses hidden and are gone already, or the dogs will tree them and we can find them when we get a new pair out. Is that simpleton of a slave still alive?"

"Yes, m'lord."

"Bring him. We'll need to get patrols out on the roads as soon as possible."

For a long time there was no sound in the forest except the soft spatter of tears running down Ashlana's face and dripping into the branches.

22

SHELTER

Bantam heard only the dogs, coming up fast and furiously behind him. Too fast; why had they loosed them? The hunters couldn't possibly find them in the dark. But there was no time to worry about it. He couldn't let them tree him like a cat, to wait for the hunters until morning. Twisting and turning in a calculated effort to throw them off his trail, he ran, dropping first the mail coif and then the body-armor to slow them down and lighten his load.

When he came to a small clearing, he decided that he could find no better place to make a stand. A large dead tree stood in the middle of the open area and the last light of dusk would give him his best vision.

They were not wardogs, but boarhounds, two of the duke's best. He could hear the menace in their growls as they held him at bay, his back to the tree. It sickened him that he might have to kill Kiam's dogs. Unless . . . could he use the Beast-Voice on them, to control them as he did horses?

"Easy, now. I'm not the one you want," he tried, in his most soothing voice. "You want rabbits. Not me, *rabbits*." He thought hard about rabbits scurrying through the brush just down the trail, trying to put the image of easier prey into the dogs' minds.

For a brief moment he thought it worked. One of them whined and put its ears back; its tail drooped slightly and it looked over its shoulder, as if to consult their absent handler. The other would have none of such nonsense—*this* was the prey they had been set on!

He stamped and feinted with the sword, trying to make them come at him one at a time. That was not their training; both of them closed in at once to take him from either side as they would a boar.

A swordsman armed with nearly three feet of steel has a longer reach than a boar armed with tusks; Bantam caught the more aggressive one with a slashing blow that cut it nearly in two. Its packmate, no longer hesitant, evaded him unharmed and closed in.

Its jaws fastened on his leg just below the knee. He frantically reversed the direction of his swing, but the dog released his leg with a ripping twist of its head, dodged, and bit him again. He scrabbled for the dagger at his belt, and grabbed the dog by its collar. The collar spikes bit into his hand as he slashed at the boarhound's throat. It gave a muffled yelp and stiffened, but drove its teeth even deeper into his leg as it died.

Bantam dropped to the ground, gasping with exertion and pain. The ripped leg was bleeding freely, but not with the spurt of a severed artery. His hands shook as he used his dagger to rip strips off the bottom of his shirt. He made a pad of one and tied the others around his leg to hold it in place. If he left a blood trail, any tracker could find him in the morning.

The river was . . . that way. He hobbled as quickly as he could in the right direction.

A half-mile downstream he heard the muffled snort and stamp of a horse. He stopped and whistled warily, three notes rising in the call of a nightbird that usually gave four notes. He counted four hasty beats and whistled again. It was answered with five notes, then four.

"Who's there?"

"It's Conal. Bantam?"

"Yeah. Problem, Conal. I got recognized and we had to break her out tonight. I'm wounded, she's barefoot, and we need your horse."

"Where is she?" demanded the other. He ripped loose the tethering reins and pulled the horse in Bantam's direction.

"Back down the trail, up a tree. You can't find her."

"I thought I heard dogs earlier."

"Taken care of for now. Look, I've got to get back to her before they bring out more. No use you trying to take a message to the captain on foot, I'll beat you there. Why don't you head back into town and get a message to Corven, then hit the taverns, see what rumors are going around.

"Damn." For the first time in his memory, he couldn't mount properly. "Give me a leg-up, will you?"

"Tavern-crawling sounds good. We're camped about three miles west, in an open field in plain sight off the main road. Luck, Bantam."

It was harder going through the darkening tangle of woods mounted, but he didn't dare dismount and lead the horse. His leg was hurting worse; he'd never get back up again. When he got back to the fir tree, his heart gave such a devastating jolt that he thought he'd be sick. The smell of trampled earth, broken bushes, and blood hung sharply in the air; had they taken her? He thought he heard a tiny noise. Ashlana, or an animal drawn by the smell of blood?

"Ashlana? Ashlana, it's Bantam."

This time the noise was definitely a human gasp. "I'm here!" A shower of bark and needles spattered down as a dark figure slithered out of the tree. She swung from the branch onto the horse's back behind him and hugged him fiercely.

"I was afraid the dogs caught you. That poor slave!"

"What slave? What happened?" His voice was sharp and she felt his body tense.

"The dog handler. He tripped and fell and let the dogs go. I thought they were going to beat him to death."

She felt him check the horse and half turn it toward the

castle. He gave a soft moan that was half a name—
"*Kiam!*"—and hesitated a heartbeat longer. Then he turned
the horse again and sent it as quickly as possible off the trail,
not heading for the river, but angling, she thought, for the
main road.

"Where are we going? I heard Duke Launart say he'd
have patrols out as soon as possible."

"My camp."

They broke from the trees and he urged the horse to a
gallop. It seemed to Ashlana no more than a few moments
before they came in sight of campfires. A sentry challenged
them as the horse swerved and bucked to a stop. "Who goes
there?"

"It's Bantam. Where's the captain?" he snapped.

"What in hell are you doing here? Where's Conal?"

"No time! *Bayard!*" Bantam howled.

"I'm here, Bantam. What's happened?" said Bayard's
voice from the shadows.

Bantam threw one leg over the horse's neck and slid off,
staggering as his feet hit the ground, then turned to help
Ashlana dismount. "This is Princess Ashlana. I was recognized and had to break her out tonight. There'll be patrols
here any moment looking for us."

Bayard would not have held his leadership if he had been
slow-witted. "Balian, up on that horse and back into town.
Get a message to Corven that the whole damned plan is
blown but we have the princess safe. Bors, she's closest to
your size, get your spare clothes. Bantam, your tent's over
there, get into your own stuff. What the hell happened to
your leg? No, tell me later. Move! Everyone else, as you
were."

Bantam headed for the tent he shared with Jehan, followed
by Ashlana. He jerked the flap down without bothering to
tie it, kicked off the too-large boots, and ripped off the ragged shirt and breeches. He burrowed in his pack for clean
clothes, hissing just a little as he pulled the breeches on over
his roughly bandaged leg.

A hand thrust another bundle of clothes through the flap
and a voice said uncertainly, "My lady?"

"Thank you, Bors, just drop them, and forget there are any ladies in this camp. Bantam, get this collar off me." Now that she could talk in a normal voice instead of a whisper, he noticed how unusual her voice was for a woman, deeper than most, like a boy's on the verge of breaking.

"Then hold still so I can." Bantam pulled the key out of the old breeches and snapped it quickly into the tiny lock as Ashlana wriggled hastily into the borrowed breeches. "No extra boots. You'll have to use these." He looked away to give her as much privacy as possible as she stripped the tunic off and reached for the shirt. Even so, he caught a glimpse of soft, round breasts as he gathered the discarded clothes and started to wrap the despised collar with them.

"No, wait, give me that shirt," Ashlana said. He handed it over with a puzzled look, mystified about why she would want another shirt, and bewildered even more when she took the ragged hem in her hand and spat on it. She rubbed the damp cloth over her eyes, spat and rubbed them again, and repeated the actions yet again on her cheeks. Dark smudges were plain on the shirt as she handed it back to him, and her eyes had lost their wide, dark, feminine loveliness, becoming only ordinary eyes.

"Well?" she asked. "Am I a good enough mercenary?"

"New recruit, maybe. Still too female." Again he burrowed in his pack and pulled out his favorite deerskin jerkin. "Here, pull this on over." He slipped his own leather browband with the howling wolf badge on her head to pull her hair back out of her eyes. "There, that'll do. Let's go."

As Bantam left the tent, Gault shoved armor at him as Bayard stood by with his helm and sword. "We've got to hide that shaved head. Here, you're standing guard duty. Give me that slave stuff. They may search the camp. We'll jam it down the latrine pit good and deep. Daveth, sing something, this is any other evening, remember."

"What?" asked the musician, glancing uncertainly at Ashlana, obviously thinking of the usual rowdy songs the warband enjoyed.

" 'Shackle and Sword,' " Bantam suggested. "What post, Captain?"

"Back would be too obvious. Left flank."

As he moved, Bantam heard Ashlana say, "No, not a song about an escaped slave turning mercenary! Sing 'Riazan Dancer.' "

Daveth gawked at her, clearly startled.

"You do know it, don't you?" She began to sing, not in a woman's soprano or alto, but a pure, clear tenor.

> *Dancer, oh dancer, come dance next to me*
> *Your sweet little toes, my love, would I see.*

Bantam was startled enough himself. The song was one that became progressively bawdier as the verses went on; the singer described what he intended to do to each part of the dancer's body as he worked his way up. Where had a princess learned it?

Daveth recovered himself enough to join her on the chorus:

> *Riazan dancer, my love, tell me true*
> *Is it true what the girls of Riaza do?*

They had reached the third verse and the song had worked its way to the dancer's calf when they heard the jingle and rattle of horses stopping. "Hello, the camp!" someone shouted.

The front sentry challenged, "Who goes there?"

"Swordguard out of Draksgard, hunting for a runaway slave and a renegade guardsman. Have you seen either of them?"

The singing stopped in a jangling discord as Captain Bayard answered. "These are Bayard's Wolves. What makes you think your runaways would try to shelter with a band of mercenaries?"

The leader of the patrol stepped into the firelight. "We have orders to question and search everybody in this area. Will you cooperate peacefully?" He was a young lordling, no more than sixteen, and not using command-voice with any certainty.

Everyone could hear the amusement in Bayard's voice. "Gentlemen, have we seen any slaves? Any guardsman other than these . . . brave warriors?"

Scattered replies of "No, Captain" answered him.

"Bantam, Jehan, Perrin, any slaves out there hiding in the grass?"

"No, sir," the three sentries chorused. Jehan added pointedly, "If they're looking for slaves, sir, they need to look closer to home. I hear tell some of these lordlings can't even piss without a pretty slave to help them hold it."

The patrol leader's face took on a look of barely controlled fury. "You men, search this camp. And you, Captain, what are you doing in this area in the first place? We're at war, you know."

Bayard made a "be-my-guest" motion with his arm as he answered coolly, "War's over, they told me. We're looking for work, to see who's offering the most gold this time."

"I will report to my warlord, then. I'm sure he will be happy to interview you, about the second or third hour after noon. You are Captain . . . ?"

"Bayard. And you are . . . ?" He deliberately omitted any honorific.

"Lord Athemar of Darkenall."

His men began to report back their failure to find anything but empty tents and tethered horses with no sign of sweat. Lord Athemar took their reports with a supercilious sneer, then glared directly at the group of Daveth, Bors, and Ashlana. "Your men want lessoning in respect, Captain."

"Perhaps, then, my lord, sometime in the future you may . . . *attempt* to teach them."

"It will be a pleasure, Captain. Mount up!"

They were gone with a great noise of jingling spurs and rattling armor.

Bantam waited a while longer before hobbling in to collapse next to the fire. He scowled at Gault, who was sitting with his knees pulled up, his face hidden in his arm, shoulders shaking. "And what's wrong with you tonight?" he said acidly.

"Your lady . . ." Gault choked out. He raised his head and

Bantam could finally see that he was laughing, silently and helplessly, tears squeezing themselves out of his eyes. "She . . . she . . ." He collapsed again, unable to control himself.

Daveth's lips twitched as well as he explained, "All the time that young snot was standing here, this lady was singing, just loud enough for him to hear." He paused for dramatic effect and Bantam scowled at him as well. "She was singing 'Mercenaries' Brag.' And if I may ask, my lady, why 'Riazan Dancer'?"

"It worked, didn't it? No lord in his right mind would expect to find a princess sitting with a warband of mercenaries and singing bawdy songs. Ladies don't even know those words." Her lips quivered in a smile and then immediately sobered. "But ladies do know how to treat wounded warriors. Bantam, off with those breeches. Do you think I didn't see that bandage with fresh blood on it?"

Bantam looked shocked and then stubborn. "I've bandaged it, that's enough."

"No, it's not," Ashlana retorted. "That's a dogbite, isn't it? Captain, you know how soon a wound like that can putrefy, as dirty as dogs' teeth can be. I'll not have him lose his leg because of me."

"She's right, Bantam. Strip or we'll hold you down and do it for you. And while she's treating it, I want a full report. Daveth, just in case our visitors left a listener, give them 'Wargames Far Away.'"

Daveth laughed and his fingers bounced over the kithara strings. This song, with its recital of the cheerful mayhem a mercenary warband could cause in wargames, was a favorite. Most of the warband joined in.

Bantam glared at Captain Bayard. Modesty was a notion long gone from his personality, but for some reason he was reluctant to strip in front of this girl. He lost that battle of will, however, when Ashlana made an impatient gesture toward him and both Bors and Gault leaped to her assistance. With a growl, Bantam kicked off one boot and shoved his breeches down far enough to free his injured leg, then pulled them back up to cover himself. Bayard passed over his own

dagger to cut the bandages loose as Ashlana studied the leg
with detached interest.

"Did it bleed well?" she asked under cover of the noise
of the raucous song. "Puncture wounds can be nasty when
they close again right away. I'll need some wine or brandy
or something like that. This is deeper than I like to use
wound-salve, and it's going to need stitches. Some honey,
then, and fresh bandages."

Bors fetched her the needle and silk thread kept for
wounds, then went to rummage in the cooking gear for the
odd things she asked for as Bantam said indignantly, "I was
trying to stop it, not let it bleed."

She ignored his protests. "I'll want to look at it again in
better light and maybe soak it in hot water, but for now this
will have to do." She uncorked the bottle of brandy Bors
handed her and dribbled it all over the ugly slashes.

Bantam's face in the firelight went utterly still and he
clamped his teeth together to keep in the yell of unexpected
pain. "Mother of *Mares,*" he hissed. "I never thought the
cure being worse than the injury was like this."

"Damn you, Bantam, give me a report," ordered Bayard.

The mercenary obeyed, watching carefully as Ashlana
smoothed the honey over the injured leg before starting to
stitch.

Ashlana's giggle interrupted Bantam's terse narration as
the words to the song crept through her concentration. "Oh,
I've *got* to learn this one! Father will—" Her voice broke
off abruptly, and she became very absorbed in carefully tying
off the last stitch.

Bayard watched her for a few heartbeats, then said gently,
"We know, my lady. All of us have lost someone and then
forgotten it for a while, until we think of something like
that."

"Thank you, Captain," she murmured in a subdued voice.

"Why honey, my lady?" Gault asked.

"It keeps infection out of a wound sometimes. I was
taught 'something sharp, something soothing.' But blue
bread mold is better if you can get it." She laid a bandage
over Bantam's leg and wrapped it snugly. "Can you move

that, or is it too tight? No, don't put any weight on it yet.''

"It's all right," he said briefly.

Bayard nodded thoughtfully. "Yeah, Bantam, judging from your report there's nothing else you could have done, although in your place I don't think I would have trusted the slave.

"After that lordling's visit tonight, we're stuck here for most of tomorrow, then. I'll have to report in and negotiate with the warlord or bring all of them down on us. Bantam, I think your new recruit will be with us until we can get back to Alnikhias' lines. That being so, what's your name, lad?''

She flashed him a smile of understanding, brilliant even in the firelight. "Alain.''

"Alain. Let me see your hands. Hm, run away from school, have you? These aren't a warrior's hands.'' The captain's eyebrow went up as he rubbed her fingertips with his thumb, and stopped at the bowstring callus on the ring finger of her right hand. "Archer, are you? Wouldn't have thought that was part of your training.''

"My father has no child now but me," she replied quietly and proudly. "I have all the training that my brother would have had, although not much swordwork of late. Yes, I'm an archer. I can hit a wand two fingers wide at fifty paces, and a man's body at one hundred. If you have a bow among your gear, tomorrow I can prove it.''

"I'd like to see that, although somehow I don't think you're just bragging, Alain. Bors, you've just been replaced as odd-jobs man.''

Bayard rose to his feet and stretched. "Bantam, I want you to go to bed now. It's early yet, but that leg has to be rested. It's bad enough that you're shaved like a slave, we can't have you limping. My lady, I will give up my tent for you tonight and tomorrow we'll break out one of the small ones for your use. 'Twouldn't be proper for you to share a tent with one of these crude mercenaries, even poor old beat-up Bantam there.''

Bantam grinned and winced exaggeratedly as he levered himself to his feet. "Captain, right now a whole troupe of Riazan dancers would be safe from me.''

"Ah, but would you be safe from them, with your reputation?"

Nevertheless, he stood alone at the edge of camp for a long time, looking back in the direction of Draksgard and mourning. He knew the dog handler had been Kiam, and he knew with equal certainty that Kiam had loosed the dogs deliberately to give his friend a better chance to escape. He remembered Kiam's hands gently rubbing wound-salve on his own lashed back, and prayed with all his soul that there was someone in that castle to care for his friend the same way. Even when he gave up with a sigh and went to his own tent, it was a long time before he fell asleep.

23

ASHLANA

At arms-practice in the morning, Ashlana proved her skill with a bow. In the space of thirty heartbeats, she clustered six arrows into a spot no bigger than a man's outstretched hand. Several Wolves watched and muttered with approval, although they shook their heads at her sword technique. Gault offered to work with her, setting Bantam off into fits of laughter. "And she didn't even have to break your arm to get you to do it!"

Captain Bayard left for Draksgard about noon, hoping to hurry his interview with the warlord. Following his orders, the on-duty half of the Wolves started to break camp, while the off-duty half left to go into town and hit the taverns.

Ashlana whistled with approval when Bantam came out of his tent dressed in his full mercenary finery. His suede jerkin was a deep royal blue, slashed in a starflower pattern on breast and back. It matched the blue and saffron embroidery of running wolves on the upstanding collar and cuffs of his wine-red shirt. His breeches, like the jerkin snug enough to display his body but loose enough to let him move freely, were a darker shade of red, and the same embroidery ran in a band down the outside of his leg, disappearing into black boots. The belt around his waist was tied in a warrior's knot rather than buckled, and silver studs shone on the black leather. The saffron-gold hat with its full rooster-tail of feathers told her how he had earned his name.

"Gawds, ain't he purty, Alain?" Bors asked in a jeering voice. His own finery he had shared with Ashlana, giving her his embroidered shirt to wear with Bantam's doeskin jerkin while he kept his own jerkin of forest-green leather. Following his lead, her hair was loose except for slender braids in front of her ears.

"You're just jealous, Bors-me-lad," Bantam replied loftily. "Never mind, you'll have a man's body to show off someday."

Ashlana felt herself blushing. She didn't know if he was deliberately peacocking like that for her benefit, but she was enjoying it anyway. Too bad those scars marred his face like that; he'd be a handsome man without them.

When they swaggered off to the horse-lines, Gault intercepted them and fixed the three with a steely glare. "And just where are you gentlemen headed this fine afternoon?"

"The lads and I thought we'd find a good rowdy tavern and waste a couple of hours."

The older mercenary gave a sigh of exasperation. "Banty, have you been fighting without a helm again? You are going to ride into a town where the castle is buzzing like a kicked-over beehive looking for you and go *tavern-crawling?*"

"Gault, if they search the camp again, and they find me looking like a slave, with my head shaved and my back the way it is, and doing slave work like breaking camp, they'll haul me in so fast my feet won't touch the ground, no matter what anybody says. Everybody knows that Free Mercenaries don't keep slaves, so how would you explain me?"

Gault looked unconvinced. "And how will we explain you in a tavern?"

"I'll wear my hat and with luck it won't come out. If it does, I'm shaved because my *sabros* pull practical jokes. I'm not collared, and I'm wearing mercenary gauds and drinking in the company of other mercenaries. It would be a really desperate slave who would hide in a tavern that caters to the likes of us.''

''All right. That explains you. What about them?'' Gault jerked a thumb in the direction of Ashlana and Bors.

Ashlana's mouth quirked into a half-smile. ''That's my idea, Gault, and the same reasoning applies as last night. The last place they would look for a gently reared princess is in a mercenary tavern drinking and pinching the serving-girls.'' Bors staggered as she swooned back against him and fanned herself with a delicate hand. ''Oh the shock, the horror of it all! I believe I shall faint!'' she squeaked in a piercing falsetto.

The sight of a mercenary, even a very young one, swooning like a fragile maiden was too funny to resist. Gault burst into laughter and shook his head. ''You three aren't going anywhere without me. Got to have an older, cooler head in the group or you'll end up breaking chairs over each other to put on a good act. Banty, where were you going to take them?''

''I've heard about the Drunken Dragon but never had a chance to go there. They shouldn't really start roistering until this evening, so I thought it'd be safe enough for the young'uns.''

Ashlana and Bors both looked indignant, although it was impossible to tell whether it was at being called ''young'uns'' or at the notion that they should be kept safe.

Gault shuddered and rolled his eyes. ''Bantam, the Dragon is always roistering. I suspect that's where most of the Wolves are heading for right now. If we take two young warriors like these in there, the dancing-girls would try to grab them, strip them, and have them right there at the tables.''

''That good, huh? All right, you suggest a place.'' Bantam grinned a little wistfully at the thought of missing a good rowdy place where he could perhaps relieve some other mercenary of coin he didn't need anyway.

''The Golden Bell. They've got some pretty little Riazan dancers, I heard.''

• • •

Bantam felt at home a short while later when they swaggered into the small tavern. It was a small, sturdy building, with an interior of whitewashed rock walls, dominated by a good-sized central fireplace. The bar curved along part of the back and side walls, and a doorway behind it obviously led to the kitchen and other nether regions. A small stage filled the rest of the back wall. A curving staircase led to the upstairs rooms.

There were a few of Launart's guardsmen identifiable by their rust-brown-and-gold surcotes, and a scattering of mercenaries in their own finery, some wearing the brown-and-gold baldrics that marked them as also in the employ of Launart. Other tables held local residents who were having their midday meal, possibly while their shops were closed.

They found an empty table near the bar, and ordered ale all around. When the serving-slave brought it, Bantam lazily reached out just as she was leaving and caught her by the skirt. "Come here, sweetheart. My lap's cold." Another slight tug pulled her onto his uninjured leg and he settled back in the chair with a sigh of contentment. She giggled and squirmed a little to make herself more comfortable.

"If you please, milord, I can't stay very long. We have to practice our dancing for this evening." She looked flirtatiously up at him from under lowered eyelashes. "If our dancing doesn't warm your lap, nothing will." Bantam laughed and kissed her, only reluctantly letting her go.

Ashlana watched them, feeling upset and angry with Bantam for flirting with a serving-slave, and annoyed at herself for reacting in such a fashion. She kept her face as impassive as possible; why should it upset her when a mercenary behaved in a way that was customary for him? This couldn't be the first time he had been tavern-crawling. He was a grown man, after all.

It appeared they were too early for any entertainment, as the musicians on the corner of the stage were rehearsing: one was running her fingers over her kithara strings and arguing with another over the suitability of a particular phrase. Someone finally picked up a tabour and started a beat for the dancers.

Ashlana watched them with open-mouthed interest and a little embarrassment. Certainly, she had seen innumerable dancers; entertainment was part of any feast she had ever attended. But never had she seen the unashamed erotic movements of these girls who moved to the drumbeat. They fanned out from the stage and posed seductively, each in front of a table as the drum fell silent.

The music started finally, a thin thread of sound, and their frozen stillness shifted imperceptibly to quivering motion. As the music built in strength, the movement of their bodies passed from sensual to alluring, from alluring to frankly provocative.

The dancers reformed into a group, a flying skein that whirled tantalizingly past the tables. As she passed, the dancer who had warmed Bantam's lap grinned mischievously and snatched his hat, tickling at his face with the feathers. He made a grab for it, but was too late.

One of the castle guardsmen and two of the mercenaries sat bolt upright and stared at him. The brown-surcoted guardsman burst out of his chair and across the room, scattering dancers out of his way, and slammed a hand down on Bantam's shoulder to push him back into his seat. "You're under arrest. Come with me quietly."

Bantam shook his hand off and snarled up at him, "Get your filthy paws off me, you six-fathered bastard! What'n bloody hell do you mean, trying to arrest a man for having an ale?"

The two Draksgard mercenaries had crossed the room with long strides to back up the guardsman. "You know why we're taking you in, slave, so don't try to play innocent," the guardsman said arrogantly.

Bantam left his chair with a deep-throated growl, ready to fight; Gault's hand clenched in his belt pulled him to a stop. "Bantam, hold it right there. Misha, what's all this about a slave?"

One of the other mercenaries, a tall, blond man with a curly beard, suddenly laughed. "Hey Gault, you flop-eared old bastard, what are you doing here? This man matches the description of a runaway slave the duke is all hot to catch. Damn big reward, too.''

Gault laughed too, but shortly and with no good humor. "Him? You've got the wrong man, Misha. He's one of mine. I'm second now in Bayard's Wolves.''

Bantam retrieved his hat from where the dancer had dropped it, jerked it back on, and glared at his adversaries, hand on his sword hilt. "You sons-of-whores call me slave again and I'll—''

"You'll shut up and sit down, you pig-headed arse,'' commanded Gault. He scowled at Bantam until he threw himself back into the chair, his face an ugly mask of anger. "Now, Misha, why do you and this guardsman think he's this slave you want?''

"He matches the description, short, shaved head, scarred face.''

"How many of us don't have scars of one sort or another, Mish?'' Gault gestured toward the scar that ran down his own cheek.

"Then why is his head shaved if he's one of us?'' asked Misha reasonably.

"Because I've got *sabros* who think shaving a drunk man is funny!'' exploded Bantam. "Gault, if I catch who it was, I'm gonna chop 'em into little bitty pieces and make 'em into soup.''

Misha ignored him. "You vouch for this, Gault?''

"Vouch, bloody hell, who do you think wielded the razor?'' Gault grinned.

Ashlana added her voice to the fray, her clear tenor rising above Bantam's growl of anger. "Damn you, Gault, you can't take all the credit! It was our idea, wasn't it, Bors? Swaggering around making cracks about 'beardless boys.' ''

"Yeah,'' echoed Bors, whose own beard was still merely a darkening along his jaw and upper lip. "You had it coming, Bantam.''

Bantam gave another wordless growl of rage and lunged across the table to cuff at both of them. Gault grabbed him in midair and tossed him to the floor. *"Bantam,"* he roared, "if you get us thrown out of this place, too—ah, what the bloody hell, Mish. You can have him. You can have all three of them, if you want. I'm sick of them stirring up a brawl everywhere we go.''

''That's the City Guardsmen's job, not mine. Call them if you want your brawlers locked up. See ya, Gault.'' Misha threw Gault a half-salute, collected the other two with a come-along motion of his head, and left.

From the floor Bantam made an insulting gesture at their retreating backs, then scrambled stiffly to his feet and resumed his chair. ''There, Gault, you see?'' he said virtuously, although he kept the angry look on his face. ''We didn't break any chairs at all.''

''Keep it quiet, Banty,'' Gault muttered. ''Now that we've established who and what you are, it's safer here than anywhere else, so we'll stay. But let's not draw any more attention than we have to.'' He fell silent as a slave came to wipe up the spilled ale, and the taverner himself hurried up.

''I regret that the actions of my dancing-girl caused you offense, milords. Do you wish her punished?'' he asked.

Bantam looked at the frightened girl standing with her fellow dancers. ''No. She didn't mean anything beyond flirting. Just have her bring up some more ale.''

''You may take her upstairs if you wish. No extra charge,'' the taverner insisted.

Bantam shook his head. ''Not today. We've got to get back to camp soon.''

''Banty, did someone hit you on the head?'' asked Gault in mock astonishment. ''You're turning down free wenching?''

''If we hire on here, there's plenty of time.'' He leaned his chair back on its hind legs and propped both booted feet up on the table. ''And with that one, I'd like plenty of time. Master Taverner, is later acceptable to you?''

''Of course, milord mercenary, of course. If I may have your name, please, so that we remember you later?''

''Bantam of Bayard's Wolves. And send the girl here.''

She knelt facing him but out of arm's reach, still looking frightened. ''Yes, master?''

Bantam brought his feet down from the table and patted

his thigh. "Come here, little dove. I won't hurt you, and my lap's still cold." When she curled up in his lap, he kissed her gently and continued, "Now look, you can't start stripping a man in front of the young'uns here. When I come back alone, you can take me upstairs and take off anything you want to. And then . . ." He whispered in her ear.

The girl's eyes widened. Suddenly she clapped her hand over her mouth to stifle a giggle. "Oh, no, master, really?"

He nodded, his own eyes sparkling with mischief. "What, you've never tried it that way? Now, go fetch us some more ale, my dove; the good stuff, mind you, not the slop you have to strain through your teeth."

Gault frowned a little when they were left alone. "Keep your ears open, lads. Something strange is going on here. That taverner should have had us tossed out on our noses, not been trying to placate us."

"Something not right at that castle, then?" Ashlana mused. "He doesn't know whose side we're on, because we don't know yet, and he wants to stay neutral maybe?" This was politics, the whole focus of her training for years, and it riveted almost all her attention. She did take a moment to think more kindly of Bantam; he might be a roguish brawling mercenary, but he had his kind side, too, or he wouldn't have bothered soothing the fears of that poor slave-girl.

Keeping their ears open proved very interesting. Though nothing was said directly, they picked up a distinct undercurrent of animosity toward Duke Launart. Though nobles were seldom popular with their people, Launart seemed to be even less favored than usual. Several tavern customers complained about last night's house-to-house search for the escaped slave, and speculation over what the slave might have done to provoke such an intensive search was both imaginative and generally bawdy, none of it complimentary to either Launart or Torkild. If Alnikhias chose to invade the lands held by the traitor duke, this city, at least, would offer only token resistance.

When they rode cheerfully back into camp, everything had been struck and packed, and when Captain Bayard came into camp a half-hour later, the warband moved out immediately.

"No work here, lads," Bayard said loudly and indignantly. "That warlord doesn't know the worth of good men. You wouldn't believe what he offered me!" In fact the offer had been very good, and Bayard had been hard-pressed to refuse it. He had finally taken offense at a chance remark that could have been interpreted as an insult, and stormed out.

Bayard's Wolves rode leisurely off to the east; not until Jehan's scouting reported no sign of followers did they pick up the pace to put as many miles behind them as they could before dark. They made a cold camp late that night, and did not bother setting up tents. It was warm enough for bedrolls on the ground.

That let them get an early start in the morning. Ashlana enjoyed that day's ride as she seldom had a chance to do. There was no tiresome protocol, no formalities, no ladies-in-waiting, servants, or bodyguards to trip over every time she turned around. The weather might have been a gift straight from the gods; the morning was cool, just enough to make breakfast's hot mint tea welcome. The sun's brightness did not make the day too warm later, for a wonderful breeze flirted with her face and ran cool fingers through her loose hair.

Many of the mercenaries seemed shy of her, but Bantam, Bors, and Gault took turns riding beside her and talking to her. They seemed as curious about the life of a royal as she was about them; none of them seemed aggressive enough to be the barbaric hired killer of the tales she had heard. Bantam especially was an entertaining companion, and she found herself liking him more and more. She wondered what his life had been like that had driven him into being a mercenary.

Bantam, for his part, was enjoying the pleasure on her face, her laughter at some outrageous story of Gault's, and her own stories that revealed a keen knowledge of human character. She readily admitted that she had been foolish to take Launart's invitation of hospitality at face value, for instinctively she had neither liked nor trusted him. His lips on her hand as he kissed it had made her skin crawl. "And when

I threw the scrying stones," she explained, "they said, 'treachery and loss.' My advisers said they meant the treachery of my father's bastard, and insisted that I should accept Launart's invitation." She remembered having dinner with him and a few other nobles; then she had become extremely sleepy. When she woke up again, it was to find herself a prisoner in Draksgard.

At this point Bors offered to go back and skewer Launart through the heart. Bantam laughed at him and pointed out that he would have to fight his way through gate guards and bodyguards first, unless he wanted to shave his head and sneak in as a slave.

Camp that night was a full setup, for Captain Bayard's weather-nose said it would rain before dawn. Bayard did not give Ashlana royalty's privilege of sitting around while others worked, either, for the captain ordered his new recruit to help with setting up the tents. Afterward she peeled carrots and onions for supper's stew while Bors rustled up firewood.

Bantam swaggered over after supper while she was trying to wash greasy pots. "Get a little bit of ash on your washrag. It'll cut through that grease better."

"You great big strong men could help a little, you know," Ashlana said acidly. "Like drying the stupid things."

Bantam grinned and shook his head. "Huh-uh, Alain. I did my stint as odd-jobs man years back. Hey, Bors, come put your strong manly male muscles to work scrubbing these pots. Alain wants to listen to Daveth singing."

Daveth didn't get a chance to do much singing; he had only sung one or two verses when a kithara string broke. He muttered a few interesting words that Ashlana pretended to ignore. While he hunted up a new string she looked around for Bantam, and found him at the horse-lines, talking quietly to his horse as he checked its hooves.

"Problem?" she asked him.

"Maybe, but I can't see or feel anything. I thought he was starting to favor that leg the last mile or so. I'll have to watch it."

She held out her hand and let the horse snuffle at it, then scratched his ears as he took a step toward her. "Oh, he's a big strong brave boy, he is," she crooned. "I'm worried about my little mare. I don't know what happened to her. I rode her to Launart's tents. . . ."

"It's a pity we couldn't check Draksgard's stables on our way out. Tell me about her, and maybe we can find her when we take the keep," Bantam suggested.

He really seemed to care that she missed her horse. Ashlana gave him a shaky smile; it was a little unnerving to have someone else know how she felt. "She's the prettiest horse I've ever seen, and our stablemaster says she's the smartest. She's a sorrel with a blond mane and tail. Do you know anything about Loarn palfreys?"

"You might say so. I was a slave in Loarn's stables for five years," he said quietly.

"Oh. Yes . . ." She could feel herself blushing at her own clumsiness. He had told her before that he had been a stable slave. Even though she had seen him so for the first few moments, it was difficult to imagine the man beside her as a quiet, subservient slave. He was so attractive, so *alive* . . . even if it was the insouciant cockiness of a mercenary. It must be his attitude of easy friendliness that was so disarming, she thought. So few people treated her as a friend, instead of a Royal Highness. So few men let their eyes linger on her as if they found her pleasant to look at. . . .

To cover her confusion she turned to the horse again. "I was saying, about my Sunbird—"

"Sunbird?" he interrupted eagerly. "One white hind foot, and a star on her forehead like a flying bird?"

"Yes . . . you know her?"

"She was born into my hands," Bantam said happily. "I named her, and had her training. She's full sister to my Whitefoot here. I'm glad she has an owner who appreciates her."

They talked about horses for a while, until Daveth fixed his kithara string and began to sing again. Ashlana noticed that as the evening wore on Bantam became quieter. Often he did not join in the singing, and when Daveth switched from bawdy songs to a mournful one about the sons of an ancient king, cruelly enchanted into swans, he slipped away from the firelight altogether.

He did not return. Ashlana waited and watched for him for some time. Gault saw her turning her head at every slight noise and asked, "What is it, Alain?"

"Bantam's disappeared. I'm worried about his leg. He was acting like he was in pain."

Gault shook his head. "If he was, you'd not know it. You've seen his back? I saw him get one of those beatings, and he never moved or made a sound. I'd say something is eating at him." He studied her face, then asked gently, "Do you want us to find him?"

"He's over there by the horse-lines again, leaning against the tree," Bors said helpfully.

"Thank you. Excuse me, please." Ashlana got up and wandered casually around the camp, trading jokes and smiles with many of the men. She could see a darker shadow by the tree; as she came closer, she could make out that he was staring back in the direction they had come.

"Bantam?" she asked softly. "Do you want to talk about what's wrong? Is there something I can help with?"

"There's nothing you can do, Ashlana. Not yet, not until we take that castle." His face was utterly still, and his voice was flat.

"I told you my worries. Can't you tell me yours? Daveth's song about the swan-children had something to do with it, didn't it?"

He looked down at a twist of grass in his hands. "Yes. I taught it to him. My friend Kiam made it."

"Kiam? Wasn't that the name of the slave you talked to in Draksgard?"

"Yes. And he was the one who let the dogs go. He did it on purpose, Ashlana, to help us—to help *me* escape. I know he did. Anything he could do to help me, he always did. When I got the lash, he would clean my back off and take care of me. And now . . . now I can't take care of him."

The last words were no more than a whisper. Impulsively she went to him and hugged him. He sighed and relaxed against her, allowing her to hold him; then his arms came up slowly and wrapped around her, pulling her close as if for more comfort.

There was nothing impulsive in her next move. Quite deliberately she raised her face to his and kissed him.

It was offered innocently, a kiss of compassion, not passion, but it did not stay that way. She realized in the first few heartbeats how distracted he had been in Draksgard, how he had given only a small part of his attention to their kissing and cuddling. This kiss had all his attention, and he rapidly changed from receiver to giver.

His hand came up to stroke through her hair and cup the back of her head. As her lips parted and their tongues met, a strange sensation washed over her. A wave of odd warmth and weakness flowed through her body, making her knees grow shaky.

He loved her. The touch-empathy that was the Gift of the D'Alriaun royal line would not let her mistake it for something else. This man who had invaded her life, heroically risking his own life to sweep her away from danger, loved her. Loved *her*—Ashlana, not the princess.

He pulled his mouth away from hers, his hand gently tracing the outline of her face. "Has no one ever warned you, little princess, how dangerous a thing that is to do to a man like me?"

"Is it?" Her voice was muffled and confused, so soft and sweet on his ears that he wanted to pick her up and carry her away into the darkness. If she kissed him again, he would do it.

"Very dangerous, my treasure," he muttered hoarsely and cupped her face in his hands, fighting hard to control himself. She was an innocent, and more; she was in his charge, to keep safely until he could return her to her promised husband.

"Bantam." That was all it took, only the one word from Bayard. Ashlana felt the quivering tension in his body as he released her.

"Alain, drag him back to the fire now," Bayard continued, a deep note of amusement in his voice. "He's been brooding long enough."

"Brooding?" someone yelled raucously. "Is that what you call it? I would have called it—" Something bawdy no doubt, but Ashlana was never to know what it was, for Conal clapped his hand over the man's mouth and grinned at her as they came back to the circle of firelight.

"Ignore Jehan, Alain. He gets like this sometimes," Conal said. "Hey Bantam, if I go hide and brood, you s'pose a princess will come along and comfort me?" He looked up at Ashlana, puppy-dog eyes wide in his tragic face, and everybody laughed.

"You want a princess to pet you, Conal, go rescue your own," Bantam jeered. "This one is mine."

"Not enough princesses to go around," Bors observed sagely, provoking another round of laughter.

"What princess, where?" Ashlana demanded, and looked around. "I don't see any princess here. Are you hiding one on me, Bantam?" She clenched her fists and stomped her foot at him, and he pretended to cower away, his face alive again with laughter.

"That's it, Alain. Whop ol' Banty upside the head. I'll help," Gault offered.

"How many arms do you want broken this time, Gault?" Bantam dropped to the ground to stretch out, feet to the fire and his head pillowed on the same log where Ashlana had just seated herself. "Sing something soothing while he decides, Daveth."

The minstrel fingered his kithara for a moment, then gave Bantam a look of wicked mischief.

> *I've heard sing of glorious battles*
> *Where heroes fight knee-deep in blood*
> *So how come when I'm in those same battles*
> *I fight knee-deep in glorious mud?*
>
> *There's mud on my hair and my mustache,*
> *And there's mud on my helm and my mail.*
> *But the worst of it all, good campanions,*
> *I've even got mud in my ale!*

"This is soothing?" Bantam asked.

"Yup," Daveth confirmed without a break in his song.

O Goddess of Rain do you hate us
To send your gifts down in full flood?
We poor mercenaries are soaking
And all our gear's covered in mud.

Ashlana was giggling at the infectious tune, but it seemed the Goddess of Rain did not appreciate the song nearly so much. The wind gusted suddenly and brought with it a heavy spatter of rain.

Bantam's eyes left Ashlana's face as he sat up. "Damn you, Daveth, you had to sing that one and make Her mad, didn't you?" He stood and pulled Ashlana to her feet, and away to her own small tent. "For your protection, my lady," and his teeth gleamed in a mocking grin as he saluted her and limped for the shelter of his own tent next door. "Until tomorrow!"

24

——◦•◦——

FAREWELL

Ashlana emerged from her tent into a cool clear morning. The rain had all blown away in the night, and the weather was a little cooler.

At times during that day's ride, she might have thought that she had dreamed the scene under the tree last night, except that Bantam looked her way more often, with a brooding look in his eyes. And then in the next instant, he was back to teasing her or jeering good-naturedly at Bors. She knew she was looking at him more often, but she couldn't help herself. The way he moved, the way he rode his horse with that easy grace, all were so curiously compelling. She thought of his fear and grief for his friend, his gentle hands on her face, the feel of his body in her arms, and the touch of his mouth on hers; now she blushed to herself at her own impulsive foolishness. That was not how a princess should behave, cuddling in the dark with a common guardsman!

But nothing she could tell herself would let her shake the flood of emotion that had washed over her. He loved her, like something out of a bard's romantic songs. And she herself—what was it that *she* felt for this dashing young hero?

• • •

That night, as they sat around the fire, they heard a wolf call, faintly and far away, and much closer another answered.

"Our brothers are singing, too," Daveth murmured.

To the surprise of the entire warband, Ashlana tipped back her head and duplicated the wolf-song they had just heard, a high, sweet ululation.

The wolf howled closer; Ashlana answered and put her finger to her lips to signal for silence. Before long they heard a whine and caught the flash of yellow eyes reflecting back the firelight before the wolf turned and ran.

Bantam released the breath he didn't realize he had been holding and asked, "How did you learn to do that, Alain?"

She grinned and blushed with pleasure that was plain to see even in the firelight. "The same way I learned to sing bawdy songs I shouldn't even know. My father . . ." Her face fell and she blinked rapidly. "My father cared about his people. He used to put on an ordinary guardsman's clothes and take a walk around his barracks or camps or towns sometimes. He'd sit at the fire or in a tavern and talk and sing. He said that way he could learn about his people's problems and complaints directly, and nobody would be too scared to speak to him, because they thought he was just one of them. He took along my brother Thorondal when he got big enough, too." She glanced around and saw several of the warband nodding. "When Thorondal died and I became the sole heir, he used to take me. I put on boy's clothes and hid my hair under a cloak and walked around with him."

The humor was back in Ashlana's face and voice. "My nurses and governesses had a cat-haired fit, but of course they couldn't stop him. And they were right. I heard many things that a gently-reared maiden wouldn't hear!" Laughter greeted this, and Ashlana laughed, too. "So just to shock them, I used to whistle the tunes I heard. I've always had a good ear for songs, so I picked up the bawdy ones along with all the others. Father wouldn't let me sing any really bad ones, but he always liked things like 'Leopard's Gard Lasses' and 'Riazan Dancer.'

"Sometimes . . . sometimes I think he forgot I was only a girl."

"Your kingdom doesn't need 'only a girl,' Alain. We need our queen to be a monarch, so that D'Alriaun doesn't become a puppet of Dur Sharrukhan," Jehan said indignantly.

She favored him with a faint smile. "I know. But somebody told me that mercenaries weren't anybody's subjects."

"We still have some loyalty to our homes, my lady. I have family there, and I care about what happens to them. I hope you'll care about your people as your father did."

"I will. But now I want to enjoy myself! Please, Daveth, sing for me?"

Bantam sat brooding and staring into the fire. More than once, his eyes went to Ashlana as she joined in the singing or teased Daveth about some song she knew and he didn't. Daveth was in a fey mood, and this night refused to sing anything bawdy or warlike. Romantic ballads of doomed lovers and dastardly deeds flowed from his kithara, and shifted gradually to songs of fair ladies, most equally doomed.

This was their last night on the road. Tomorrow about midday they would meet up with the forces of Alnikhias, and Bantam's mission would be over. He realized with a gut-clenching shock of dismay that he didn't want it to be over. He wanted Ashlana across the fire from him every night, or even better, cuddled up next to him under his cloak. He didn't want to just bed her, he wanted to cherish her and make sure she was safe with him always.

It was the first regret he'd ever had for the life that he had chosen. There was no way she could share it with him, for she would not be safe, and no way for him to share her life. What queen would have a common brawling bastard mercenary for a lover? And even if, unimaginably, she should, what would he do out of her bed? He had no skills other than fighting and horsemanship; if she had the peaceful happy life he wished for her, what place would there be for him?

As Daveth finished his last song, about a maiden dying of grief over her brave lord treacherously slain in battle by his jealous brother, Captain Bayard rose to his feet, his face unaccountably grave. "My lady," he began, and looked at Ashlana, who made a sound of protest.

The captain shook his head. "Tomorrow, it must be my lady, and not Alain. I think I'm not alone in being of two minds, relieved to bring Princess Ashlana to His Majesty, and regretful that we can't keep Alain with us."

There was a murmur of agreement. Ashlana glanced Bantam's way to see if he agreed, but he was staring expressionlessly into the fire.

Bayard continued, "That being so, I want to say that while Alain is our *sabro*, Ashlana will always be our queen. Daveth, if you will, 'Queen of Summer'?"

For a moment, Daveth's face mirrored Bayard's solemnness, then he looked broodingly down at his kithara and began to play softly. After a moment he began to sing.

> *I kissed my love in a summer meadow*
> *With garlands of flowers her hair was entwined*
> *She smiled, and she kissed me,*
> *And I fell in love for all time.*
> *I swear by the goddess you worship*
> *Byela's grain and vine,*
> *If you'll be my queen of summer,*
> *No other will ever be mine.*

One or two of the other mercenaries who knew the song joined in, although to most of them it was unfamiliar. Sentiment was an emotion most of them believed they had forsaken a long time ago. Bantam knew it only slightly, and yet every word seemed to come out of his own heart.

The song went on in the way of its kind as the singer offered to fight a dragon to prove his love, steal the treasure from its very lair, and drop the crown of a queen in his lady's lap.

In the old tongue Draksgard meant "Dragon's Stronghold." Did that count as a lair? He had fought to give her a crown, though before this, as he had said to Alnikhias, she had been only his employer. *My queen? Yes.*

> *Though summer's sun may vanish,*
> *And winter's winds blow cold,*

If you'll be my queen of summer,
Our love will never grow old.
Our love will never grow old.

The last notes of music died in the still air, and he realized that he had been singing softly also, had sung the last line alone. Bors was staring at him open-mouthed. *Bantam* singing something that didn't involve fighting or wenching?

His *sabros* would likely needle him for weeks about this, Bantam knew. He might as well give them more to use. "I wish you could have seen her when she looked like a princess instead of a mercenary," he said quietly, not willing to break the mood. "She was standing by the window, and the sunlight brought out red glints in her hair. It was wound around her head like a crown, with golden ribbons woven into it, and she wore a long gown of some shimmery red stuff. I don't even know what it was, only that it felt like swansdown under my hands." He shifted his gaze from the fire to her eyes. "And she was so regal I hardly dared touch her."

She gave him a tender smile that made his heart leap, then glanced at the men around them, quirked her mouth in her devilish half-grin, and said quite deliberately, "Hah! Who was it who grabbed me from behind, then?"

His eyes widened briefly with shock at the breaking of his fey mood before he understood. This put them back where they were, and with luck no one else caught that he had just declared in so many words that he loved her.

He flashed her a quirked grin of his own, and replied with a shrug of his shoulders, "Hey, I've got a reputation to uphold!"

Ashlana laughed out loud at that, and he continued, "I'm still proud of her, *sabros*. She fought like an ice leopard before I could make her understand who I was. And later when I had to cut all that beautiful hair, she didn't waste a moment in regrets."

"Not like you, Banty?" Gault asked innocently. "He's been mourning for days about his hair, Alain."

"At least mine will grow back," Bantam retorted.

Gault rubbed his thinning hair. "Yeah, I wish you could have seen him when he looked like a mercenary, Alain," he said dreamily, to the laughter of the Wolves. "Purty blond hair in side braids like yours and a decent beard and mustache instead of scuzz. Now none of the tavern girls will want to kiss him until it grows back."

They broke camp early the next morning, and were soon on the road. About midmorning, a courier from Alnikhias brought them a message. They were to stop at a sanctuary of Byela, so that the priestesses there could offer the Princess Ashlana rest and refreshment, and she could be suitably garbed as befitted her rank before she met her bridegroom.

Bayard tapped the paper with a disgusted flick of his finger. "I suppose we have to follow orders. But damn, I was looking forward to riding in there bringing Alain instead of Ashlana."

The priestess who answered their ring at the high barred gate of the sanctuary's walled compound must have been warned of their coming. She didn't flick an eyelash at the sight of a warband of armed men at her gates, nor at an apparent young mercenary claiming to be the Princess Ashlana, but took her inside without a murmur.

Men were not usually allowed into the sanctuary, so a young novice directed them to the wayfield where they were to wait and showed them the stream where they could water their horses. Other young women, some novices and some slaves, brought them food. It was a measure of both their awe at the sacredness of this place, and their pride in being the escort of the princess, that the mercenaries did not even try to leer at the slaves.

They had been there for about an hour when an older priestess, disapproval clear in her rigid body and the thin pinched line of her lips, approached them. "Her Gracious Highness wishes to speak to the one called Bantam," she said loudly. Clearly she had no wish to permit a scruffy mercenary inside her gates, but the wishes of royalty overrode everything.

Inside the compound Bantam found that they did maintain

guards, female ones. Remembering Anya, he had no doubt that they were fully as capable as any Wolf. He resignedly handed over his sword and daggers, and followed his guide to a small bare room.

Ashlana stood next to the window, eerily reminding him of his first sight of her, although this time she was wearing a simple blue gown. Her hair was caught up in a net of gold threads, and she looked like a princess again instead of a mercenary.

"You sent for me, my lady?"

"Yes, I . . . have Bors' clothes here, if you would give them back to him with my thanks." She seemed about to say something else, then fell silent.

"As you wish, my lady." So there was nothing to his imaginings after all. No doubt she merely wished to thank him as well in a little more privacy than in front of all the Wolves. Surely she hadn't sent for him just so that he could deliver a package? A slave could have done that.

The silence stretched out between them, until at last, even knowing that Ashlana, royalty and his employer, should speak first, he asked, "Is there anything else, my lady?"

"Yes. I . . . I'm going to send a message to Alnikhias. To tell him that I can't marry him."

There wasn't anything he could say about that, so he didn't. Who his lady married was her affair. But, by all the gods, he wished it could be him!

She sat down, and her voice became firmer. "I will thank him for his assistance, but I am Queen of D'Alriaun by right of birth and arms, and I reserve the right to choose my own consort. And I choose *you*."

Think before you ask something of the gods, Bantam thought. They just might give it to you. His heart stopped in his chest, and he couldn't breathe. "Me?" he managed to squeak.

"Why not? You can't deny that we love each other. I don't want to let you go, to know I'll never see you again."

For him, her warrior's courage, and her sweetness, and her love? More than anything in the world he wanted to believe that it could be true. But for all the reasons he had accepted so bitterly last night, he couldn't.

Formality be damned. This was his love and he wouldn't hurt her by a cold, stilted refusal. It was bad enough that he had to hurt her by refusing her at all.

He sat down facing her and took both her hands in his. "Ashlana." His voice made her name a caress. "Yes, I love you. But I can't change who and what I am, nor can you. No matter what we feel for each other, your Council of Nobles would never accept a baseborn bastard half-breed mercenary freedman as your consort." He tried to smile wryly but more than a tinge of bitterness crept into his voice. "One or two out of the five, maybe, but all five blows at once? I know what they think of me. They made that very clear when we were planning your rescue. I'm not fit to crawl on my belly to lick your feet."

"Then . . ." she said in a trembling voice, "would the Wolves accept an ex-princess as a mercenary?"

She would do that for him? Throw away everything she was, everything she owned, even her kingdom? The kingdom so many men had died for? And how many more men would die if she abandoned it? A war among her nobles to take her throne would make the war just past look like a children's quarrel.

"Gods, don't tempt me, Ashlana! Do you think I haven't thought of it? Every night of my life I'll sit by a fire and see your face in the flames and wish you were there next to me.

"But I know, and if you think about it as it really is, you'll know that you wouldn't be happy with our kind of life. A day or two was a wonderful adventure for you, but you don't know the kind of hardships we live with. Very seldom is it the pleasure of riding in the sunshine during the day and singing around the fire at night.

"Were you warm and dry in a castle this campaign, or in a tent with the rain pouring down week after week until the few little things you owned were soaking wet and covered with mud? Have you ever gone to bed in your boots so they aren't frozen solid in the morning? Or hauled a drunken tent-mate outside so he won't puke all over your bed? Or looked into a man's eyes before you kill him so he doesn't kill you? Or listened to a woman scream as other men rape her and you know you can't do anything to stop it?"

He thought he saw her wince; the brutal truth was rapidly pulling down her illusions, and he pressed on. "And if you're wondering, the answer is *no*. Bayard doesn't tolerate rape, and I like my partner to enjoy what I'm doing to her.

"I know you've heard stories about what mercenaries are like. Most of them are true. Take Bors, for instance. You thought he was a sweet boy, didn't you, like a younger brother?"

She looked puzzled. "Yes."

He chuckled softly. "And Bors thought it was funny and played along. There's a lot of words I might use for Bors, but none of them would be 'sweet boy.' He's been a mercenary a year longer than I have. He killed his first man at twelve, and he's a cold, mean fighter that I wouldn't want to face. When he turned fourteen this last spring and could legally sign with us, the Wolves took him to a tavern like the Drunken Dragon to celebrate. He celebrated so much that he swived one of the dancers right there on the table, and all of us stood around and cheered him on. All of us, Ashlana. Me too. And judging from the performance he gave, he was no virgin.

"Did you know that we guarded you every moment you were with us? Bayard told everyone to watch over you, just in case one of us tried to give in to the impulse we all had to tumble you. You wouldn't have that protection if you joined up, nor could I protect you all the time. Oh, the Wolves wouldn't bother you, but we wouldn't be with them. I'd have to renege on my contract, cut and run from Alnikhias and try to find some other warband, maybe in Sargada, that would accept us. You'd have to have eyes in the back of your head and the willingness to slash up a few men until word got around that you weren't a whore available to everyone. I know a few female mercenaries and that's what they said they had to do. And if you couldn't do that—well, I hear gang rape isn't pleasant."

She couldn't look at him now; he took a deep breath to make his voice gentler.

"We're not the heroes in disguise of sentimental ballads, my darling—we're brutal, crude men who fight hard and die young. We take our pleasures where and when we find them because maybe tomorrow we'll be lying on a battlefield with our guts ripped out and the ravens picking at our eyes.

"Add all those things together, and you would be miserable. And after a while, you would begin to hate me as the cause of it all. I can live somehow without your love but I couldn't live with your hate."

She couldn't answer him, for her voice didn't seem to work. The tears she had been fighting to control spilled out of her eyes to make dark spots on the front of her gown.

Bantam fought his own private battle and won. He wanted to pull her into his arms and do anything, say anything that would stop such misery in the woman he loved. Instead he didn't move, but sat looking down at her hands still in his, his thumb idly caressing her knuckles. Where had he seen someone do something like that before? It was something else about Ashlana . . . yes, that was it.

At last she pulled her hands away from his and fumbled for a kerchief to wipe her face. "I'm s-sorry to do this to you, Bantam. And thank you for keeping this on a personal level, and not reminding me of my royal duties. I shouldn't have inflicted my romantic fantasies on you."

"They were my fantasies, too, my darling. And fantasies are what they must remain." With an effort he kept his voice even and gentle, as if she were a frightened filly that needed soothing. "Ashlana, how old are you?"

"S-seventeen."

Seventeen. Gods, when he was seventeen, he'd been hopelessly in love with the kitchenmaid who'd dished out his food every night. He had never looked into her eyes, never spoken to her beyond "thank you, mistress," for she was free and he was a slave. Now he couldn't even remember her name.

"When they wanted you to marry Alnikhias, how did you feel about him?" he asked.

"After . . ." She swallowed hard and began again. "After

we wrote to each other for so long, I was certain that I was in love with him. But that was before I saw you. . . .''

"Do you know that he loves you?"

She shook her head. "He never said so."

"In a letter that might pass through a dozen hands before it got to you? A warrior just can't lay himself open that way. But when we were planning your rescue, he sat the whole time holding something in his hands, rubbing his fingers over it as if it were a talisman, as if it were something very precious to him. He finally showed it to me so that I could recognize you.

"It was your picture. He refused to let that little picture out of his hands, Ashlana. If you give him a chance, he will love the real princess much, much more.

"I can't stay any longer, my love. Always remember it's because I love you that I'm letting you go." As both stood, she lifted her face to him and looked at him with tear-filled eyes. Gods, she was so tempting. *Just one kiss, one last embrace . . . no! Make a clean break. She'll get over it.* "Gods be with you, Ashlana." He tore his eyes away from her face and vanished out the door.

An hour later, the Free Mercenary Warband of Bayard's Wolves escorted Her Gracious Highness the Princess Ashlana of D'Alriaun into the roadside encampment of His Majesty King Alnikhias of Dur Sharrukhan. Sharrese and D'Alriaun troops and the nobles leading them swept into a wave of bows as Her Highness passed. They drew rein in front of the royal tent; Bantam kicked his feet loose of the stirrups and slid to the ground before they stopped moving. He gravely assisted Ashlana from her mount and escorted her to where the king waited.

Alnikhias did not look like a calm, regal, self-possessed king. He looked like a man who had been worried sick over someone he cared for deeply. There were no formal greetings from the king to his betrothed; instead he gathered her into his arms and held her tightly for an instant. Only Bantam was close enough to hear him whisper "my beloved" before he released her.

Bantam thanked the gods then for the years of schooling his face. His expression, he hoped, was one of suitable satisfaction over a job well done, touched with just a hint of interest in the affairs of his betters. It wouldn't have mattered, however, if the jealousy that was ripping his guts had boiled over onto his face. Alnikhias barely acknowledged his presence. Instead he spoke to Bayard.

"Thank you, Captain, for your care of Her Highness. You will be suitably rewarded. My aide will show you where to camp."

"Thank you, Your Majesty. Your Highness, all of us wish you well."

One by one they came before Ashlana to pay their respects. One by one she held out her hand to them. And one by one each Wolf went to one knee, took her hand in his, and raised it to his forehead in the formal guardsman's salute. Ashlana's insides were in turmoil. Captain Bayard had not been making just a pretty speech. From all of them, Sharrese and D'Alriaun alike, came varying amounts of love and respect and fierce loyalty.

That was not what had shaken her so badly. When her betrothed husband had taken her in his arms for the first time, the intensity of *his* love for her had nearly made her faint. Dearest Byela, was it love or infatuation that she felt for Bantam? If it was love, then what was this intense emotion she felt for Alnikhias?

The Wolves had set up camp, somewhat surprised at the choice site they were shown to, when a messenger came from the king. He brought Bantam's pay and their "suitable reward." Her Royal Highness the Princess Ashlana had appointed the Free Mercenary Warband of Bayard's Wolves as her personal honorguard.

23

KIAM

"**O**ut! *Out!* Every one of you sneaking little backbiting snakes in the grass get *out* until I give you permission to come back!" Crashes followed the shouting as if someone had thrown something.

Bantam winced at the noises coming through the door. Her Highness was in a terrible mood, from the sound. The King's Elite who was serving this guard-shift with him looked appalled. So did the slave who carried a basket and was about to open the door. "God oh god, *help*," she murmured almost inaudibly.

"No gods here, sweetling, just us. Give me that cloth," Bantam said cheerfully. He reached out and plucked off the white cloth covering the breadrolls that were the basket's contents.

As the room fell silent he eased open the door and stuck his hand through the opening, waving the cloth vigorously. "Hey in there. We surrender!"

There was a moment of silence and then a bark of reluctant laughter. "Is that you, Bantam?"

"Yes. If it's safe, there's also a young woman out here with food. If you don't want it, can we eat it?"

"No, you can't, you abominable mercenary. Send her in," Ashlana said, not with any graciousness.

The door closed behind the slave-girl and Bantam resumed his slouching position against the wall. He ignored the indignant sidelong glance of the Elite, who was standing properly at attention. *Might be a good thing I never made it to the King's Elite after all. All that rigid spit-and-polish formality would have driven me crazy. That poor bastard next to me can't even talk on duty. Or scratch.* He rubbed absentmindedly at the healing bite on his leg as he propped it against the wall to take his weight off it.

He wasn't sure how long he could tolerate being an honorguard, either. True, it was the kind of job a mudslogger dreamed of when it was pouring rain, but a pretty red silk baldric with the three gold roses of D'Alriaun looked odd over his battered dull scouting armor, and they hadn't done any fighting in days. Draksgard City had fallen to Alnikhias' forces with only token resistance. Now it was all siege, sitting outside the keep's walls while Launart sat tight and thumbed his nose at them.

Guard-duty bored him enough that when a quarter of an hour later a very young, hard-faced mercenary stomped out of the royal apartments, he was ready to burst out laughing at the bewildered look on the Elite's face. He didn't, of course. The Elite was a friendly enough young man, and it wasn't his fault nobody had told him about Alain.

Bantam did watch with a grin as the other grabbed Ashlana's arm and growled, "Here now, lad, what were you doing in there? I know neither of us let you in."

Her Royal Highness the Princess Ashlana picked his hand off as if it were a bug crawling on her sleeve and proceeded to tell him, in her unmistakable voice, just who she was and what she intended to do. And he could either do his duty and come along tavern-crawling or stand there guarding an empty room.

"B-but—please, Your Highness, I'm on duty," the poor Elite stammered.

"If I wanted to go riding or walking in the garden, would it be your place to object?" Ashlana asked sweetly.

"N-no, my lady, of course not."

"It would be your duty to accompany me, would it not?"

"Yes, my lady."

"Then while you are on duty, you will accompany me wherever I wish to go, will you not?" She turned imperiously to Bantam. "And you. Do *you* have any objections to tavern-crawling?"

"Whether he does or not, I do." The king came around a corner and stopped. Only a tiny flicker in his eyes showed his surprise. Bantam stiffened to attention, put on his blank face, and pretended that he didn't see any princess disguised as a mercenary.

"Not exactly regal garments, my dear," Alnikhias remarked.

Ashlana turned her dangerously sweet smile on him as well. "No. But quite effective, as my father taught me, for doing some listening on my own. I'm going mad, cooped up in those rooms with that pack of females who don't have anything better to do than gossip, backbite, and bicker about the color of embroidery silks!"

"No. I can see embroidery silks are not to your taste. But tavern-crawling is not on the schedule, either. We have a visitor whom I think we both need to hear. If you would care to change, my love?" He opened the door and gestured her inside.

Bantam spent the next quarter of an hour grinning evilly at the other guardsman and thinking about the dancing-girl at the Golden Bell. He had gone back the night before to collect his free wenching, and the girl had remembered him. She'd turned out to be an imaginative little wench, lively as a ferret, and a giggler. He'd always liked that; passion could be faked, but delighted laughter couldn't. The Elite looked as though he was speculating on what the royals were discussing in such low voices. Only murmurs came through the door.

Ashlana looked female again when they emerged, if not particularly regal. She wore a simple embroidered blouse and divided riding skirt, and her hair was back in its gold net.

Her hand was tucked firmly into the crook of Alnikhias'
elbow.

Bantam and the other bodyguard trailed along after them
to the room that had been set up as a reception hall, and took
their places beside the chairs.

Other guardsmen showed in their visitor. When he
straightened from his deep bow, Bantam's eyes widened
fractionally. It was Roldan.

Alnikhias eyed him suspiciously. "So, Lord Roldan. I understand you have an offer for us that will break this siege."

"Yes, Your Majesty."

"Why have you not come forth with this offer sooner?"

"It is a difficult thing, Your Majesty, having to make a
choice between kinsmen and king. What I have to tell you
is a secret known only to the family."

The king nodded thoughtfully. "I see. And this secret
is . . . ?"

Roldan hesitated, looking distrustfully at the armed
guardsmen at the royals' backs. "A concealed exit to Draksgard Keep."

"An exit that could become our entrance, hm? You will
forgive me if I doubt your sincerity, Lord Roldan. There are
many who would call you a traitor, no matter which of us
you supported."

"I know. What else can I do, Your Majesty, to prove my
loyalty to you?"

There was a soft sound from Bantam's position, like a
word chopped off before it could leave someone's mouth.

Ashlana twisted her head to look at him. The blank mask
that a guardsman should keep was missing; he was staring
at the lord as if he had seen a ghost. "Bantam? What is it?"

"Your Majesties, I know him. If I may speak?"

"You again, mercenary?" Alnikhias asked. "How did we
run our kingdoms before you came along?"

Bantam chose not to rise to the bait. " 'If you would know
the worth of a man, ask his slaves.' Some proverbs have the
truth behind them, sir."

"And that truth is?"

"That I was this man's slave for five years. In all that

time, he never treated me or any other slave with anything other than strict fairness and honesty. I don't know how rare a thing that might be among nobles, but I do know how rare it is for a master. I would trust him with my life.''

"Well, Lord Roldan?'' Alnikhias asked. "Is Her Majesty's guardsman telling the truth?''

Roldan stared back at Bantam in honest perplexity. Evidently the week's growth of beard and the face-concealing properties of the helm were enough to disguise him. "One of my slaves, Your Majesty? His voice sounds familiar, but I have to say I don't recognize him.''

Bantam pulled off his helm. "My name was Farris then, sir. And one of the first things you said to me was that you liked to think of yourself as a fair and honest man. You were, so I'm returning that favor.''

"Farris? What—I—Your Majesty, much as I would like someone to confirm my integrity, I have to tell you this man is a renegade, an escaped slave; Launart sentenced him to death for rape.''

"We are aware of that. We have manumitted and pardoned him.''

Ashlana looked thoughtfully at Roldan. "Doesn't this prove his integrity, Alnikhias? If he wasn't honest, he would never have revealed that, just said, 'Yes, I remember him now.' ''

"You persist in having intelligence as well as beauty, my dear. I think we will make an excellent team. Well, my lord, details please. I will call a full council if I think your information warrants it.''

Alnikhias did call a full war council. Roldan's information revealed that there was a secret exit, leading from a storage room in the central keep to an abandoned shrine outside the castle walls. The king hammered out a plan with his nobles and other warleaders. A small group would infiltrate the castle through the passage, disguised as Launart's warriors, and attempt to open the main gate. At the same time, other forces would proceed with conventional siege warfare, using catapults to bombard the castle with rocks and spears and attempting to use siege towers, while sappers secretly started digging tunnels to undermine the walls.

Bantam was not an infiltrator this time. As her bodyguards, Bayard's Wolves were assigned to protect Ashlana, who took her place fighting with the archers. He was sorry to have missed the battle between Ashlana and Alnikhias that had settled that; Daveth, who had the duty then, told his *sabros* that it was a treat to see the king's face when he realized that his bride was a fighting ice leopard instead of a pretty little kitten.

Alnikhias' reputation as a tactician was well deserved. The distractions of normal siege warfare were enough to allow the infiltrators to reach the main gate undetected, and open and jam both portcullis and gate. It was pure luck, however, that the sappers struck an old tunnel from some past and forgotten siege and put it to use. The ancient timbers that held the shaft open were already rotting; when they filled the passage with oil-soaked brushwood and fired it, the collapse of the tunnel brought a huge section of the wall down with it.

With his castle walls breached in two places, Duke Launart had no chance. His sworn forces fought fiercely, knowing that the king would condemn them as traitors; they preferred to die fighting rather than wait for the gallows. They were outnumbered, however, and soon it was clear that the besiegers would win the day. Launart and Torkild disappeared from the fighting and attempted to use the escape tunnel, only to run straight into the arms of a waiting detachment of King's Elite. Both of them were captured.

Bantam found all this out later; the battle for him was as it always was, a screaming chaos that he survived by wits and sword-skill and luck. The surrender of the garrison, when it came, was not a surprise, nor was the reward granted later to all the besiegers. Alnikhias released them to loot as they pleased, their only restriction being that they had to turn any sort of document over to the king and Ashlana's palfrey Sunbird over to her.

Let the others go after treasures or pretty slave-girls; Bantam had a friend to claim.

Where was Kiam likely to be? How badly had he been beaten, and where would they dump an injured slave? Slave barracks, or kennelmaster's office? Either one was not here in the castle proper, but in the outer bailey. The barracks was more likely, but he didn't know exactly where it was. He'd try the kennelmaster's office first, then.

A voice called "Hey, Bantam!" as he crossed the bailey, and Bors loped after him. "What's up, you're not looting? Me and Balian hit the stables, got a couple of damn good horses."

"I'm after a slave, an old friend," he said without stopping. Bors grinned, assuming that the old friend was female, and trailed along after him.

The kennelmaster's office was not locked on the outside, but the door didn't give. "Kiam?" Bantam yelled. "Kiam, it's Farris! Let me in!" There was no sound from inside.

"Bors, help me break it down." The weight of two armored bodies hitting it made the door give slightly. A second blow brought it suddenly open all the way, revealing a dim room.

"Kiam? Oh, gods—*no.*" He approached the figure lying on its belly on a folded blanket in one corner, not wanting to believe what his eyes and nose told him. But the body was Kiam, and it was gangrene that he smelled as he knelt beside him. His friend's back was worse than any wounds he had ever seen. The unhealed cuts of the lash oozed pus, and red streaks led away from areas that were already black with dead flesh.

Kiam moved his head slightly. "Who . . . ?" The word was a barely audible breath.

Bantam's voice was hard and cold when at last he forced words out. "Bors. Go find Ashlana, can you? I think she's with the healers now."

"Why, Bantam? There's nothing she can do with wounds like that."

"Because I need her, that's why! He's like this because of me, and he's going to die a free man, free by royal command!" His voice broke as he added, "I . . . promised him, Bors. Please, find her!"

Bors retreated without another word. Bantam stripped off his helm and gauntlets. "Kiam? It's Farris, Kiam."

Kiam's eyes slowly opened. His hand was hot with fever when Bantam took it gently in his grasp. "Not dreaming?" he whispered.

"No, I'm here. I said I would be. We've taken Draksgard. Roldan let us in the back way. You're loot now, my friend, my share."

The corner of Kiam's mouth moved in an attempt to smile. "New master?"

"Not me. You get to be your own master now."

"No." His head moved slightly in negation, and long pauses broke up his words. "I'm dying . . . someone said. I know."

"Bantam?" said Ashlana's low voice. She slid into the room and knelt beside Bantam. Bors and Gault followed her in and stopped just inside the door.

"You are Kiam?" she asked softly. "Then I have you to thank for my rescue and my kingdom, too." Her fingers brushed his forehead gently. "You are free, not a slave any more. Is it witnessed?"

"Yes, my lady, it is witnessed," Gault rumbled from the door, echoed by Bors, but Bantam could only nod as his throat tightened. This wasn't the freedom he had wanted for his friend, not the freedom to die.

Ashlana moved her hand over Kiam's back, not quite touching him, then put her hand on Bantam's arm. Her eyes full of pity, she shook her head.

Bantam had known it since he entered the room and the smell had hit him in the face. There was nothing they could do. No healer could cure massive infection like this; the best they could do would only prolong Kiam's death. In an arm or leg amputation might work, but not on a man's back. Even as he watched, the red streaks of blood poisoning seemed to grow longer.

There was only one thing he could do now for Kiam. His fingers searched blindly in his boot, and the hilt of his mercy-dagger slid into them.

He balanced the long slim blade on his palm and held it

in front of Kiam's face. His own voice was as strained as his dying friend's when he choked out, "Kiam? Do you want it?"

Kiam did smile this time. "Yes ... but not ... you. Not ... my blood ... on your hands."

"Too late, Kiam," he whispered. "Already, your blood is on my hands."

And how did he kill a friend the easiest way? He had used his mercy-dagger on the battlefield before this, on ally and enemy alike. A mortally wounded warrior deserved that last kindness, the quick merciful slash of a blade across the throat. But do it to Kiam, send his blood spurting from a severed artery with the quick pumping of his heart? No. Through the heart itself, quick and clean.

Ashlana slipped her arm under Kiam's neck as they eased him onto his side. He gasped with pain until she slid around to support his head in her lap.

Bantam never took his eyes off Kiam's face. Kiam's eyes were dim with pain, but steady on his as he set the naked blade in the right place. "Tell Haral ... now, Farris."

"Likarion keep you, my brother." And he drove the dagger into Kiam's heart, and his own.

Bantam remembered only bits and pieces of that day and the next. He remembered carrying Kiam's body in his arms out through the gates, to the place where the priests of Likarion were preparing the bodies of the dead for the pyres; he remembered facing down the Master Priest, who was not willing to accept that a slave deserved the honor of a warrior's end. He remembered his Wolf *sabros* appearing by ones and twos to back him up, until at last the whole warband was ranged at his back; he remembered Her Royal Highness the Princess Ashlana adding her persuasion where even she could not compel obedience.

And finally, he remembered Kiam's blood on his fingers as he drew the ritual red lines of a warrior's mourning down his face, as if he wept tears of blood, remembered the roaring fire. The bodies of the dead were dark outlines against the flames; before they caught fire the scaffolding that held them fell in with a crash as it was designed to do, and the smoke lifted in a dark column to carry the souls of warriors into the heavens.

26

---❖---

SEARCH

Year 420 D.S.: Autumn

Ashlana of D'Alriaun, daughter of King Corleon, was crowned in her capital city of Alria on the Sacred Day of the Equinox, the thirty-first day of Harvestend. As one of her first official acts, Her Majesty confirmed Bayard's Wolves as the Queen's Shields, an honor that had never before been given to men not sworn in fealty to the monarch.

A week later, Her Majesty traveled in state back to Dur Sharrukhan's capital of Ardesana for her marriage to her betrothed. Both kingdoms erupted into an orgy of celebration as she passed. Village maidens threw flower petals to carpet the ground in front of her horse, and noble houses vied for the honor of hosting her. Her entourage stretched for nearly a mile, giving the peasantry of the two kingdoms a glimpse of rich pageantry few had ever dreamed existed.

Ardesana put on its most festive face for the marriage of the king. Flags and flower garlands were hung from every available place, feasting and revelry entertained the masses, and merchants and pickpockets relieved the excited and unwary of their coin.

For another week Queen Ashlana lodged in the Royal Castle while her Council of Nobles conferred with their counterparts, arguing all over again points that had been settled years ago, points of protocol and precedence, bargains of land and inheritance, and a thousand other petty details.

It was during one of those days that Bantam belted on his dagger and slipped the sword-baldric over his shoulder, as carefully and grimly as if he prepared for battle. He had a job to do now that he was back in Ardesana, one that he had left far too long.

Gault fell into step with him as he left the guardsmen's barracks. "Where are you headed to in such a hurry and with such a grisly look on your face?"

"I'm looking for revenge and my sister."

"What did your sister do to you?"

"Not revenge against my sister, you bonehead," Bantam said impatiently. "My stepfather sold her, too. I want to find her and buy her free."

"Oh. I see what you mean." Gault shook his head. "I wouldn't leave my sister as a slave, either. If I had a sister, that is. Where does the revenge come in? You can't chop up a slaver for conducting his legal business, you know."

"Jared had no right to sell either of us. I'm going to find him and cry blood-debt on him."

"One moment Ashlana's hero, and the next a marauding mercenary, huh? You want some company?"

"Come if you want." Bantam's lip curled in an expression that was not quite a smile. "It might be handy to have a man along who can read."

When at last they came to the fountain that marked the Slavers' Quarter, he stopped for a moment to run his hand over the granite figures of a boy and a girl in chains, kneeling at the feet of a man in the simple tunic and breeches of an earlier day. The little statue was Amethyst, was all slaves in their helplessness.

It took them almost an hour to find the slaver's establishment that matched Bantam's drug-hazed memory. He had never run these streets as a boy, nor did any other child. Too many stories of unscrupulous slavers snatching up children and selling them kept them far away.

A slaver came forward to meet them at the door, clearly uncertain why two armed and unwelcome Free Mercenaries were patronizing his business. It was unlikely that they were in the market for slaves, but not impossible.

Bantam's fingers itched to put sword to the man's throat and demand his sister. Only the knowledge that she was ten years gone from the place kept him in check.

"I'm trying to trace a particular slave sold from here. I want to see your records," he said, surprised to find his own voice rasping in his throat.

"You want, mercenary?" The slaver didn't quite sneer, now that he knew the two were not customers. "Our records are private, not for the view of any scum who wanders in off the street."

Bantam's hands shook as he fumbled in his belt-pouch and pulled out a paper. "You see this, slaver? This is a royal warrant, signed by the king's own hand, authorizing me to see your records and instructing you to aid me in any way possible." He handed it over with a half-sneer of his own, his voice gone soft and threatening.

The slaver took the paper as if it were a dead mouse and scrutinized it carefully. "Very well," he said coldly as he returned it. "If you will come this way, please."

Bantam, with a cold set face and firm step, once again walked halls that had haunted his nightmares for ten years. Crimson hatred seethed in him, and his body insisted that he had to draw his sword, run, do *anything* that would keep them from locking a collar around his neck again. Only the iron control learned during long years as a slave kept him moving forward.

They came finally to a room that he did not remember, a room that had walls covered with shelves full of lidded boxes. With cold formality, the slaver turned to him. "Royal warrant or no, we will not allow you to rummage at random through our records. If you will tell him the approximate date," and he motioned to a silent slave standing quietly and waiting, "and the slave's sex, age, and name, we will find the appropriate paperwork."

"The day I don't know. About mid-Yellowgrain, 410. Her name is Amethyst. She was thirteen."

The slaver's face grew even angrier. "Why are you wasting everybody's time, mercenary? The law requires that we keep records for only seven years. We would have destroyed anything older at the appropriate time."

Destroyed. The word echoed through his head, and a cold pit opened in his belly. *Destroyed.* Around him the room turned black; only the blade of the sword in his hand pierced through the darkness clouding his vision. A voice, Gault's voice, yelled something, and a weight pulled down on his arm.

Gradually Gault's voice became clearer in his ears, and Bantam vaguely realized that Gault was frantically wrestling him for control of the sword. "Bantam, no, you can't! It's not his fault—if you kill him we'll both get the gallows!"

Two large guardsmen, summoned by the slave-master's loud cries for help, burst into the room.

"Bantam, put away the sword. We'll find her, I promise. We'll go back to Ashlana—she can send out messages to both kingdoms." Gault blurted, torn between coaxing and ordering.

Something in his face or voice finally broke through to Bantam. He shook his head sharply as if he were awakening from a nightmare and looked with stunned surprise at the menacing guardsmen and at the bared blade in his own hand. "Gault?"

"Come on, Banty, give me the sword. No one blames you for being angry. Put her away and we'll leave. There's nothing more we can do here." Gault pulled the sword out of Bantam's unresisting hand and slid her back in her scabbard.

The guardsmen, swords still drawn, escorted them back to the street. Bantam let Gault take the lead as they left the Slavers' Quarter. He was lost in his own head still, still hearing the word "destroyed" in the slaver's cold, angry voice. *Only the papers,* he kept reminding himself. *Not Amethyst, only the records.* But it didn't help. He was alone, more lost and alone than at any time since his mother died. First Ashlana, then Kiam, and now Amethyst, his twin, was gone. She could be anywhere in the kingdom, anywhere in the world. If the records were gone, not even Ashlana could help him track her down.

At last Gault's voice broke into his thoughts again. "Banty, I don't know where the hell we're going, and I need a drink. Look." He held out a hand still visibly shaking. "Where's a good tavern?"

Tavern. Inn. He still had a job to do. With an effort he brought himself back to the present, this cool, clear autumn day, not the hot summer one that haunted his memory.

"Uh, yeah, let me get my bearings." He scanned the streets around them. They were a long way from the Slavers' Quarter. "How the hell did we get clear over here?"

Gault shrugged. "I've just been walking to get you away from there. I was beginning to think I was going to have to lead you by the hand back to the castle."

Bantam snorted. "Wouldn't that have made a pretty picture! Two mercenaries hand in hand like a pair of little girls. This way."

These streets were so familiar he could have run them in the dark. One thing he was certain of—if he couldn't find Amethyst, he would not come back here again. This part of the city was too haunted by old memories. He felt drained already by the events of the morning and was tempted to . . . to what?

Run? Hide? Put off facing down the man who had sold them, the man who was responsible for every scar on his back, every drop of blood that he'd shed in those eight years of slavery? *No.* He wasn't that drugged helpless boy anymore.

The inn looked older and shabbier than he remembered it. It needed a good coat of whitewash and new thatch. The door squeak was the same, though, as they entered the common room and paused to allow their eyes to adjust to the darker room after the bright sunlight outside.

It was perhaps not unexpected that the two mercenaries received even less of a welcome here than they had at the

slaver's business. Bantam remembered his mother's insis-
tence that she ran a respectable family inn, not a rowdy tavern for the likes of brawling, uncivilized mercenaries.

A thin scarecrow of a woman moved to intercept them as
they looked for an empty table. Her crowd of regular customers watched with anticipation as the taverner began to
scold and attempt to shoo them out like stray dogs. "You
mercenaries get out of here!" she squawked. "I'll not have
your kind getting drunk and throwing ale mugs and mauling
the serving-girls. This is a decent, respectable place!"

"We have no intention of doing that," said Gault in an
uncertain, soothing voice. "My good woman, we only want
a mug or two of ale and something to eat."

She stood with hands on hips and surveyed them contemptuously. "I know your kind. I'll feed you, but just you
be warned that my son is downstairs in the cellars and will
be up here in a heartbeat if you so much as burp loud."

Bantam asked hastily, "If you please, I'm looking for
someone, the man who owned this place about ten years ago?
His name is Jared. He was a big man, brown hair and little
piggy blue eyes."

"Jared, yes, we bought the place from the old drunkard.
He comes around every day for his usual afternoon drink.
That was part of the bargain."

"I see," said Bantam. "May we have the common meal
while we wait, please?"

She sniffed, still angry. "You'll pay in advance. I'll not
have the likes of you starting a fight and then skipping out
without paying."

"Of course." He followed meekly as she led them to a
table, clearing out those already seated there with a fierce
glare.

Gault glared at him also as she turned her back and stalked
off to her kitchen. "Look, Bantam, why here? There have to
be places around that will welcome our money if not our
presence."

"I grew up in these rooms, Gault. My mother used to own
this place, and her father before her. When she died, it should
have been mine. That filthy swine who married her owes me

more than blood-debt. He owes me the life I should have had." His eyes roved around the room, all so familiar and yet not.

"I thought you were headed for the King's Elite, and I don't blame you. Somehow I can't see you on the other side of the bar, Banty. You belong out here, and in a rowdier place than this."

Somehow he couldn't see himself behind that bar, either. The room was smaller and grubbier than he remembered. Live here, all his life? Hustle up drinks for any man with a copper in his fist? No, it wasn't for him. He would take his revenge and be gone.

He ate the food and drank the ale that the serving-girl put in front of him, and brooded. Beyond a quick glance at everyone coming in the door, he didn't look up as Gault talked for the pleasure of hearing his own voice.

The serving-girl bent over him as she refilled their mugs. "You wanted to see Jared, sir? He just came in."

He stared in disbelief at the man she indicated. This was the ogre of his childhood, the bull-like man that had dragged them away and sold them? This man was shrunken and shaky and looked to be at least sixty years old, not the mid-forties that Bantam knew Jared should be.

Gault turned and looked at him with an odd mixture of anger and pity. "Bantam? That old sot is the one you're looking for?"

He reached for the anger again, the lust for revenge that had once been the only thing keeping him sane. It was there, fanned by the frustration of the morning. Feeble old sot or no, Jared was the man who had sold him, had sold Amethyst.

He was off the bench and across the room, pinning Jared to the wall with his right hand before anyone else could move. Bantam found his eyes were on level with the older man's; the piggy blue eyes he remembered were full of drunken incomprehension.

Out of the corner of his eye he caught a flicker of movement; the innkeeper's son, perhaps. His voice rang through the room. "I cry blood-debt on you, Jared!" A piece of his mind noted that Gault had his blade bared now, holding the rest of the room at bay in frozen silence.

He drew his sword and put the point under Jared's chin, stepping back so that he stared coldly down the length of the blade. "You don't remember me, do you, old man? Oh, but I remember *you*. You sold me, and my sister, into slavery ten years ago." Bantam watched dawning understanding come to Jared's face, and terror with it.

"Every time they sold me again, Jared, every time they lashed me, every time they forced me to my knees, I remembered you and swore that someday I would have you just where I've got you right now. I wanted to watch you squirm and beg, and then I would push the blade home. Beg, Jared. Beg for your miserable life."

Jared's eyes met his cold amber stare, and the older man's mouth opened. No words came out, only a thin yammering whine. A dark stain grew on the front of his breeches, matching the trickle of blood that snaked its way down his throat.

Bantam's voice grew even softer. "So I come home to find a weak feeble old drunkard who pisses his breeches like a babe when he sees a free man draw steel. Take a good close look at warrior steel, Jared." The sword shifted from Jared's throat to just in front of his eyes; he crowded back as if he would melt through the wall, whimpering in terror as the blade licked his cheeks and left behind flowing red lines. "She's Sargadan steel, sharp enough to cut a feather floating in midair. I killed a D'Alriaun noble to get her. She talks to me, she does. She says she's thirsty for blood, Jared, hungry for her next kill.

"And now . . ." As he shifted the sword back to Jared's throat the old man closed his eyes in submission and stood trembling.

"Not a cold-blooded killer, Ydona?" Likarion gloated. *"Watch this."*

Abruptly the heat of anger deserted Bantam and bleak cold logic took its place. There would be no satisfaction for him in killing this helpless old drunkard. Jared's death would not

bring back Amethyst, or the lost years. Nothing he could do
to this man would be retribution enough for the pain and
shame he had suffered. Revenge was not a dish best served
cold—it was too bitter.

"Now I won't shame my sword with the worthless life-
blood of a sniveling coward like you." He slammed the
sword back into her scabbard. "Mistress Innkeeper, I apologize for disrupting your day. Let's go, Gault."

They were a good way down the street before Gault said,
"Next time I take a notion to come with you, remind me
that I'm too old to take on the kind of trouble you stir up."

Bantam snorted loudly. "The day you can't take on trouble is the day we push you over and toss you in the pyres."

"Yes, Likarion? You were saying?" Ydona asked sweetly.

Likarion's face drew into a scowl and his humanoid form
vanished in a sheet of flame. *"It's the influence of that princess. Damn Byela and Her notion to give humans love. It
always make them soft."*

*"Nonetheless, you've lost the bet—again. He's mine
now."*

Bantam served his duty shift that afternoon, and returned to
barracks to find most of the Wolves preparing to hit the taverns. "Hey, Bantam," Conal said cheerfully. "My pockets
are feeling too light. Where are you going brawling tonight?"

"My own bed. Your pockets aren't my problem."

"Come on, Banty," Gault coaxed. "You'll feel better
once you get outside of some ale and inside of some wench.
When have you ever turned down an opportunity to brawl?"

"There's a first time for everything," Bantam said sourly.
"I think you can handle yourselves without me. Maybe I'm
not in the mood, all right?"

"Who tied a knot in your tail?" asked Bors. "Or doesn't
the queen's dashing hero want to go roistering with common
mercenaries?"

His only answer was the growl that floated over Bantam's
shoulder. As always when he was in a bad mood, Bantam

turned first to working it out. Whitefoot got a grooming that even surpassed that of the previous day, and so did any other animal remaining in the stable allotted to them. Bantam was finishing Bayard's roan when a hand reached over his shoulder and tweaked away the brush.

"Maybe you don't care about your own condition," said Bayard firmly, "but I have to. You're favoring that right shoulder again, and I think you don't even know it. I'm ordering you to relax and rest and get that shoulder worked on. Go to those public baths just west of the Grand Plaza, ask for Nolema, let her give you a massage, and then soak in the hot pool. What you do after that is your business, but I want you gone for at least two hours, understand?"

"Yes sir." When the captain talked like that, everybody obeyed without question. Now that Bayard pointed it out to him, Bantam was aware that his right shoulder was aching abominably. Bayard's orders would be a pleasure to follow.

Nolema's hands were strong and sure and skilled on his shoulder. The massage there felt so good that he did not resist when she suggested a full back massage as well. He nearly fell asleep under her soothing ministrations, so relaxed that he did not even worry about his lack of desire for her tempting body.

The small hot pool also felt good. Only the growling of his stomach reminded him that he needed to eat as well. He tried to ignore it and let his head loll back, his eyes half-closed. Nolema's greeting to another customer was a barely heard buzz.

"Bantam! Well met!" said a voice from above him.

He opened his eyes and looked into a face that he knew, even upside down. "Thought I heard you were married, Corven. What are you doing here ogling the bathgirls?"

Corven laughed. "Getting clean, so my wife doesn't throw me out of my own home. She's up at the castle with Varian's lady while we poor warriors are stuck in camp outside the walls. No room, you know!" He sloshed down the steps and sat down across from him.

Bantam settled deeper into the hot water and sighed. He

could let his guard down with Corven. Maybe Corven's lord
would be around long enough to get to know him better. "It
must be nice to have a home to go to."

"No family at all, Bantam?" Corven said sympathetically.

He shook his head. "My mother died years ago, and while
I was a slave I lost my sister. No wife, and as far as I know,
no kids. So my home's a barracks and my family a band of
jug-headed mercenaries."

Corven felt a quick burst of empathy with the mercenary.
He had been a slave once, and alone, too, except for Varian's
friendship. Impulsively he offered, "Come home with me
for the evening. My wife will feed us supper and my kids
will be happy to crawl all over you."

"It won't put her out—an unexpected mouth to feed?"
Bantam asked uncertainly. Mother of Mares, he was tempted!
And it would let him enjoy Corven's company for a while
longer.

"Not at all. We're part of Baron Varian's household, you
know, so we all get served out of the same pots. All she has
to do is find another plate. Varian and Cathlin are attending
on the royalty, so we're alone tonight. Come on. Please?"
He stood up, dripping water as he held out his hand to pull
Bantam to his feet.

"Home" turned out to be one of a suite of rooms in the
castle, where Corven explained Varian's household was staying for the coronation. A small brown-haired woman flew to
meet Corven at the door. He swept her up and spun her off
her feet, while a little girl and a slightly older boy clamored
for their turns. As he released her and gathered in his children, she turned to greet her husband's guest.

A man changes much from thirteen to twenty-three, but
the face of the woman is already recognizable in the girl. As
a girl she had been pretty, and now in the happy greeting of
her husband she was beautiful. Bantam knew her immediately.

She saw a lean, scarred man somewhat shorter than her
husband, wearing the finery and short-clipped mustache and
beard of a mercenary, although his hair was much shorter

than mercenaries usually wore it. Strangely, she felt as if she ought to know him, but couldn't remember where she might have seen him. He was staring at her with an odd, almost tender half-smile on his face.

"My love, this is Bantam, the mercenary I was telling you about. Bantam, my wife is—"

"I know her name, Corven. Amethyst. I thought I'd never see you again." His voice was husky, and his amber-brown eyes very bright.

"Do I know you?" Amethyst asked with puzzlement. Why did he seem so familiar—and why was the aura of his emotions trembling between the sky-blue of love and the bright golden yellow of sheer joy?

He smiled then, and sparks of mischief danced in his eyes. "You do, although it's been about ten years since I saw you last. It was a couple of weeks after you hit me and gave me *this*," and he turned his head to show her a faint white scar over his left ear.

Amethyst gasped indignantly. "I never hit anybody in my life but my brother Far . . ." Her voice died and she stared at him in disbelief. *"Farris?"*

He nodded silently and held out his arms. She threw herself into them, crying and laughing at the same time as he held her in a most unbrotherly embrace.

Corven tactfully ignored the suspiciously wet eyes of a certain mercenary and sat down in a chair by the fire, his children on his lap.

"Dada, why is that man hugging Mama?" his daughter asked.

"Because he's her brother that we thought she lost. And he wouldn't have been lost quite so long if he'd ever told me his real name."

The little girl considered this information thoughtfully. "Oh. Did he get lost when he ran out into the street?"

"Something like that, sweetheart. Farris, can you let her go sometime tonight so we can eat? I did promise you a meal."

Bantam hugged his sister tightly again before he did as his brother-in-law requested. "It's still 'Bantam' to you,

Corven. Only my sister gets to call me Farris. There are too many bad memories that go with that name.''

Once Amethyst had settled a squabble between her children over who got to sit next to Uncle Bantam, they ate without making any more reference to the past. Bantam was unwilling to discuss what had happened to him in front of innocent little children, and was of two minds whether or not to tell Amethyst anything. He was willing, for the present, to listen to their stories of life attending on a lord baron and his lady.

True to Corven's word, the children crawled all over Bantam afterward. His nephew Vadaris wanted to see his sword, and his niece Beronia wanted to sit on his lap. He agreed to the last request somewhat dubiously at first, but found that having a little girl on one's lap was an entirely different feeling from having a big girl in the same place. When she fell asleep snuggled up against him, he felt fiercely protective. This child was blood of his blood, the closest he would likely ever have to a daughter of his own, and he was reluctant to give her even to his sister to take her off to bed. Vadaris went on his own feet, but only after a promise from his father that they could go to see his uncle at swordpractice with the other Queen's Shields in the morning.

With the children gone, they caught up on each other's history. Bantam was relieved to know that none of his fears for his sister had been justified; Lord Varian had bought her at her first sale and freed her immediately. Corven had married her two years later.

''As soon as we could,'' Corven said quietly, ''we tried to find you. But the slaver wouldn't tell us anything or let us see the records. I finally had to go to Alnikhias and ask for his favor. Well, this was right after his accession to the throne, and there was a lot for him to settle first. It was several months before we got his orders for the slaver to open the records. By the time we found your first master, he had died. All his heirs knew was that he'd sold you a couple of weeks earlier. Because it was a private sale, there were no records. We just couldn't get any further.''

Bantam sighed. ''I'm grateful you tried, anyway, Corven.

I couldn't do anything about trying to find Amethyst until this morning, and then they told me that the records were destroyed.

"I'm . . . not going to describe the years I spent as a slave. The friends I made were the only good parts, and the closest one of those is dead. For the rest—" he spread his hands and shrugged slightly, "well, I lived through it." He fell silent and stared at the fire.

"What will you do now, Farris?" Amethyst asked. "I suppose we could ask Varian to give you a job as a guardsman."

He smiled ruefully at her. "Have you forgotten, little sister? I'm a Queen's Shield now, contracted for the next two years. And after that? Well, we'll see if any of us Wolves are still sane or if we've gone crazy with no fighting to keep us out of trouble."

Corven laughed. "Just like a merc. Wishing for a nice warm dry guard room and when you get one, grumbling because you're not out on the field fighting."

"What can I say? I'm a fighter, I was even as a slave, and I like it. It's more or less honest work, and I'm good at it. Oh, maybe someday all these lords will stop fighting each other and be peaceful, and I'll really be out of a job, but then we'll all be, won't we, Corven?"

Corven snorted. "That's as likely as Alnikhias abdicating to take a job as a peaceful shepherd herding his happy little flock. Still, keep it in mind, Banty. Now that we've found you, I know we'd like to see more of you."

"You bet I will."

When he went to take his leave, Amethyst came into his embrace again, and he hugged her hard as Corven grinned at them. "By the way, Banty, just how *did* you get that scar over your ear?"

Bantam looked embarrassed although he continued to keep his arm around Amethyst. "You won't let it get out? I'd hate to have my *sabros* know I got my first battle scar from my little sister." He grinned at her and she wrinkled her nose at him and stuck out her tongue.

"She clobbered me with an ale mug."

27

REWARD

On the fifteenth day of the month of Redleaves the king, resplendent in crimson velvet and cloth of gold, paused for a moment beside the captain of his bride's honorguard. His eyes ranged up and down the line of mercenaries, waiting to take their places in the procession that would escort Her Gracious Majesty Queen Ashlana to the shrine of Byela for her wedding. "You seem to be missing a few, Captain Bayard."

"Yes, Your Majesty. Not all of the men are on duty today."

"That young man who brought Her Majesty out of Draksgard, for instance? I don't see him here."

"No, sir. He does not have duty today."

"Indeed? And if I specifically require his presence?" Alnikhias asked coolly.

"I would have to tell you, sir, that it is impossible. I really can't say where Bantam might be right now. I believe he said he was going to rut his way through every brothel in the city."

Bantam, at that moment, would have been easy to find. He was in one of his favorite taverns, wishing that for once in his life he could get drunk. The serving wenches walked carefully around him, eyeing him with definite uneasiness. He did not savor the mead in his mug as he usually did, but was steadily putting it away in a manner that certainly should have made him drunk.

The taverner eyed him watchfully, too. Drunken warriors were one of the hazards of his trade, but not usually so early in the day. His bouncer did not come on duty until early evening, and this man's reputation as a fighter was formidable. He himself had seen him take on two men at once in a match fight just last week, and put both of them down in a matter of heartbeats.

After whispered orders from the taverner, one of the girls hesitantly approached him. "Master?" she murmured as she knelt just out of his reach.

"What?" he growled without looking up.

She paled with fear, but orders were orders. "Master, I . . . since you visited me last week, master, I've been lonely. Please, will you come upstairs and let me give you pleasure?"

He looked at her then—tiny, dark-haired, and dark-eyed as he preferred his bed-partners. And frightened to death, as he did not. She put her head down as he stared balefully at her and went utterly still, as a bird does under the mesmerizing gaze of a serpent. The fall of her hair past her cheeks reminded him unbearably of Ashlana in the corridors of Draksgard.

"No. If I want one of you, I'll tell you." He motioned with his head to dismiss her, and she fled silently. His fist tightened on his mug as he pictured taking her to bed. Taking her roughly, forcing her with thought only for his own release. Taking her gently, loving her with hands and mouth and body until she cried out with pleasure. Which of them would Alnikhias try to do to Ashlana tonight in the privacy of their wedding chamber? Which would she let him do? True rape she would not tolerate, and Alnikhias loved her, Bantam would grant him that. But the other possibility was almost worse.

With a curse he hurled the mug across the room to shatter

against the stones of the fireplace, threw a silver piece on the table, and stalked out.

He walked for a long time, not noticing that people celebrating their king's wedding faltered when he came near, fell silent, and moved out of his way. Briefly he considered finding Joy Street and rutting his way through the brothels as he had told Gault he would do.

He stopped in the shade of a building, only then noticing that it, too, was one of the places that had become his regular haunts. The Black Fox—hah! That picture on the tavern sign was no fox, but a vixen, a teasing smile on her little pointed face and a flirting brush of a tail. He pushed through the door and nearly collided with a serving-slave. She gave a small startled squeak and then smiled at him. "Master Bantam! Welcome back! We didn't look to see you until this evening, with your friends."

He stared at her for a moment until his lips curled back in a grimace that made her suddenly aware that he called himself a Wolf. Ah, this one. She was perfect. His own height, a pale blonde with ocean-blue eyes so deep a man could drown in them, long legs that wrapped oh so enticingly around a man's waist, and a feline sensuousness that must have given her her name.

"How could I stay away from a temptation like you, Fela?" Putting a hand under her chin to draw her face closer, he kissed her fiercely.

Her eyes were wide and startled when he released her. He turned away to shout for Vardon, the taverner. "I want a room and exclusive rights to this girl until I'm ready to leave. How much?"

Vardon looked startled, too, and a little unhappy. Fela was his own favorite, and he had intended to reserve her for himself tonight. Ah well, but money was money, and the girl wouldn't wear out from this mercenary's use. He named a daily price that was twice as much as the normal rental of the room. Again he was startled when the mercenary only nodded, with no bargaining.

"Done. Send up some mead and some food, then nobody disturb me until I call for something. Is that clear?" Bantam

didn't wait for the taverner's answer, but pulled Fela away
by the hand.

Two mornings later Fela woke him by nuzzling at his ear
and smiling down at him. He smiled lazily back and pulled
her down so that he could kiss her and stroke her breasts.

She laughed softly. "Don't you men ever think of anything else?"

"What else is there worth thinking about?" *Ashlana,* his
mind told him, then rebuked, *Not for you, Bantam. Accept
it.*

Fela's company had not been quite the cure for his fever
of jealousy that he had expected. Last night, while she
moaned in pleasure under his hands, the thought of Ashlana
doing the same thing with her new husband had nearly driven
him insane with envy and despair. Even taking Fela in a
desperate violent frenzy of mindless lust had not forced the
thoughts from his mind for very long.

And yet he did find consolation and a sort of ease in her
arms. Even as he lay on top of her, shaking and spent, she
cradled and comforted him with her body. Her kisses for him
had not been erotic then, but tender. She was too wise to ask
him his troubles; that something tormented him she knew,
but by both nature and training she was content to wait until
he chose to unburden himself.

Now she smiled at him, a spark of mischief in her eyes.
"You could try thinking of food. Someone just put a tray
down outside the door."

"Oh yeah, food," he mused, then looked down at his suddenly growling stomach in surprise. He looked even more
surprised when hers answered, growling even louder.

Fela dissolved into laughter, and after a moment he joined
her. "What do you keep in that pretty belly to make it growl
so loud? Bears?" he asked playfully.

She shook her head. "Wolves. *You* ought to know that."

Bantam rolled onto his side and propped his head up on
his hand to watch as she walked to the door to bring in the
tray of food, suddenly feeling vaguely guilty. There was a
bruise on her hip that he hadn't noticed before. "Fela, did I

make that bruise, that last time? I'm sorry. Hurting you is not what I wanted.''

"I know, and you didn't. I bumped into something in the dark.''

Vague guilt blossomed suddenly into full guilt. Though she had given every evidence of enjoying what he had done to her, she had not been free to refuse him. He had treated her, and all the other girls he had bedded, no better than his masters had treated him. "How can you stand it? Having to take bastards like me to bed every night?''

Fela cut him off by stuffing a piece of bread in his mouth. "You were hurting. If giving you my body helped you, I'm happy," she said firmly. "All the other girls are jealous because you chose me. We pray that we get a man like you, a decent, kind man. It's even better that you're a damned good lover. Is it because you're half-fai, like me?''

"You are? If I'd known that, I'd have made Vardon take that damned iron collar off you.''

She smiled and kissed him again. "There, you see? You're not a brutal bastard who cares only for himself. It doesn't hurt me, not like they say iron hurts full fai.''

"Even so, I'd like it off.''

This time Fela pushed a handful of grapes in his mouth.

A horrendous pounding on the door interrupted them. "Bantam, are you in there?'' a familiar voice yelled.

"No!'' Bantam bellowed back. "And if I was, I'd kill you for interrupting me, Balian.''

"Finish with the wench and get dressed. Bayard has the whole warband looking for you. The royals have called another damned parade for this afternoon, and *you* are specifically commanded to appear.''

He remembered the parade from a long time ago and his old dream of riding in one as a King's Elite. Now instead of an Elite's blue-and-red surcote he wore a plain white shirt and new brigandine armor, polished so that the brightwork was actually bright. The red silk baldric was new, too, an eye-blinding scarlet, and he felt as conspicuous as a cat in a birdcage. Only his hat was his own, worn in a wordless and prideful message that he was still a mercenary.

The horse under him was not one of the Elite's matched blacks, but his own Whitefoot, curried until he gleamed almost as satiny as one of his palfrey kindred. Bayard rode on one side and Gault on the other. Behind him, ranged around the royal carriage, rode the rest of the Wolves, self-consciously aware that they were on display to the cheering crowds.

In the central square of the Grand Plaza he took a moment to look at the Griffin Fountain; sure enough a gang of young boys was in possession of it for the best viewing in the city.

They pulled to a halt in front of the raised dais where the thrones for the king and queen waited. The rest of the long line of the parade was waiting as the royals took their seats with the King's Elite standing guard behind them, and the heralds' trumpets squawked out brassily.

"All attend to Their Majesties Alnikhias and Ashlana, Monarchs of Dur Sharrukhan and D'Alriaun!" the heralds called, in voices as loud and strident as their own trumpets. "Their Majesties call before them Her Majesty's Shields, the Free Mercenary Warband of Bayard's Wolves!"

The crowd fell nearly silent as they dismounted and walked toward the thrones, spreading out into a wedge formation on the steps of the dais in a movement they must have rehearsed. Bantam found himself nudged into place at the point of that wedge, on the top step with his captain and second just behind him. With his comrades he dropped to one knee in the manner proper to a guardsman.

The heralds cried, "Let honor be given where honor is due. Hear now the words of Her Majesty!"

Ashlana rose, smiling down at the men before her. Her voice rang out as Bantam had never known a woman's voice could. "All here have heard of the events of the last months, how my half-brother sought to take my throne and thwart the efforts of peace between our two lands. You have heard also how the traitor Launart sought also to bend these events to his own will, holding me prisoner in Draksgard Keep. That he did not succeed is due to the efforts of one man, the man before me now, known as Bantam of Bayard's Wolves.

"This man, at great risk to his own life and liberty, alone and in the guise of a slave, made his way to where I was being held and brought me away unharmed. He and this warband sheltered me until they could bring me safely to my lord the king. For this, all of them have my most profound thanks, and these gifts, above and beyond their pay and position." She signaled to part of the King's Elite honorguard behind her; they carried two large boxes forward and from them began to distribute new swords in carved and gilded scabbards.

When they were done and had carried the boxes away again, Ashlana took two steps forward to stand in front of Bantam where he still knelt at the top of the dais.

"Bantam of Bayard's Wolves, I have thought long and hard what I can give you besides my gratitude. Know all of you assembled that this man has my favor, now and forever. In recognition of this my Lord the King Alnikhias and I do jointly create him a Lord Baron and grant him arms, these arms being 'Argent, a bantam cock rousant proper perched on a slave-collar fracted sable.' He may bear these arms as he chooses, without let or hindrance, that all may know him and honor his deeds."

She signaled again, and a guardsman brought out of concealment a shield gleaming with new paint. On the shield's white background, a rooster in all the glory of his natural colors flapped his wings and crowed proudly in challenge. Under his feet the black of the broken slave-collar looked grim and sullen.

Ashlana fitted around his head a soft black leather browband bearing the same arms. "Not a coronet," he heard her soft whisper for his ears only, "but the best I could do. And Bantam . . . you were right about Niko."

Mother of Mares! Me? A lord? He heard an echo in his head, his own sullen voice saying, *"Nobody's subject. Not yours, not Alnikhias', nobody's!"*

Ashlana had gathered her skirts in preparation to back the two steps to return to her throne when he heard his own voice saying "My queen, please, wait."

In the silence everyone near enough heard the soft *shfff* of his new sword leaving its sheath and saw him balance the naked blade across his open palms. Only he knew how the bright steel burned in his hands.

"From this moment forth I am thy man; from this moment forth I pledge life and limb to thy service, as long as I have breath in my body. This I vow on the sword I hold; if I dishonor or break faith with thee, may it twist in my hand to slay me as I stand."

Swiftly her hands flew to cover the sword also, squeezing both of their hands together hard enough to cut their fingers, staining the blade clasped between them with their mingled blood.

"From this moment forth I am thy queen; thou art mine to command or release, mine to protect with my power as thou defend me with thy body. This I vow on the sword between us; if I break faith with thee may the gods above deal with me as an oathbreaker deserves. In sign and token of this I give to thee this sword and shield which thou hast dedicated to my service. May they forever be a reminder unto thee."

Ashlana bit her lip as she resisted the impulse she had had all afternoon, to reach out and caress his scarred cheek. She could imagine the rest—how the sword in his hand might slip down to rest on his knee as he moved to capture and hold her wrist, just long enough for him to turn his head and kiss her palm. No. Not for them, ever. This man had been wise enough to know that what she had felt for him was half hero worship, half romantic infatuation, and left her free to build a loving relationship with her husband.

That he loved her had not been her imagination; better to let him show that love in the only way he could, in the loyalty he had just pledged, and let the rest of it go.

As Alnikhias stepped forward and took her hand, Bantam rose to his feet. Before he sheathed his sword, he raised it in momentary salute to the king, the salute of one warrior to another. He heard Alnikhias laugh softly, and knew the king had understood him; he had pledged personal fealty to *her*, not to the royal couple.

Bantam bowed and stepped back the required three steps,

and thankfully turned to go. Her voice arrested him in mid-step. *"Sabro!"*

He whipped his head around to face her again. "Command me, my queen!"

She laughed and tossed him a soft leather bag that chinked when he caught it. "The first round of drinks is on me!"

The senior herald, though caught off guard by this distinctly unregal behavior, nevertheless raised her staff to lead the cheers. "For Lord Bantam and the Free Mercenary War-band of Bayard's Wolves—Vivant!"

And the assembled people, who had already fallen in love with their new queen, roared their approval. "Vivant! *Vivant! VIVANT!"*

Alanna Morland

"Exciting and fast-paced."—Anne Logston,
author of *Firewalk*

Leopard Lord

**For fifty years, the barony of Leopard's Gard has suf-
fered brutal rule, under a series of barons in league
with a dark power. Now the latest of these is dead,
and his son Varian has inherited his father's lands.
But with the lands he also inherits his father's power
to shapeshift, and the demands that the dark god
makes in return. Varian will be forced to ravage his
own subjects as his father did before him.**

**In desperation, Varian strikes a terrible bargain. He
promises that the woman he chooses to marry will be
a gift to the dark god, in exchange for the land's freedom. When Varian marries the lovely Cathlin, he
knows he will feel guilty about her fate, but convinces
himself that one woman's life is a small price to pay for
the release of thousands of his countrymen.**

But Varian didn't count on falling in love...

☐ 0–441–00606–X/$5.99

ACE
SCIENCE
FICTION